MARGARET DRABBLE

A Day in the Life
of a Smiling Woman

Edited with an Introduction by
JOSÉ FRANCISCO FERNÁNDEZ

PENGUIN BOOKS

PENGUIN CLASSICS

Published by the Penguin Group
Penguin Books Ltd, 80 Strand, London WC2R ORL, England
Penguin Group (USA) Inc., 375 Hudson Street, New York, New York 10014, USA
Penguin Group (Canada), 90 Eglinton Avenue East, Suite 700, Toronto, Ontario, Canada M4P 2Y3
(a division of Pearson Penguin Canada Inc.)
Penguin Ireland, 25 St Stephen's Green, Dublin 2, Ireland (a division of Penguin Books Ltd)
Penguin Group (Australia), 250 Camberwell Road, Camberwell, Victoria 3124, Australia
(a division of Pearson Australia Group Pty Ltd)
Penguin Books India Pvt Ltd, 11 Community Centre, Panchsheel Park,
New Delhi – 110 017, India
Penguin Group (NZ), 67 Apollo Drive, Rosedale, Auckland 0632, New Zealand
(a division of Pearson New Zealand Ltd)
Penguin Books (South Africa) (Pty) Ltd, Block D, Rosebank Office Park, 181 Jan Smuts Avenue,
Parktown North, Gauteng 2193, South Africa

Penguin Books Ltd, Registered Offices: 80 Strand, London WC2R ORL, England

www.penguin.com

First published in Great Britain by Penguin Classics 2011
Published in paperback by Penguin Classics 2012
001

Copyright © Margaret Drabble, 1966, 1967, 1968, 1969, 1970, 1972, 1973, 1975, 1989, 1993,
1999, 2000
Introduction copyright © José Francisco Fernández, 2011
All rights reserved

The moral right of the author and the author of the introduction has been asserted

Set in Sabon
Printed in England by Clays Ltd, St Ives plc

ISBN: 978-0-141-19643-5

www.greenpenguin.co.uk

MIX
Paper from
responsible sourc
FSC
www.fsc.org   FSC™ C01817

ALWAYS LEARNING   PEARSON

For Pat Kavanagh

Contents

Introduction

When Margaret Drabble's short story 'The Caves of God' was published in Nicholas Royle's *Neonlit: Time Out Book of New Writing*, Volume 2 (1999), Michael Moorcock, in his introduction, termed her contribution 'a rarity'. The sense of having found an anomaly was reinforced by the editor's comments in the foreword: they were just as excited, Royle wrote, about publishing some promising writers' first short stories 'as we are about featuring a rare excursion into the short form by Margaret Drabble'.

The truth of the matter, however, is that, before 'The Caves of God', Drabble had published a dozen stories in a number of journals, magazines and anthologies. Moorcock and Royle's comments are mentioned here merely to demonstrate the general lack of awareness surrounding the author's short fiction, despite her having written such small gems as 'Hassan's Tower' and 'The Gifts of War', which have been reprinted and anthologized several times. These two and her other pieces are fine examples of well-made stories: neatly constructed, carefully contextualized, focused, unified in tone, elegantly climactic, and at times tinged with the seriousness of a moral dilemma. At the same time they are so very *English*; they encapsulate values and ideas that, for better or for worse, have been associated with England, or with a kind of England Drabble admires: restraint, moderation, common sense, intolerance of snobbishness (which was the main topic in Drabble's first published short text, the sketch 'Les Liaisons Dangereuses', 1964), wit and seriousness.

Perhaps it was the Englishness of her stories that impelled a lecturer at an English university in the mid-eighties to distribute 'The Gifts of War' to a group of foreign students, myself included, who were engaged in an informally arranged exchange programme in those pioneering days before the extension of the celebrated Erasmus scheme. What did we see in that story? What did we learn from that exposure to Englishness? The silent dignity of Kevin's working-class mother, for example, watching her son going to school along the narrow back alleys of terraced houses; the self-deceit of Frances Janet Ashton Hall, ready to move to a southern university, accosting distressed passers-by, trying to convince them on the banning of all armaments; the mazy introspection of female conscience that Drabble developed in novels such as *The Waterfall* (1969), a reasoning, self-assured, if slightly severe narrative voice, which would in time step out of the printed page and address the reader directly, reaching high levels of intimacy in *A Natural Curiosity* (1989) with such well-known remarks as 'What do *you* think will happen to her?'

None of the stories in this collection are autobiographical in the strictest sense, although many are based on Drabble's own experiences, on places she has been to and people she has met. Some of her friends are taken as characters, like the lichenologist in 'Stepping Westward', while the coastal village in Somerset where she keeps a house appears in one of the stories. Drabble did visit the island of Elba when she was seventeen, while studying Italian in Perugia, and she took material from that experience to write 'A Pyrrhic Victory'. She certainly made a journey to Morocco with her husband in the mid-sixties, crossing the length of Spain by car to reach their destination, and this provided details for the story 'Hassan's Tower'. Drabble was pregnant with her second son at the time, and this may account for the willingness on the part of the protagonist to consider the common bonds of humanity at the end of the story. In these and other journeys Drabble surely took precise notes on the English abroad, a persistent topic in the early stories. The English are shown to be an interesting subject of study, afflicted with a mixture of fear and admiration, halfway between neurosis caused by the threat of foreigners and fascination with new experiences. 'What you would like,' says newly wed Chloe to her groom, Kenneth, in Marrakesh, 'is a country without any people in it. With just places. And hotels.' Kenneth and Chloe, the protagonists of 'Hassan's Tower', are too polite to ask if the food that has been offered them along with their drinks is for free, and yet at the same time they feel outraged in case the price turns out to be exorbitant.

In these early stories there is a longing for an exotic life – as with Helen in 'A Voyage to Cythera', who 'could get excited by the prospect of any journey longer than thirty miles' – a life of travelling on the continent and beyond, a desire to apprehend a more dazzling life elsewhere. Helen maintains the illusion that she can change just by travelling. No matter how far they go, however, the protagonists of these initial pieces cannot truly escape England. They are haunted by their English upbringing in a time of drabness. Their handling of space outside their homes is problematic: that is why they compare their new surroundings with their homeland as the only way to appropriate the foreign landscape. In 'A Pyrrhic Victory' Anne remembers childhood excursions to the beaches on the Yorkshire coast while contemplating a sunny rock pool on the island of Elba. In 'Hassan's Tower', what first comes to Kenneth's mind when he looks at the people at the top of the monument is the image of grandmothers on a beach in England. When he reconciles with mankind and accepts them as human beings, with their little lives of worries and joys, he sees 'all of them, alive and separate as people on a London street'.

If the characters of the stories written in the sixties cannot escape the constraints imposed by England – either the reality or illusion of England – they also inhabit a different time-frame, where the effects of the war are still present in the geography of cities. These pieces refer to a past time, when people still kept fourpenny stamps in their wallets, used pens to write letters and boxes of matches to light cigarettes on trains.

The short stories written in the seventies, however, suggest a change of attitude. No more longing for distant places or deep states of contemplation caused by the struggles of love. Brisk, busy, highly efficient professional women enter the stage: Kathie Jones in 'A Success Story', Jenny Jamieson in 'A Day in the Life of a Smiling Woman' and the unnamed TV presenter and mother of four in 'Homework' are representatives of the woman who has to divide her time between her duties at home and the demands of a job, usually, in Drabble's stories, one related to the media. There is usually a husband and children too, and the stories of this period encapsulate Drabble's attempt to draw a picture of the modern woman trying to reconcile all the pressures put upon her and, at the same time, maintain an independent voice. The influence of Doris Lessing, whose work Drabble had discovered during the previous decade, can be clearly seen here.

In the last group of stories, from 'The Merry Widow' onwards, a period that roughly covers the late eighties and most of the nineties, the female protagonists, usually middle-aged, having paid their dues to society, escape the burden of

mundane obligations and retire to a corner of England, seek-
ing peace and solitude, and gaining time for themselves,
becoming more interested in the wonders of nature than in
the paradoxical workings of love. They let their hair go undyed,
abandon diets and happily put on weight, driving their cars
themselves to places of their own choosing. A kind of circle
has been completed from the solipsistic young women of the
first period: forgiveness has been granted, a serene conscience
has been achieved.

My contention is that Margaret Drabble's short stories
constitute an essential complement to understanding her work:
not only do they establish a fruitful dialogue with her major
novels, but they also contain clues that point to lesser-known
aspects of her art. This makes all the more surprising the fact
that a substantial part of the literary imagination of one of
the most important writers of postwar Britain has not been
studied in depth. With the exception of the odd article, there
is no thorough study of Drabble's short fiction. Perhaps her
work as a novelist has eclipsed her production of short stories,
here collected for the first time in book form. Perhaps the
dispersion in time and space of her short stories, mostly
published in Britain and America over a period of more than
thirty years, has not allowed a proper assessment. Research
on the interwoven lines, preoccupations and topics shared
between her stories and novels remains a task yet to be
completed. The fascination that Helen, for example, the
protagonist of 'A Voyage to Cythera', feels for the perfect,
harmonious family picture she glimpses through the window
from the street corresponds with the sophisticated world that
Clara experiences in the Denham household in *Jerusalem the
Golden* (1967). While, in order to achieve the final version of
the protagonist in *The Realms of Gold* (1975) – independent,
self-confident and respected archaeologist Frances Wingate

– Drabble probably needed to gain the necessary practice drawing the profile of the main characters in 'A Success Story' and 'A Day in the Life of a Smiling Woman'. In this last story, TV presenter Jenny Jamieson's savoir-faire marks a relevant precedent for future heroines: 'she never offended and yet never made people dull. She was intelligent and quick, she had sympathy for everyone she talked to, and all the time she looked so splendid [. . .]'

Liz Headland was unable to find Stephen Cox, the man who could have been her lover, in the jungle of Cambodia in *The Gates of Ivory* (1991), but the interested reader has an opportunity to imagine how such a meeting would have fared in 'The Caves of God', when Hannah Elsevir finally finds her ex-husband, Peter, or rather the reincarnation of her husband in Turkey (Drabble had been impressed by the dream-like landscape of Cappadocia during a British Council visit). The similarities between the two men (humane, compassionate, calm) are remarkable. It would be interesting to analyse, incidentally, why her mature and intelligent women fall for elusive, ambiguous, evanescent men, such as Stephen Cox, or Bill Elliot in 'The Dower House at Kellynch'. Perhaps they need a respite after disentangling themselves from the turmoil of a life with the likes of Nick Gaulden (*The Peppered Moth*, 2000), that attractive and remorseless rolling stone who leaves behind a trail of families and children.

When one reads the stories in this collection, certain motives and places acquire special relevance, as if one were seeing the hidden threads that make the writer's oeuvre, like the reverse of a tapestry. The rock pool that Anne spoils with her sacrilegious deed in Drabble's early story, 'A Pyrrhic Victory', finds its final significance in her most recent novel, *The Sea Lady* (2007). By swimming in a rock pool on the North Sea coast at the end of the novel, Ailsa Kelman is almost gaining redemption for young Anne's sin on that distant Mediterranean shore so long ago. The author herself stressed the importance of these connections in a 1991 lecture, aptly named 'In Search of a Future': 'For the past is not fixed: it changes as we change, and we look back and perceive in it different messages, different patterns. Our past selves speak to our future selves. We are part of a continuing process.' Just as is common in her novels, so too in her stories fate and chance exert a pull that impels or diverts human efforts towards happiness. It is because of luck, therefore, that Viola meets her former lover in that particular restaurant in 'Faithful Lovers', although perhaps she was destined to go there because of their past affair. Giles Reader meets by chance his old friend Peter Elsevir in Turkey in 'The Caves of God', thus procuring the encounter that Hannah so badly needs with her ex-husband, a reunion that was meant to take place.

The stories in this collection are, of course, worth reading on their own, even if one is not acquainted with Drabble's longer fiction, and details concerning their publication are themselves truly enthralling narratives. It is now known, for instance, that Nobel Prize-winner Saul Bellow wrote a prickly letter of complaint to Drabble, rightly suspecting that he was the model for womanizer and woman-hater Howard Jago in 'A Success Story'. By reading this story one also has privileged access to the sort of parties that publisher George Weidenfeld used to give. And, on one occasion, the Woodcraft Folk even took legal action against the author when she had some children in 'Homework' make the naïvely funny remark that their organisation was 'a kind of guerrilla warfare training for Marxist boy scouts'. The Mill House, which appears so prominently in 'The Merry Widow', was rented by Drabble herself in the mid-eighties. Just like the protagonist of the story, the author went to Dorset to recover from a period of distress.

Unlike Elsa Palmer, however, Drabble had recently experienced her mother's, not her husband's, death.

Although imbued with Drabble's characteristic themes – her cautious feminism, class conflicts, a fascination for those chosen by grace, metafictional devices ('You must not imagine me as speaking to you in my own person,' writes the authorial voice in 'Stepping Westward') – in Drabble's short stories the social concerns are more subdued, the tone is more relaxed than in her longer works. Drabble the social anthropologist is less obviously at work here. Occasionally, though, she still lets it be known that she is aware of the class abyss that separates people in modern Britain: old and new money, property . . . These are issues that she does not abandon completely: 'The Elliots of old would not have acknowledged the existence of my category of person', reflects Emma Watson in 'The Dower House at Kellynch' on her unexpected rapport with a member of the landed gentry. There is an authorial tut of displeasure for those who forget their origins, those who pretend that they have been affluent all their lives and that round the corner does not lurk a lower-middle-class past, as with the Palmer offspring in *The Witch of Exmoor* (1996) ('They have turned themselves into members of the English middle class by sleight of hand'), an attitude also represented in Drabble's short fiction by Kenneth in 'Hassan's Tower', who believes that being rich is something natural: 'he sometimes found himself wondering how his own parents had so dismally failed to have it [money].' Drabble may despise the network of contacts between the upper classes and make passing remarks on the falseness of committees which give an appearance of democratic procedures to a system of nepotism in stories such as 'A Day in the Life of a Smiling Woman' – she occasionally expands on the merchandising of the past in England, now labelled as 'Heritage', as in 'Stepping Westward' – but, generally speaking, as perhaps befits a genre such as the short story, in Drabble's short pieces there are fewer global concerns and many more intimate portraits. Less political strain and more tranquil pleasures.

Much of the sensuousness in these stories comes from the contemplation of the English landscape, in particular Drabble's adopted territory of the West Country: 'It is the most beautiful place in England', as Esther Breuer says about Somerset in *The Radiant Way* (1987). In short stories such as 'The Merry Widow', 'The Dower House at Kellynch' or 'Stepping Westward' the author shows, as she puts it in *A Writer's Britain* (1979), an almost mystic devotion to the land itself, a pure affection that eases her painful love for England. Most readers will probably share Elsa Palmer's grief in 'The Merry Widow' when the old man from the village destroys her private Eden in Dorset, her little paddock at the back of the Mill House, which had been her source of healing peace. There is certainly moral strife in the story, a personal betterment achieved through suffering, but the watercolour of wild flowers growing in profusion makes up for the misery Elsa endures.

A luxurious and lustful delight in the overpowering landscape can also be found in 'Stepping Westward', as seen by the twenty-year-old who had once been the schoolteacher Mary Mogg:

Ferns sprouted like orchids from the trunks of vast oaks overhanging the rapid rivers, ivy with berries like grapes rampaged up ash and beech in tropical splendour, and hollies soared towards the sky. Primeval lichens of grey and sage green and dazzling orange encrusted bark and twig and stone, and the red earth broke into bubbles of scarlet and purple and bright spongy yellow.

This is an interesting angle from which to consider someone labelled as the moral conscience of her generation. Drabble does indeed surprise the prejudiced mind in these stories: a woman rekindles an adulterous old flame in a public bar; an intelligent female writer relishes the sexual longing that she provokes in a man of worldly fame; a famous TV presenter heroically speaks about the future to a school audience of children and parents while bleeding profusely, due to a gynae-cological examination. There is certainly a dialogue with the tradition the author hails from – Wordsworth's voice, for instance, can be heard in 'Stepping Westward' – but Drabble has always been able to supersede that same tradition ('How I dislike Jane Austen', Jane Gray had said in *The Waterfall*) by an exploration of different kinds of consciousness, revising from the inside old forms of writing.

After the trilogy of the late eighties and early nineties (*The Radiant Way, A Natural Curiosity, The Gates of Ivory*) her novels have, in their own quiet way, endeavoured to open new paths for fiction, entering the realm of the supernatural and flirting with uncertain areas of the occult in *The Witch of Exmoor*, or courting the underworld and revisiting myths of a dark nature in *The Seven Sisters* (2002). Similarly, the unex-pected comes up in her short stories, where she convincingly portrays a mentally unstable character in 'Homework' or when she chooses a geneticist as the protagonist of 'The Caves of God', anticipating her interest in genealogy, DNA research and matrilineal descent in *The Peppered Moth*. The lack of closure in 'The Dower House at Kellynch' is intriguing too, as is the intersection of this narrative with 'Stepping West-ward', when the protagonist of the first story appears in the background of the second one as an old acquaintance of the reader, thus adding elements of playful intertextuality to conventional storytelling.

It has to be said that Margaret Drabble has never disowned the tradition of the social realist novel and has always admitted the powerful influence on her work of the great English novelists of the nineteenth century, George Eliot among them. She has often stated that in her writing she is arguing back, continuing *their* story. But as her novels of the nineties and the new millennium show, only a short-sighted and uninformed critic could maintain old clichés, as that of Drabble being a 'typical' woman novelist of the 1960s and 1970s or that she is a writer clinging to the past. Even a cursory reading of Drabble's 2004 novel *The Red Queen* will show that her work has followed a steady pace of innovation. Following the British tradition of long rambling books (she is a great admirer of that rambling constructor J. C. Powys and his *A Glastonbury Romance*, 1932), she takes the story of the Red Queen of Korea of two centuries ago, whose ghost tells the tale of her past to readers across continents and cultures. Current global issues are discussed as well and an intricate plot is developed, with the very English character of Dr Barbara Halliwell, 'an archetypal middle-class grammar-school girl from Orpington', as its protagonist. In this novel Margaret Drabble appears as a character, too, and is able to tell Dr Halliwell with postmodern irony that novelists 'are not to be trusted. They steal; they borrow; they appropriate. You should never tell them anything, if you want to keep it a secret.'

One, of course, should not underestimate the power of a perfectly balanced syntactic structure: 'I'd rather be at the end of a dying tradition, which I admire, than at the beginning of a tradition which I deplore.' This statement, casually expressed by Drabble in a radio programme when she was starting out as a writer, and later reproduced in Bernard Bergonzi's *The Situation of the Novel* (1970), has done much to pigeonhole her as a writer out of touch with the fresh winds of change buffeting the English novel, and this stamp has been difficult to rub away. Take for instance her authorial interventions, a common feature in her novels since *The Realms of Gold*. Reviewers of her books have frequently viewed these asides as manipulative and irritating ticks in her style, suffocating intrusions by the author, and not as attempts by the writer to bridge the gap that separates her from her readers. It is time for a re-evaluation of Drabble's work as a whole and for taking into consideration its multifaceted nature. Perhaps the publication of her short stories will stimulate new approaches to her writing.

No one should really expect contemporary literature to make positive declarations of intention or to have an unquenchable faith in humankind. And Margaret Drabble's stories do not offer such things either. Many stories in this collection, however, contain their own epiphanic moments, taking bold steps into the future and searching for inner light, and that makes them appropriate for any attempt to find meaningful narratives for our time. Furthermore, and perhaps at the most intimate level, there is a pure and simple pleasure to be found in reading these survivalist, questioning, belligerently intense short stories.

José Francisco Fernández
University of Almería, Spain

Note on the Texts

The stories collected here are arranged chronologically according to their dates of publication. Some of them, however, may offer a variation as to their dates of composition. 'A Pyrrhic Victory' was probably the first story that Margaret Drabble wrote, when she was a student at Cambridge University in the late 1950s, but it was not until she was an established writer that it was finally published, in the magazine *Nova* in 1968. 'Stepping Westward' was written on commission for the Wordsworth Society in 1994. In actual fact, however, Drabble read it aloud at the annual meeting of this association in the Lake District at Grasmere, but it was not published until the year 2000 in the Massachusetts literary magazine *The Long Story*. In this volume, therefore, it appears as the last of the stories Margaret Drabble has published so far.

Other stories were kept for a time in a drawer for different reasons. 'The Caves of God', for example, was not destined for the *Time Out* anthology; Drabble wrote it for a book about 'secrets' which was never published. She rescued it when Nicholas Royle asked her for a story for his collection.

Two fragments from two of her novels, not included here, were published as short fiction in magazines: 'The Dying Year', an excerpt from *The Radiant Way*, was published in *Harper's* magazine in July 1987, and 'The Dinner Party', taken from *A Natural Curiosity*, appeared in *Harper's* in

September 1989. 'Les Liaisons Dangereuses', Drabble's first published short text, appeared in *Punch* in October 1964.

The details of publication of the stories are as follows:

'Hassan's Tower', *Winter's Tales* 12, A. D. Maclean (ed.), London: Macmillan; New York: St Martin's; *Nova*, June 1966; Los Angeles: Sylvester and Orphanos, 1980.

'A Voyage to Cythera', *Mademoiselle*, December 1967.

'Faithful Lovers' (published in an early version as 'The Reunion'), *Winter's Tales* 14, K. Crossley-Holland (ed.), London: Macmillan; New York: St Martin's, 1968; *The Saturday Evening Post*, 6 April 1968.

'A Pyrrhic Victory', *Nova*, July 1968.

'Crossing the Alps', *Penguin Modern Stories*, Volume 3, J. Burnley (ed.), Harmondsworth: Penguin, 1969; *Mademoiselle*, February 1971.

'The Gifts of War', *Winter's Tales* 16, A. D. Maclean (ed.), London: Macmillan, 1970; New York: St Martin's, 1971; *Women and Fiction: Short Stories By and About Women*, S. Cahill (ed.), New York: New American Library, 1975.

'A Success Story', *Spare Rib* 2, 1972; *Ms.*, December 1974; *Fine Lines: The Best of Ms. Fiction*, R. Sullivan (ed.), New York: Scribner's, 1981.

'A Day in the Life of a Smiling Woman', *Cosmopolitan*, October 1973; *In the Looking Glass: Twenty-One Modern Short Stories by Women*, N. Dean and M. Stark (eds.), New York: Putnam, 1977.

'Homework', *Cosmopolitan*, November 1975; *The Ontario Review* 7, Fall–Winter 1977–8.

'The Merry Widow', *Woman's Journal*, September 1989.

'The Dower House at Kellynch: A Somerset Romance', *Persuasions* 15, 1993.

'The Caves of God', *Neonlit: Time Out Book of New Writing*, Volume 2, N. Royle (ed.), London: Quartet, 1999.

'Stepping Westward: A Topographical Tale', *The Long Story* 18, 2000.

A Day in the Life of a Smiling Woman

I

Hassan's Tower

'If,' she said, 'I could be sure they were free, then I would eat them.' 'They must be free,' he said, 'when you look at the price of the drink.' 'But supposing, just supposing,' she said, 'they turned out to be as ludicrously expensive as the drink? If you can pay twelve shillings for one gin and tonic, just think what you might have to pay for those.' He was silenced, for he too had been thinking this thought, though unwilling to admit it to her, unwilling to display before her the full extent of his mercenary fear; and he was annoyed with her for voicing it, for in her such thoughts were merely niceties, whereas to him they were daily bread. He stared glumly at the little squares of toast, with their sadly appetizing decorations of sardine, shrimp and olive, and wondered how much, in the fantastic and unreal financial system which he had entered, they could possibly cost. What, he wondered, was the absolute ceiling for each of those squares? Five shillings? Ludicrous, ludicrous, but alas surely not impossible? Seven and six? Now seven and six was truly impossible. By no stretch even of the Moroccan five-star imagination could they possibly cost seven and six each. So if she were to eat them all (and be assured that she would eat them all, if any, her appetites being as it now appeared insatiable), that would cost him over three pounds. But what was three pounds, after all, amongst friends? Or between bride and bridegroom, rather? Nothing, it would

3

appear. To his continuing amazement, even he thought that it was nothing. Although, of course, so much too much for the article. And then, of course, there was the chance, the probability, that they might be free, thrown in, as it were, with the shocking price of the gins. It would be a shame to leave them, if they were free. But then again, if they weren't free, and she ate them, and then set off towards the lift and the hotel bedroom on the assumption of non-payment, what would happen then? Would the barman in his foolish fez nip deftly out from behind his bar and pursue him? Or would the cost be added, discreetly, within the price of sundries on their anyway colossal hotel bill? Really, he was caught by inexperience between two brands of meanness: he hated to leave them if they were free, and he hated equally to eat them if they cost more than they ought. And he was moreover irritated by her luxurious, gratuitous hesitations: what had he married her for, but to decide about such things?

He reached out and took one, then pushed the little plate over to her. She took one, to his annoyance, independently, almost absent-mindedly, showing no gratitude for his decisive action, her face blank as though her mind had left his trifling crisis far behind. As indeed, when she spoke, he found that she had.

'I do so wish,' she said, in her quietly strident, heavily over-inflected tones, 'that you wouldn't get in such a panic when people try to sell you things. I mean, that man in that souk place this afternoon. There was no need to get so worked up about it, surely?'

'What do you mean, worked up?'

'Well, there was no need to shout at him, was there?'

'I didn't shout,' he said. 'I hardly raised my voice. And anyway, if you don't shout, they go on pestering.'

'You should ignore them,' she said.

'How can I ignore them, when they're hanging on to my coat sleeve?'

'Well then,' she said, changing her tack, 'why don't you just laugh? That's what other people do, they just laugh.'

'How do you know they laugh?'

'Because I see them. That French couple we saw in Marrakesh, with all those children pestering them, they were just laughing.'

'I don't find it funny,' he said. 'I wish they'd just leave me alone, so I could look at things in peace.'

'They don't mean any harm,' she said. 'They're just trying it on.'

'Well, I wish they wouldn't try it on me.'

'What you would like,' she said, 'is a country without any people in it. With just places. And hotels.'

'Nonsense,' he said. 'I don't mind people, I just wish they'd stop trying to sell me things I don't want. I just want to be left alone.'

'I find them all quite amusing,' she said, with a determined little lift of her chin: and he hated her for saying it, because he knew they didn't amuse her at all. On the contrary, they scared the life out of her, all these foreign jugglers and mountebanks, these silent hooded robed men, and the only reason she did not like him to shout at them was that she was afraid he would provoke some reciprocal violence or offence. She wanted him to laugh in order to placate them: she was so nervous that if he left her to herself she would buy their horrible objects, their ill-stitched toy camels, their horrid little woolly caps, their rings set with fake, crude-faceted stones. And yet, if he were to buy them, she would despise him for it, as she would have despised him had he left, through fear or ignorance, the shrimps and the olives. It was just like her, to accuse him of her own fears; yet there had been a time, surely, when they might have in some way shared their alarms, and a time not so far distant at that. Even during their long and grinding engagement there had been moments of unison, moments when he could sneer at her family and she could mock at his with some forgiveness, but in the last two weeks, since their wedding, their antagonism, so basic, so predictable, had found time to flower and blossom, and their honeymoon had been little more than a deliberate cultivation of its ominous growth. He had hoped that in leaving England they would have left behind some of their more evident differences, differences that should be of no importance in a foreign setting, but instead they had found themselves steadily isolated in a world of true British conflict, where his ways and hers had become monstrously exaggerated, as though they were on show, a true British couple, for all of Morocco to observe. Things which he had been able to tolerate in her at home, and which he had seen merely as part of her background, now seemed part of the girl herself: and similarly, in himself, he could feel his own defects magnified beyond all proportion, his behaviour distorted by foreign pressures into a mockery of itself. He began to see some reason for leaving sex until the honeymoon, for at least its problems would have diverted him from other more gloomy forebodings. It was a mistake to come to Morocco, but where else could they have gone, in their position, with so much money, and in so cold a month?

It was the money, truly, that created the worst of their problems, and it was Morocco that cast so nasty a shade upon the money. He knew quite well that were he not earning what he himself daily considered to be a truly astonishingly high salary, he would never have dared to marry a girl with so much money of her own, because of what people might say: and thus between them, she with a small inherited fortune, and he with money earned by the sweat of his brow writing idle articles for a paper, they were really rather well off. And the subject of their finances was an endless source of bitterness. Both suffered from guilt, but hers was inherited, his acquired: when he attacked her for hers, he could not but see how much more guilty he himself was, for he had had a choice. It was no defence to say that he had not sought the money but the job itself, for there were certainly less lucrative branches of journalism than the one into which he had, however respectably and innocently, drifted. He must have wanted it, just as he had wanted her, although, like the money, she had so many connotations which he despised. But in England the money had at least seemed necessary as well as wickedly desirable: all her friends had it, all his friends, being clever, were beginning to acquire it, and in fact he sometimes found himself wondering how his own parents had so dismally failed to have it. Here in Morocco, however, things were very different. To begin with, every penny they spent was pure unnecessity (although he had hopes of recovering a little on the tax by writing a judicious article). Nobody saw them spending it, and the conditions of expense he found sickening in the extreme. He had not bargained for such poverty and squalor, and the rift between rich and poor, between hotel and medina, made his head split in efforts of comprehension. As a student, years ago, he had travelled in a different style, and almost as far afield as this: he had been to Tangier, with a few pounds in his pocket, suffering from appalling stomach disorders, hunger, filth and painful blisters, and he had sat in dirty cafés with seedy expatriates, staring at the glamour of more elegant tourists, and desiring their beds and their meals, and yet at the same time confident that he was happy, and that they were not capable of seeing, as he had seen, the city rising white in the morning out of the sea, in the odourless distance, and all

7

the more beautiful for the cramped and stinking night. In those days, he had been permitted to see, and because he now could not see, was it not logical to suppose that the money had ruined his vision?

The truth was that perhaps in those old days he had been able to pretend that he too was poor, as these Arabs were poor, and he had seen that their life was possible. He had not winced at the sight of their homes, and nobody had thought it worthwhile to pester him with toy camels and fake rubies. But now, on this painful honeymoon, every time he went out of the hotel a boy at the door would leap jabbering at him, jabbering about his shoes, and could he clean the gentleman's shoes, and please could he clean the gentleman's shoes, and he could speak English, for listen, he could sing the songs of the Beatles. He lay there in wait, this boy, and every time Kenneth ventured through the great revolving doors – and they even swung the doors for him, they wouldn't allow him the pleasure of revolving his own exit – this wretched, grinning, monkey-faced, hardly human creature would pounce on him. He was unbelievably servile, and yet at the same time increasingly brazen: when Kenneth had declined for the tenth time to have his shoes cleaned, the boy had pointed out the fact that his shoes needed cleaning, and that they were a disgrace to any respectable, hotel-dwelling tourist. And Kenneth, gazing at his own feet, could not but admit that his shoes were dirty, as they usually were, for he disliked cleaning them, he disliked the smell of polish, he disliked getting his hands dirty. And yet he could not let this hatefully leering, intimately derisive child do them, for it was not in him to stand while another pair of hands dirtied themselves for money on his behalf. So that each time he entered or departed from the hotel, the boy at the door would chant some little jingle in French about the English miser with muddy shoes, and Chloe would stiffen coldly by his side.

He looked at her now, as she sat there, sipping her gin, and eating idly the pricy small squares: her face, as ever, was plain in repose, a little blank and grim, and the fatigue of sightseeing let the coarse dullness of her skin show through her make-up. He was continually amazed by how plain she really was, how featureless, for when he had first known her she had seemed to him beautiful, exotic and obviously to be admired: now, knowing her better, he could see that it was animation only that lent her a certain feverish grace. The grace was real enough, but more rarely bestowed him. When still, she was nothing, and her face, which had once dazzled and frightened him, now merely touched him. One day, months ago, at the beginning of their engagement, she had shown him in a moment of confidence a photograph of herself as a schoolgirl, and the sight of her stolid, blank, fat face peering miserably at the camera from amongst her smaller-featured, more evidently acceptable schoolfriends, had filled him with despair, for she appeared to him for the first time as pathetic, and if there was anything he hated it was the onslaughts of pathos. But by then it was too late, and he was no more able to refuse the temptations of pity than he had been able, earlier, to refuse those of an envious admiration. More and more, as his first clear impressions of her dissolved into a confusing blur of complications, he found himself harking back to what others had said of her, as though their estimate of her value must be more just, as though it could not be possible that he should have married such a woman through a sense of obligation. Others found her beautiful, so beautiful she must be, and it was his fault only if he had ceased to see it.

When she had finished the gin, and all but one of the little squares (he could not even to himself call them canapés, so deeply did the word offend his sense of style, but then there was no word in his background for such an object, for in his background such objects did not exist, so what was one to call them but canapés?) she leant back in her chair, letting her headsquare fall to the ground, and not even acknowledging it when a hovering uniformed boy handed it back to her. She looked tired, the gin had affected her; she had a weak head. He was not surprised when she said, 'Let's have dinner here in the hotel tonight, I haven't the strength to go out again. Let's have dinner in their panoramic restaurant, shall we?'

And he agreed, relieved that he would not have to pass once more that day the grinning familiar boot boy, and they went up to their room and changed, and then they went up to the vast glassy restaurant on the top floor, and looked out over the city as they silently ate, and she complained about her steak, and he got annoyed when the head waiter came and wrenched him from his orange, saying that he would prepare it, as though a man could not peel his own orange (and in fact he disliked peeling oranges, almost as much as he disliked cleaning his own shoes, he disliked the juice in his fingernails, and the pith that he was obliged through laziness to devour) and she got annoyed with him for getting annoyed with the head waiter, and they silently left the restaurant and went silently to bed, disturbed only by the uncontrollable whine of the air-conditioning, which neither of them had been able to subdue. In Marrakesh, oranges had hung upon the trees by the roadside, and thudded warmly from time to time at their feet, and the walls and buildings had been orange too, and beautiful against the distant icy snows of the Atlas mountains, where lions walk, but not beautiful to him, and they had quarrelled there, quarrelled bitterly, because they could not find the Bahia Palace, and because he would not take, not trusting any, a guide, and because they had both been frightened of the mobbing children.

In the morning they went to Rabat. They did not particularly want to go to Rabat, but it was necessary to go somewhere, and they had heard that Rabat was worth a visit. When they got there, they did not know what to see, so they looked at the tediously modern-looking palace, and wondered at the vast numbers of local sightseers, until they bought a paper and discovered, though imperfectly, that there was some day of national holiday in progress. They sat in a French café, and looked at the paper, and wondered where to have lunch, and he thought once more that money, instead of enlarging prospects, confined them and made choice pointless. There seemed to be an expensive enough restaurant called after something called the Tower of Hassan, so they went and had lunch there and he was foolishly taken in yet again by the charm of the idea of eating horrible semolina, which remained horrible however cooked, and then they wondered what to do next, and she said, 'Well, let's go and see Hassan's tower.'

'Do you really want to go and see Hassan's tower?' he asked irritably. 'You know what it'll be like, just some crumbly great incomprehensible lump of brickwork, crawling with guides and postcard sellers and pick-pockets. And on a festival too. It'll be even more horrid than usual.'

'It might be nice,' she said, 'you never know, it might be nice.' Though he could see that she took his point, and that she too quailed.

'It won't be nice,' he said, 'and anyway we'll never find it.'

'It must be on the map,' she said, and produced from her handbag the little chart which the hotel had given her, on which all the streets were misnamed, and which was so badly drawn that it was impossible to follow. And it was not on the map.

'Oh Lord,' she said, 'if we just drive around a little we're sure to see it. I mean to say, it must be important, or it wouldn't have restaurants named after it.'

'That's what you said about the Bahia Palace,' he said.

'But this is different,' she said. 'It's a tower. It must, well, it must kind of stick up. One ought to be able to see it over the top of things.'

'What do you expect me to do, then?' he asked. 'Just get in the car and drive around until I see something that might be the Tower of Hassan? Eh?'

This, it turned out, was just what she did expect, so, with a suspension of disbelief, of much the same order as when he would embark, at home, so continually to drive through the London rush hour, he got into the car and they started to drive around looking for a tower. Driving was hazardous, because he had not grasped the principle that those making right-hand turns have the right of way, and consequently his estimate of the Moroccan character could not but be lowered by his experiences at junctions. However, somewhat to his surprise, they did very shortly locate something that could only be the tower after which their restaurant had been named, and so they parked the car and got out to look at it. It was, as he had foretold, incomprehensible: a square red block, decorated in some system which they did not understand, and baffling in its solid lack of beauty.

'Well,' she said, after they had stared at it in silence for some time from the safety of the road, 'I suppose it must be very old.'

'It looks old,' he conceded.

'There must be a good view from the top,' she ventured. 'Look, there are people on top.'

And there were, indeed, people on top.

'We could go up,' was the next thing she said.

'What?' he exclaimed, with a violence that was only half assumed. 'What? All the way up that thing? And I bet there isn't even a lift. I'm not climbing all the way up there just to get my pocket picked. And I bet it'd cost us a fortune even to get in.'

She did not answer, but wandered slowly forward onto the short scrubby turf of the surrounding open space. He followed her, watching her movements with a grudging pleasure: she was wearing a navy wool skirt and jersey, and in the bright light they had a heavy absorbent matt dull warmth that curiously suited her skin. On the turf, she stopped, without turning to him, and said, 'I should like to go up.'

'Nonsense,' he said, but he followed her to the foot of the tower, nonetheless. He knew that she had made her mind up, and he was too alarmed by the country to let her go alone, and also ashamed that she, though afraid, had the bravado to continue. It annoyed him to know that although she was wholly impelled by timidity, her actions would belie her motives: she would climb the tower, though trembling in every limb through fear of rape, whereas he, alone, and afraid only for his pocket and his sensibilities, would probably not venture.

There was no lift, and no doorkeeper or entrance fee either; access was free. She stepped first out of the sunlight and into the gloom of the doorway: there was just a broad, square, mounting path, without steps.

'Come on,' she said.

'It'll be a long way,' he said, 'and probably smelly.'

'I don't mind the smells,' she said. 'If you wait for me here, I'll go up by myself. I want to see what it's like.'

'There won't be anything to see,' he said, but he started to follow her just the same, being genuinely unable to let her go alone; and moreover, having got so far, there was something irresistible about the idea of ascent. So, with a sense of humiliating risk, he began to climb. They had made several turns of the tower, and had already risen a good few yards above ground level, before he became nervously aware that none of the other people either ascending or descending were tourists: they were all Arabs, and there was not a guide book in sight. It was worse than he had expected. He closed his hand tightly in his pocket over his passport and his wad of traveller's cheques, and wondered whether he should draw Chloe's attention to the situation, but she was a yard or two ahead of him, walking slowly and evenly, and not apparently suffering from the breathlessness that threatened him. So, not wishing to make himself conspicuous by calling out in his foreign tongue, he was obliged to follow. None of the Arabs so far, it was fair to say, seemed to be paying him much attention, and nobody had so much as offered him a packet of postcards, so he relaxed a little, as much as the rigour of climbing would allow, and concentrated on watching the glimpses of gradually increasing panorama through the arrow slits on each side of the wall. He wondered if there might, after all, be a view from the top. There were certainly enough people coming and going, and they must be coming and going for something, he assumed: they all seemed to be in a happy holiday mood. He began, gradually, to feel pleased that there had been no lift, no rich man's way up, no European approach. His pleasure was marred at one point by sudden panic, as he heard above and ahead of him a great deal of high-pitched screaming: he looked anxiously for Chloe, but she was out of sight, round the next bend, and he started to run up the absurdly high incline after her when the source of the screaming hurled itself harmlessly down the tower, and proved to be nothing but a group of very small children, who had climbed to the top simply in order to run breathlessly and hilariously down. Down they rushed, banging into people as they came, losing their footing, falling, rolling, scrambling up again, to be met by amused indulgence from the ascending adults. The men shook their heads and smiled, the women laughed behind their veils. It was clearly a well-established pastime, such usage of Hassan's tower, and welcomed in the dearth of parks, fairs and playgrounds.

When he reached the top, the sudden glare of the sun dazzled him, and he could not at first see Chloe. She was standing at one corner of the wide square block, gazing out over the estuary towards the sea: the view was, as she had foreseen, breathtaking. In silence they stared at it, and he thought that it was very beautiful but somehow depressing because totally, totally unimportant, and pointless in a way that beautiful landscapes somehow are, and yet there was Chloe staring at it in exaggerated affected passion as though it mattered, as though it meant something, staring in fact as he had stared at early-morning Tangier ten years ago, and after a moment or two he could stand the sight of her rapture no longer, and he went and sat down on one of the stone parapets, his knees weak from the climb, his breath short, and his spirits unbelievably low from some dreadful bleak sightless premonition of middle age. And as he sat there, at first seeing nothing, his eyes gradually began to take in the other people on top of the tower, who were, in their own way, astonishing enough as a view. The whole of the top of the tower was covered with people: small children were crawling about, mothers were feeding babies, young men were holding the hands of girls and indeed the hands of other young men, boys were sitting on the very edge and dangling their feet into space, and old women who would need a day to recover from the climb were lying back in the sun, for all the world as though they were grandmothers on a beach in England. And a beach in England was what the scene most of all resembled: he saw there the very groups and attitudes that he had seen years ago as a child at Mablethorpe, and as he gazed he felt growing within him a sense of extraordinary familiarity that was in its own way a kind of illumination, for he saw all these foreign people keenly lit with a visionary gleam of meaning, as startling and as breathtaking in its own way as Tangier had once been. He saw these people, quite suddenly, for what they were, for people, for nothing but or other than people; their clothes filled out with bodies, their faces took on expression, their relations became dazzlingly clear, as though the details of their strangeness had dropped away, as though the terms of common humanity (always before credited in principle, but never before perceived) had become facts before his eyes. It was as though he had for a few moments seen through the smoky blur of fear that convinces people that foreigners are all alike, and had focused beyond it upon the true features and distinctions of separate life: there they stood, all of them, alive and separate as people on a London street, brothers and sisters, cousins, the maiden aunt with the two small children, the pretty fast girl with nylons under her long gown and pale green lace veil, the fat woman with her many operations, the student with his Arabic Dostoyevsky. Even their garments, hitherto indistinguishably strange, took upon themselves distinctions. And with the vision, a sense of overwhelming relief settled heavily upon him, for he had been afraid, afraid for years that he had come to the end of the new and the interesting in life: he sat there and watched, watched all those people being, and took pleasure in their being, and as he watched he suddenly became aware that one of the young men at whom he was staring was none other than the boot boy from the hotel. And he stared at the boot boy, and the boot boy stared at him, and their eyes met with recognition, but with no acknowledgement: neither of them smiled, neither of them moved, for there was no way, in that place, of expressing their mutual knowledge. And he saw, too, that the boot boy was with a small woman who was his mother, and that by one hand he held his little brother, who was wearing a best red shiny holiday shirt, and who was about four years old.

(1966)

2

A Voyage to Cythera

Beloved,
lost to begin with, never greeted,
I do not know what tones most please you.
No more when the future's wave hangs poised is it you
I try to discern there. All the greatest
images in me, far-off experienced landscape,
towers and towns and bridges and unsuspected
turns of the way,
and the power of those lands once intertwined
with the life of the gods:
mount up within me to mean
you, who forever elude.

Oh, you are the gardens . . .[1]

Rainer Maria Rilke

There are some people who cannot get onto a train without imagining that they are about to voyage into the significant unknown; as though the notion of movement were inseparably connected with the notion of discovery, as though each displacement of the body were a displacement of the soul. Helen was so much this way, and with so little lasting justification, that she was continually surprising herself by the

---

1 From an untitled poem. Used by permission.

intensity of her expectation; she could get excited by the prospect of any journey longer than thirty miles, and the thought of travel to the Continent was enough to reduce her to a state of feverish anticipation. The mere mention of the names of certain places would make her tremble, and she was addicted to railway stations, air terminals, ports, motorways, travel brochures, and all other points and emblems of departure. A phrase in a novel could make her feel weak with desire, and when once at the Gare de l'Est in Paris she saw a train with Budapest written on it, she felt her skin tighten and her hair stand on end. Her most erotic dreams were not of men but of places; she would dream of piazzas and marble fountains, of mountains and terraces with great lumps of baroque statuary, of great buildings abandoned in green fields, and she would wake from these dreams cold with the sweat of fading passion. There was a certain angle of road that never failed to affect her, whenever she approached it: a rising angle, with a bare empty curve breasting infinity, the blue-sky space of infinity. She always felt that the sea might lie beyond such rising nothingness, and sometimes it was the sea, but more often it was the Caledonian Market or a row of Hampstead houses; though whatever it was was somehow irrelevant, for it was that tense moment of expectation before revelation that she so much cherished.

Once she talked of this preoccupation of hers to a much-travelled old man, and he said that she felt this way because whenever she went to a new place she hoped to fall in love. He had been the same, he said; restless, expectant; and she knew that he was telling the truth, for his life illustrated his explanation. 'When I was young,' he said, 'I thought there was a woman waiting for me in every railway compartment, on every airplane, in every hotel. How can one not think this? One thinks the plane will crash, and that one will die, and that one must die in the arms of the woman in the next seat. Isn't that so?'

And she had, in a way, thought that it was so, though the truth was that she herself would never fall in love in any of these temporary places, for she could not speak to strangers. Though that in itself proved nothing, for she supposed that nevertheless she might one day do so, and that it might be for this one moment of sudden communication that she so persistently sought. People spoke to her, from time to time, but always the wrong people, always the motherly women and the fatherly men and the dull irrepressible youths. Her own kind did not speak to her, nor she to them. She travelled once overnight from Milan, alone in a compartment with a girl who was reading the same book she herself was reading; a book both of them might have been proud to acknowledge and not a word did they exchange. Another time, in a crowded train from Edinburgh, she sat opposite a woman who started to weep as the train left the station; she wept silently and effortlessly for hours, great tears rolling down her white cheeks into the neck of her emerald-green sweater, and at York Helen offered her a cigarette, and she declined it, and ceased weeping. On another occasion a man kissed her in a corridor as they drew into Oxford; she liked him, he was a lovely man, but he was drunk and she turned away her face and turned up the collar of her coat.

And yet despite these wasted opportunities she continued to expect. Truly, she thought to herself, as she got onto the London train at Reading Station late one cold night, truly, it is a proof of madness that the prospect of this journey should not appal. It is cold, the train is half an hour late, I am hungry; this is the kind of situation about which I hear my friends most tirelessly and tiresomely complain. And yet I am looking forward to it. I shall sit here in the dark and the cold, with nothing to watch but the reflection of my own face in the cold pane, and I shall not care. As soon as the train moves, I shall sit back, and feel it move with me, and feel that I am moving, although I know quite well that all I am doing is going back home again to an empty flat. There will be rain and steam on the glass of this window by my face, and I shall look at it, and that will be all. What a hardened case I am, that such dull mileage should recall those other landscapes, those snowy precipices, those sunny plains, those fields of corn, those gritty swaying breakfasts in the pale light of transient Switzerland or angel-watched Marseilles. I am a child, I like to rock and dream, I dream as if I were in a cradle.

And she shut her eyes, waiting for the whistle and the metallic connections of machinery; so with her eyes shut she did not see the man come into the compartment, and could never know for certain whether he had seen her, whether he had joined her because he had wanted to join her. All she knew was that when she opened her eyes, aware of the intrusion, aware of the draught from the opened door, he was already there, putting his overcoat up on the rack, arranging his books and papers on the seat next to him, settling himself in the empty compartment as far away from her as he could, on the corridor side, diagonally opposite, where she could not fail to watch him. She turned her fur collar up defensively against her face, and arranged her legs more tidily together, and opened her book upon her knee, disclaiming all threat of human contact, coldly repelling any acknowledgement of her presence, and all the time she watched him discreetly through her half-shut eyes. Because the truth was that not since she was seventeen, more years ago than she cared to think, had she sat on a train so near to such a man. When she was seventeen she had sat in a compartment with an actor, on the late-night train to Brighton, and he had talked to her all the way, and amused her by imitating Laurence Olivier for her and other famous men whom she did not recognize, and when they had parted on the station he had kissed her soft and girlish and impressionable cheek, and murmured, 'Bless you, bless you,' as though he had a right to bless. She had subsequently followed his unremarkable career, catching sight of his name in the *Radio Times*, admiring him once on the television, glimpsing him as he passed on the cinema screen; she felt quietly possessive about him, quietly amused by her sense of intimacy with one who must so long ago have forgotten her, and who would hardly now recognize her from what she then had been. Sometimes she wondered idly whether her preoccupation with journeys might not date from this experi-ence; but chronologically this was not so, for her preoccupation had long preceded it. She had been this way since childhood, when she had shrunk and trembled at the sight of the huge pistons, when she had stopped her ears in delighted terror as she heard the roar of the approaching seaside train.

This man, this night, did not look as though he wished to amuse her with imitations of Laurence Olivier. He looked preoccupied. In fact, the more she watched him, the more she realized that he was almost grotesquely preoccupied. He was restless; he could not sit still: he kept picking up one book from this pile, then another, then turning over the pages of his *New Statesman*, then staring out into the corridor and onto the dark platform. At first she thought that he might be waiting for someone to come, half expecting somebody to join him, but she decided that this was not so, for she could perceive no augmenting of his anxiety as the time drew on, no sudden start when the loudspeaker apologized for the delay and said that the train would leave in two minutes; nor did his nervousness seem to be directed towards the door and the platform, as it would have been had he been waiting. She recalled that she herself had once developed a dreadful pain in the neck from sitting with her neck to the window through which she knew that she might glimpse the first sign of a long-awaited arrival. But this man's nervousness was as it were diffused, rather than directed; it attached itself to nothing and to everything. She could not take her eyes off him, and not only because of the nakedness of his condition, which in another might have appeared merely ludicrous; indeed, embarrassment would have turned away her eyes, had it not been for the extreme elegance of his gestures, and the lovely angles into which each struggle against immobility brought him. There was the way he had of clutching his eyebrows with one wide-spanned long nicotine-fingered hand that filled her with an intense delight; the hand covered the eyes, bringing to him no doubt an illusion of concealment, but she could see beneath it the anxious movement of the lips, trembling with some expression that she could not catch, with speech or smiling or perhaps with a sigh. And as he made this gesture, each time, he tossed his head slightly backward, and then again forward, so that his long hair fell tenderly over his fingers. It was the colour of his hair that moved her most. It was a colour that she had always liked, but she had never before seen it adorning such vexed, haggard and experienced features: for it was a dark gold, the colour of health and innocence. It was a dark golden yellow, and it was streaked with grey. It was soft hair, and it fell gently.

When the train moved off, he flung himself back into his corner, and shut his eyes, with an appearance of resolution, as though his own restlessness had finally begun to irritate him: as though he had decided to sit still. Helen looked out of the window by her face, into the lights and darkness of the disappearing town. In one piece of glass she could see the reflection of his face, and she watched it, quite confidently aware that he would not be able to keep his eyes shut, and after a few minutes he was leaning forward in his seat once more, his elbows on his knees, staring at the ground. Then, even as she watched, she saw a thought strike him: she saw the conception of the idea, she saw him reach into his pocket and take out a pack of cigarettes and a box of matches, and abstract a cigarette, and light it, all with the dreamy movements of a habitual smoker, and yet with a kind of surprise, for the truth was, as she could so clearly see, that he had even in his abstraction forgotten the possibility of such a trivial solace. As he drew on the cigarette she could see his relief, his gratitude towards his own recollection. The smoke consoled him, and she who had rarely in her life smoked a cigarette could feel in her the nature of the consolation: for she herself, when tormented by love, had found comfort in the repetition of small and necessary acts, in washing cups and emptying bins and fastening her stockings and remembering that it was time to have a meal. It seemed clear to her that it was love that was tormenting him: she knew those painful symptoms of disease.

And indeed, ten minutes later, when the ash of his last activity lay scattered all over the floor and all over his trousers, he stood up and got a packet of letters out of his overcoat pocket, and began to read them. He could not more clearly have indicated his malady if he had turned to her and told her what was in his mind. She watched the reflection of his face as he read, ashamed now to watch him directly, though she knew that he could not know that she so keenly watched him, that she was so expert in the intimate language of his state. She felt that she could tell everything from the way he handled those letters: he was still rapt in the first five minutes of love, that brief and indefinite breathless pause before familiarity, affection, disillusion, rot, decay. The number of letters in his hands supported her divination, as well as the quality of his attention; there were five of them, only five, and the paper of them was new, although they were crumbling wearily at the folds from overuse. She felt such pangs, in his presence, of she knew not what: of envy, of regret, of desire. At his age, with those greying strands and those profound wrinkles, he must surely know the folly of his obsession, and the inevitable tragic close before him; and she found such a wilful confrontation of pain almost unbearably moving. She herself, enduring daily the painful death of such an attitude, the chilly destination of such deliberately romantic embarkations, could hardly prevent the tears from rising to her eyes; and in fact, they rose, warm in the cold skin of her lids, making her nose prick and her eyes ache, yet warm, coming from within her, and chilling only at the touch of the outside air. Absurd, she said to herself, absurd: absurd to weep. His image turned into a blur, and it was like the image of time itself, human, lovely, perishing, intent.

When he had read and reread his letters, he stood up again, and got a pen out of his coat pocket, and tore a piece of paper off a block of typing paper, and started to write. He wrote slowly, after the first three words, hesitantly, as though what he was saying was of no interest, as though all the interest lay in the way of saying it. She wondered what he was, who he was, what his woman was, and jealously whether she were worth such care. He took a quarter of an hour to write his letter, and when he had finished it he had covered only half a page. She wondered whether he would have an envelope, and saw that he had; it was a brown business envelope. He folded his letter up and put it in the envelope, and then sealed it up. She waited for him to write the address, but he did not write the address: he sat there looking down at the small brown oblong, and as he looked at it she became in some indefinable way aware that he had become aware of her own presence, that he was at last considering her, in some significant way. Later, she wondered how this shadowy and delicate intimation could ever have reached her – for reach her it did, and she was one of those who believe that no intimations are too delicate to exist – and she concluded that it could only have been a sudden stillness on his part, a sudden fading of restlessness, as he returned from whatever other place he had been in to contemplate her in her proximity. She felt his attention: she endured it, for five minutes at least, before he spoke.

She was pretending to read when he spoke to her. He said to her, 'I wonder, I wonder if you would do something for me?' and she looked up and met his eyes, and found that he was smiling at her with a most peculiar mixture of diffidence and vanity: he was truly nervous at the prospect of speaking to her, and those five silent minutes were a measure of his nervousness, and yet at the same time he had taken the measure of her curiosity and helpless attraction: she knew that he knew that she would like to be addressed. And his tone enchanted her, for it was her own tone: a tone of cool, anxious, irresistible appeal. She knew that he too did not speak often to strangers.

'It depends what it is,' she said, smiling back at him with his own smile.

'It's a very simple thing,' he said, 'not at all incriminating. Or at least, not for you.'

'It would be, then, for you?' she said.

'Of course it would,' he said. 'That's why I'm making the effort of asking you to do it.'

'What is it?' she said.

'I wondered if you would address this envelope for me,' he said.

'Well, yes,' she said. 'I don't see any harm in that. I'd do that for you.'

'I thought you would do it,' he said. 'If I hadn't thought that you would, I wouldn't have asked you. I wouldn't have liked it if you had said no.'

'I might ask you what it was about me that made you think I would say yes,' she said, 'but such a question might embarrass you.'

'Oh,' he said, 'oh, no,' rising to his feet and crossing to her with the envelope, 'oh, no, I don't mind answering, it was because of that book you're reading, and the kind of shoes you're wearing, and the way your hair is. I liked that book when I read it.'

And then he sat down by her, and handed her the envelope, and said, 'Look, I'll write it down for you and you can copy it. It's hard to hear when people dictate things, isn't it?'

And he wrote the name and address on another piece of his block of paper. He wrote:

Mrs H. Smithson,
24 Victoria Place,
London NW1

And Helen dutifully copied it out, on the brown envelope, then handed it back to him.

'I hope,' she said, 'that my handwriting is sufficiently unlike yours.'

'I was just thinking,' he said, 'that after all it's rather similar. But dissimilar enough.'

Then he said no more, but he remained sitting by her. She would in a way have preferred him to move, because where he now was she could not really see him, either overtly or covertly. And she had nothing to say to him: for she could hardly have said, I was right about you, I guessed right. He said nothing to her, for a while: he got a wallet from his pocket, and took out a sheet of fourpenny stamps, and tore one off, licked it, and stuck it on. She liked watching his hands, and the way they moved. Then, still holding the letter, he said to her, 'Where do you live?'

She must have recoiled slightly from the question, because immediately he followed it up with, 'Only, I was meaning, from the point of view of postmarks.'

'Oh,' she said. 'I see. Yes. I live in SW7. You want me to post it, do you?'

'Would you mind posting it?' he asked.

'No, I would post it for you,' she said.

'You take my point very quickly,' he said, then, with some difficulty, looking downward and away from her, hardly able to bring himself to thank her more formally.

'I've had to make such points before myself,' she said.

'I thought, somehow, that you would not mind about such things,' he said.

'You wouldn't have asked me if you'd thought I minded. Tell me, do you really trust me to remember to post it?'

'Of course I do,' he said. 'One wouldn't not post a stranger's letter.'

And this was so exactly the truth that it silenced her, and they said no more to each other until the train drew into Paddington; and as they walked together off the platform, he said, 'Thank you, and goodbye.'

And she said, 'Goodbye,' and she carried the letter in her hand all the way home, and dropped it into the letterbox on her block. Then she went down the basement steps to her dark flat, and she knew that the name and the address, written there in her own writing, so strangely, were imprinted upon her memory forever.

And indeed, over the next month, she sometimes fancied that she thought of little else. She knew that this was not the truth, that it was merely a fancy, because of course she did think of other things: of her job, of her friends, of her mother, of what to buy for supper, of whether she wanted to go to the cinema on Wednesday night. But she did not think of these other things in the mad, romantic, obsessive way that she thought of Mrs H. Smithson, and the nameless man, and the whole curious, affecting incident: in a sense she resented the incident, because it did so much to vindicate her own crazy expectancy, her foolish faith in revelation. She knew, in her better, saner self, that such faith was foolish, and she suspected that such partial hints of its validity were a delusion, a temptation, and that if she heeded them she would be disabled forever, and disqualified from real life, as Odysseus would have been by the Sirens. And yet at the same time she knew, in her other self, that it was that man she was thinking about, however unreasonably. She looked for him as she walked along the streets of London, and she could not convince herself that it was not for him that she was looking. She speculated about the identity and appearance of Mrs Smithson, and supplied her endlessly with Christian names, until she remembered that the H. might well have stood for her husband's name, not hers. She speculated about the deceived husband. Although most of her own friends were married and had children, she still found it hard to acknowledge that Mrs Smithson might well be a woman of her own generation, for the prefix Mrs invariably supplied her with a maternal image, the image of her own mother: and she would realize from time to time, with a start, that the women that she thought of as mothers were in fact grandmothers, and that the young girls she saw pushing prams on Saturday mornings and quarrelling with vigorous toddlers on buses were not in fact elder sisters but mothers. Mrs Smithson, Mrs Smithson. She could not give form to a Mrs Smithson.

It was in the week before Christmas that she decided to go and have a look at Mrs Smithson. The idea occurred to her at lunchtime one day, in the middle of a lunchtime business Christmas party. She stood there, drinking too much and not getting enough to eat, defeated as ever by the problems of buffet technique, and as she listened to a very nice man whom she had known and liked for several years describe to her the felicities of his new central heating, she suddenly decided to go and look at Mrs Smithson. After all, she said to herself, what could be more harmless, what more undetectable? All I need to do is to knock on her door and ask, say, for Alice. And then I would know. I don't know what I would know, but I would know it. And she smiled at the man, and allowed her glass to be once more filled, and then told him politely all about some other friends of hers whose central heating had entirely ruined all their antique furniture, and split all the antique panelling of their rather priceless house. And as she talked, she was already in her heart on her way to Mrs Smithson's, already surrendering to the lure of that fraught, romantic, painful world, which seemed to call her, to call her continually from the endurable sorrows of daily existence to some possible other country of the passions, a country where she felt she would recognize, though strange to it, the scenery and landmarks. She thought often of this place, as of some place perpetually existing, and yet concealed: and she could describe it to herself only in terms of myth or allegory, unsatisfactory terms, she felt, and perniciously implanted in her by her classical education. It was a place other than the real world, or what she felt to be the real world, and it was both more beautiful and more valid, though valid in itself only: and it could be entered not at will, but intermittently, by accident, and yet always with some sense of temptation and surrender. Some people, she could see, passed most of their lives in its confines, and governed by its laws only, like that old man, himself a poet, who had first defined for her the nature of her expectations. There were enough of such people in the world to keep alive before her the possibility of a permanent, irreversible entry through those mysteriously inscribed and classic gates: a poet, a drunken Frenchman, a girl she had known who said one day: 'I will go to Baghdad,' and went. They crossed her path, these people, or their names came to her, garlanded with wreaths of that unfamiliar foliage: Yves was seen in Marseilles carrying a lobster, Esther was seen in a bookshop in New York wearing a fur coat and with diamonds in her hair, Esther was in Marrakesh, living in one room with an Arab, Yves had gone to Ireland and started a lobster farm. Oh, messages from a foreign country, oh, disquieting glimpses of brightness. Helen gulped down the remains of her fourth glass of wine, and looked at her watch, which said that it was five past three; and said to the central-heating man that she must go.

She walked to Victoria Place, pausing dazed at traffic lights, stumbling at each irregularity of the pavement, running her hand idly along grimy railings. It was cold, but she could not feel the cold: her face was burning. She knew her way because she had looked Victoria Place up a month ago, the day after she had posted the letter, in her *A to Z Guide to London*: she remembered the moment when she had done so, because she had pretended to herself that she was doing no such thing, and her mind had not known what her hands and eyes were doing. But her mind now remembered what it had then refused to acknowledge, and she took herself there as though entranced, the trance persisting long after the effects of walking had dispelled the effects of so much drink on so empty a stomach. I must be mad, she said to herself more than once: I must be mad. And at the very end of the journey she began, very slightly, to lose her nerve: she thought that she would not dare to knock upon the door, she thought that perhaps after all only insignificant disaffection could await her, that she could do no more than dispel what had already in its own way been perfection.

But there was no need to knock at the door. Victoria Place, when she reached it, was a short main street of tall terraced houses, either newly recovered or so smart that they had never lapsed: the number 24 was brightly illuminated, shining brightly forth into the gathering darkness. She walked slowly towards it, realizing that she would be able to see whatever there was to see without knocking: realizing that fate had connived with her curiosity by providing a bus stop directly outside the house, so that she could stand there and wait without fear of detection. She took her place at the bus stop, and stood there for a moment before she gathered her courage to turn around, and then she turned. The lights were on in the two lower floors, and she could see straight into the basement, a room which most closely resembled in shape the one where she herself lived. The room seemed at first sight to be full of people, and there was so much activity that it took some time to sort them out. There were two women, and four children; no, five children, for there was a baby sitting in a corner on a blue rug. The larger children were putting up a Christmas tree, and one of the women was laying the table for tea, while the other, her back to the window, one elbow on the mantelpiece, appeared to be reading aloud a passage from a book. It was a large, bright room, with a green carpet, and white walls, and red-painted wooden furniture; even the table was painted red. A children's room.

It shone, it glittered. A mobile of golden fishes hung from the ceiling, and the carpet was strewn with coloured glass and tinsel decorations for the tree. The plates on the table were blue and white, and the silver knives caught the light; on the mantelpiece stood two many-faceted cut glasses and an open bottle of wine. Two of the children had fair hair, and the other three were dark: and the woman laying the table had red hair, a huge coil of dark red hair from which whole heavy locks escaped, dragging down the back of her neck, falling against her face at each movement, and she moved endlessly, restlessly, vigorously, taking buns out of a bag, slicing bread, pouring blackcurrant juice into beakers, turning to listen to the other woman, and suddenly laughing, throwing back her head with a kind of violence and laughing: and the other woman at the mantelpiece laughed too, her thin shoulders shaking, and the children, irritated by their mother's laughter, flung themselves at her, clinging angrily onto her knees, shouting, until the red-haired woman tried to silence them with slices of bread and butter, which were rejected and flung around the floor: so she followed them up with the iced buns, tossing them round and yet talking, all the time talking, to the other woman and not to the children, intent upon some point, some anecdote too precious to lose, and the children chewed at the buns while she scooped up the torn pieces of bread and bestowed them all, with a smile of such lovely passing affection, upon the baby, a smile so tender and amused and solicitous that Helen, overseeing it, felt her heart stand still.

And as she stood there, out there in the cold, and watched, she felt herself stiffen slowly into the breathlessness of attention: because it seemed to her that she had been given, freely, a vision of something so beautiful that its relevance could not be measured. The hints and arrows that had led her here took on the mysterious significance of fate itself: she felt that everything was joined and drawn together, that all things were part of some pattern of which she caught by sheer chance a sudden hopeful sense: and that those two women, and their children, and the man on the train, and the bright and radiant uncurtained room, an island in the surrounding darkness, were symbols to her of things too vague to name, of happiness, of hope, of brightness, warmth and celebration. She gazed into that room, where emotion lay, like water unimaginably profound. The red-haired woman was kneeling now, on the green carpet, rubbing with a corner of the tea towel at a buttery mark on the carpet, and at the same time looking up and listening, with an expression upon her face in which vexation with the children, carelessness of her own vexation and a kind of soft rapt delight in the other woman's company were inextricably confused; and the other woman had turned slightly, so that Helen from the window could see her face, and she was twisting in her hands a length of red-and-silver tinsel, idly pulling shreds from it as she spoke. And Helen thought of all the other dark cold rooms of London and the world, of loneliness, of the blue chilly flickerings of television sets, of sad children, silenced mothers and unmarried girls; and she wondered if so much delight were truly gathered up and concentrated into one place, or whether these windows were not windows through which she viewed the real huge spacious anterior lovely world. And it seemed possible to see them so, because she did not know that house, nor those women, nor their names, nor the name of the man who had led her there: the poetry of inspiration being to a certain extent, as she knew, the poetry of ignorance, and the connections between symbols a destructive folly to draw. She did not even know which of these women was Mrs Smithson, whom she had come to see, for if one woman had laid the table, the other cleared it, equally at home. She knew nothing, and could therefore believe everything, drawing faith from such a vision, as she had drawn faith from unfamiliar cities: drawing faith from the passionate vision of intimacy, where intimacy itself failed her; as Wordsworth turned from his life to his keener recollections, and Yeats to lions and towers and hawks.

By the time that one of the children was sent to draw the curtains, she was stiff and white with cold. She turned away, as the child, a small girl with straight dark hair and a face suddenly grave with the weight of her task, began to struggle with the heavy floor-length hangings, shutting inch by inch away from her the coloured angles of refracted light, the Christmas tree, the airy fishes, the verdant green, the small angelic innocent faces, the shining spheres of glass and those two young worn women: and as she turned she felt the first snowflakes of the year settle softly on her skin, and looking up, she saw the dim blue sky full of snow. She glanced back, to see if the child had seen it, but the curtains were already drawn, and she saw nothing but her own image, pale in the glass. So she started to walk down the street, away from the house, away from the bus stop, but before she had taken ten steps a car drew up, just by her side, a slow yard from her, and there was the man from the train, sitting there and looking at her. She paused, and he opened the door, and sitting there still he said to her, 'I don't know what to say to you, you look so fragile that a word might hurt you.' And she smiled at him, a slow dazed smile, knowing that as he for her, so she for him was some mysterious apparition, some faintly gleaming memorable image:

and she turned away, and walked down the street away from him into the snowy darkness, and he got out of his car and went into the house.

She walked carefully, because her ankles were so brittle from the cold that she feared that if she stumbled, they would snap.

(1967)

3

Faithful Lovers

There must have been a moment at which she decided to go down the street and around the corner and into the café. For at one point she was walking quite idly, quite innocently, with no recollection or association in her head but the dimmest shadow of long-past knowledge, and within ten yards she had made up her mind that she would go and have her lunch in that place where they had had lunch together once a fortnight or so over that long and lovely year. It was the kind of place where nobody either of them knew would ever see them. At the same time, it was not impossibly inconvenient, not so very far from Holborn, where they both had good reason to be from time to time. They had felt safe there – as safe as they could ever feel – yet at the same time aware that they had not allowed themselves to be driven into grotesque precautions.

And now, after so long, after three years, she found herself there – and at lunchtime, too. She was hungry. There is nothing more to it than that, she said to herself. I happened to be near, and the fact that I wanted my lunch reminded me of this place, and moreover, there is nowhere else possible within a five-minute walk. She had done enough walking, she thought – from the Old Street tube station to the place where they had made her new tooth. She ran her tongue over the new front tooth, reassuringly, and was slightly ashamed

by the immense relief that she felt at being once more present-
able, no longer disfigured by that humiliating gap. She had
always made much of caring little for her beauty, and was
always disturbed by the accidents that brought her face to
face with her own vanity – by the inconvenient pimple, by
the unperceived smudge on the cheek, by the heavy cold. And
that lost tooth had been something of a test case ever since
she had had it knocked out, while still a child at school. Her
dentist had made her the most elaborate and delicate bridge
then, but the night before last she had fallen after a party
and broken it. She had rung up her dentist in the morning,
and he had promised her a temporary bridge to last her until
he could make her a new one. When he had told her the name
of the place she should go to collect the bridge, she had
noticed in herself a small flicker of recollection. He went on
explaining to her, obliging yet irritable. 'You've got that then,
Mrs Harvey? Eighty-two St Luke's Street? You go to Old
Street Station, then turn right . . .' And he had explained to
her that she should express her gratitude to the man at the
laboratory, in view of the shortness of the notice. And she
had duly expressed it to the man when, ten minutes ago, he
handed her the tooth.

Then she had come out and walked along this street. And
as she paused at the café door, she knew that she had been
thinking of him and of that other year all this time, that she
could not very well have avoided the thought of him, among
so much familiar scenery. There they had sat in the car and
kissed, and endlessly discussed the impossibility of their kissing; there they had stood by that lamp-post, transfixed, unable
to move. The pavement seemed still to bear the marks of their
feet. And yet it was all so long ago, so thoroughly slaughtered
and decayed. It was two years since she had cared, more than
two years since she had suffered.

She was content, she was occupied, she had got her tooth back, everything was under control. And in a way it made her almost happy to be back in this place, to find how thoroughly dead it all was. She saw no ghosts of him here; for a year after their parting she had seen him on every street corner, in every passing car, in shapes of heads and hands and forms of movement, but now he was nowhere any more, not even here. For as long as she had imagined that she saw him, she had imagined that he had remembered. Those false ghosts had been in some way the projected shadows of his love; but now she knew that surely they had both forgotten.

She pushed open the door and went in. It looked the same. She went to the side of the room that they had always favoured, away from the door and the window, and sat at the corner table, where they had always sat when they could, with her back to the door. She sat there and looked down at the red-veined Formica tabletop, with its cluster of sugar bowl, salt and pepper, mustard and ketchup, and an ashtray. Then she looked up at the dark yellow ceiling, with its curiously useless trelliswork hung with plastic lemons and bananas, and then at the wall, papered in a strange, delicate, dirty flowered print. On the wall hung the only thing that was different. It was a calendar, a gift from the garage, and the picture showed an Alpine hut in snowy mountains, for all that the month was May. In their day the calendar had been one donated by a fruit-juice firm, and they had seen it through three seasons; she recalled the anguish with which she had seen its leaves turn, more relentless even than those leaves falling so ominously from real trees, and she recalled that at the time of their parting the calendar showed an appalling photograph of an autumn evening in a country garden, with an old couple sitting by their ivy-covered doorway.

They had both been merciless deliverers of ultimatums, the

one upon the other. And she had selected in her own soul the month, and the day of that month, and had said, 'Look, on the twenty-third, that's it, and I mean it this time.' She wondered if he had known that this time it was for real. Because he had taken her at her word. It was the first time that she had not relented, nor he persisted; each other time they had parted forever, a telephone call had been enough to reunite them; each time she had left him, she had sat by the telephone biting her nails and waiting for it to ring. But this time it did not ring.

The menu, when it was brought to her, had not altered much. Though she never knew why she bothered to read menus, for she always ate the same lunch – a cheese omelette and chips. So she ordered her meal, and then sat back to wait. Usually, whenever left alone in a public place, she would read, and through habit she propped a book up against the sugar bowl and opened it. But she did not look at the words. Nor was she dwelling entirely upon the past, for a certain pleasurable anxiety about that evening's show was stealing most of her attention, and she found herself wondering whether she had adequately prepared her piece about interior decoration for the discussion programme she'd been asked to appear on, and whether David Rathbone, the producer, would offer to drive her home, and whether her hair would look all right. And most of all, she wondered if she ought to wear her grey skirt. She was not at all sure that it was not just a little bit too tight. If it wasn't, then it was perfect, for it was the kind of thing that she always looked marvellous in. Then she said to herself: The very fact that I'm *worrying* about it must mean that it must be too tight after all, or the thought of its being too tight wouldn't have crossed my mind, would it? And then she saw him.

What was really most shocking about it was the way they

noticed each other simultaneously, without a chance of turning away or in any way managing the shock. Their eyes met, and they both jerked, beyond hope of dissimulation.

'Oh, God,' he said, after a second, and he stood there looking at her.

And she felt at such a loss, sitting there with her book propped up against the sugar bowl, and her head full of thoughts of skirts and false teeth, that she said, hurriedly, throwing away what might after all have been really quite a moment, 'Oh, Lord, oh, well, since you're there, do sit down.' And she moved up the wooden bench, closing up her book with a snap, averting her eyes, confused, unable to look.

And he sat down by her, and then said quite suddenly and intimately, as though perfectly at home with her after so many years of silence, 'Oh, Lord, my darling Viola, what a dreadful, dreadful surprise. I don't think I shall ever recover.'

'Oh, I don't know, Kenneth,' she said, as though she too had discovered exactly where she was. 'One gets over these things quite quickly. I feel better already, don't you?'

'Why, yes, I suppose I do,' he said. 'I feel better now that I'm sitting down. I thought I was going to faint, standing there and looking at you. Didn't you feel some sort of slight tremor?'

'It's hard to tell,' she said, 'when one's sitting down. It isn't a fair test. Even of tremors.'

'No,' he said, 'no.'

Then they were silent for a moment or two, and then she said, very precisely and carefully, offering her first generous signal of intended retreat, 'I suppose that what *is* odd, really, is that we haven't come across one another before.'

'Have you ever been back here before this?' he asked.

'No, never,' she said. 'Have you?'

'Yes,' he said. 'Yes, I have. And if you had been back, you might have seen me. I looked for you.'

'You're lying,' she said quickly, elated, looking at him for the first time since he had sat down by her, and then looking away again quickly, horrified by the dangerous proximity of his head.

'No, I'm not,' he said. 'I came here, and I looked for you. I was sure that you would come.'

'It's a safe lie,' she said, 'like all your lies. A lie I could never catch you out in. Unless I really had been here, looking for you, and simply hadn't wanted to admit it.'

'But,' he said with conviction, 'you weren't here at all. I came, but you didn't. You were faithless, weren't you, my darling?'

'Faithless?'

'You forgot me quicker than I forgot you, didn't you? How long did you remember me?'

'Oh, how can one say?' she said. 'After all, there are degrees of remembrance.'

'Tell me,' he said. 'What harm can it do to tell me now?'

She moved a little on the seat, away from him, but settling at the same time into a more comfortable pose of confidence, because she had been waiting for years to tell him.

'I suffered quite horribly,' she said. 'Really quite horribly. That's what you want to hear, isn't it?'

'Of course it is,' he said.

'Oh, I really did,' she said. 'I can't tell you. I cried all the time, for weeks. For at least a month. And whenever the phone rang, I started, I jumped, like a fool, as though I'd been shot. It was pathetic, it was ludicrous. Each time I answered and it wasn't you I would stand there listening, and they would go on talking, and sometimes I would say yes or no, as I waited for them to ring off. And when they did ring off I would sit down and I would cry. Is that what you want me to say?'

'I want to hear it,' he said, 'but it can't, it can't be true.'

'It's as true as that you came to this place to look for me,' she said.

'I did come,' he said.

'And I did weep,' she said.

'Did you ever try to ring me?' he asked then, unable to resist.

'No!' she said with some pride. 'No, not once. I'd said I wouldn't, and I didn't.'

'I rang you, once,' he said.

'You didn't,' she said, and became aware at that instant that her knees under the table were trembling.

'I did,' he said. 'It was just over a year ago, and we'd just got back from a party – about three in the morning it was – and I rang you.'

'Oh, God,' she said, 'oh, God. It's true, it's not a lie, because I remember it! Oliver went to answer it, and he came back saying no one was there. But I immediately thought of you. Oh, my darling, I can't tell you how I've had to stop myself from ringing you, how I've sat there by the phone and lifted the receiver and dialled the beginning of your number, and then stopped. Wasn't that good of me?'

'Oh,' he said, 'if you knew how I'd wanted you to ring.'

'I did write to you once,' she said. 'But I couldn't bring myself to post it. But I'll tell you what I did do: I typed out an envelope to you, and I put one of those circulars from that absurd poetry club of mine into it, and I sent it off to you, because I thought that at least it might create in you a passing thought of me. And I liked the thought of something from my house reaching your house. Though perhaps she threw it away before it even got to you.'

'I remember it,' he said. 'I did think of you. But I didn't think you sent it, because the postmark was Croydon.'

'Oh,' she said, weakly. 'You got it. Oh, Lord, how alarmingly faithful we have both been.'

'Did you expect us not to be? We swore that we would be. Oh, look, my darling, here's your lunch. Are you still eating cheese omelettes every day? Now, that really *is* what I call alarming consistency. And I haven't even ordered. What about some moussaka? I always used to like that; it was always rather nice, in its own disgusting way. One moussaka, please.'

After her first mouthful, she put down her fork and said reflectively, 'From my point of view, at least, the whole business was quite unnecessary. What I mean is, Oliver hadn't the faintest suspicion. Which, considering how ludicrously careless we were, is quite astonishing. We could have gone on forever, and he'd never have known. He was far too preoccupied with his own affairs.'

'You know,' he said, 'all those continual threats of separation, of ending it – that was really corrupt. I feel bad about it now, looking back. Don't you?'

'How do you mean, bad about it?' she said.

'I feel we ought to have been able to do better than that. Though, come to think of it, it was you that did nearly all the threatening. Every time I saw you, you said it was for the last time. Every time. And I must have seen you six days in every week for over a year. You can't have meant it each time.'

'I did mean it,' she said. 'Every time I said it. I must have meant it, because I finally did it, didn't I?'

'You mean *we* did it,' he said. 'You couldn't have done it without my help. If I'd rung you, if I'd written to you, it would have started all over again.'

'Do you really think so?' she said, sadly, without malice, without recrimination. 'Yes, I suppose you might be right. It takes two to part, just as it takes two to love.'

'It was corrupt,' he said, 'to make ourselves live under that perpetual threat.'

'Yes,' she said, 'but remember how lovely it was, how horribly lovely, each time that one relented. Each time one said, "I'll never see you again . . . all right, I'll meet you tomorrow in the usual place at half-past one." It was lovely.'

'Lovely, but wicked,' he said.

'Oh, that sensation,' she said, 'that sensation of defeat. That was so lovely, every time, every time you touched me, every time I saw you. And I felt so sure, so entirely sure that what you felt was what I felt. Lord, we were so alike. And to think that when I first knew you I couldn't think of anything to say to you at all; I thought you came from another world, that we had nothing in common at all, nothing except, well, except you know what; I feel it would be dangerous even to mention it, even now. Oh, darling, what a disaster, our being so alike.'

'I liked it, though,' he said. 'I liked breaking up together. Better than having it done to one, better than doing it.'

'Yes, but more seriously incurable,' she said. And silence threatening to fall once more, she said quickly, 'Anyway, tell me what you're doing round here. I mean to say, one has to have some reason for coming to a place like this.'

'I told you,' he said. 'I was looking for you.'

'You *are* a liar,' she said, smiling, amazed that even here she could allow herself to be amused; indeed, could not prevent herself from smiling.

'What are you doing here, then?'

'Oh, I had a perfectly good reason,' she said. 'You know that false front tooth? Well, yesterday morning I broke it, and I've got to do a programme on television tonight, so I went to my dentist and he made me a temporary new bridge, and I had to come round here to the laboratory to pick it up.'

'Have you got it in?'

'Look,' she said, and turned to face him, smiling, lifting her upper lip.

'Well, that's convincing enough, I guess,' he said.

'You still haven't told me what you're doing here,' she said. 'I bet you haven't got as good a reason as me. Mine is entirely convincing, don't you think? I mean, where else could I have had lunch? I think my reason clears me entirely of suspicion of any kind, don't you?'

'Any suspicion of sentiment?'

'That's what I meant.'

He thought for a moment, and then said, 'I had to call on a man about my income tax. Look, here's his address.' And he got an envelope out of his pocket and showed her.

'Ah,' she said.

'I came here on purpose,' he said. 'To think of you. I could have had lunch at lots of places between London Wall and here.'

'You didn't come here because of me; you came here because it's the only place you could think of,' she said.

'It comes to the same thing,' he said.

'No, it doesn't,' she said firmly. She felt creeping upon her the familiar illusion of control, created as always before by a concentration upon trivialities; she reflected that their conversations had always followed the patterns of their times in bed, and that these idle points of contention were like those frivolous, delaying gestures in which she would turn aside, in which he would lie still and stare at the ceiling, not daring to touch her, thus merely deferring the inevitable. Thinking this, and able to live only in the deferment, for now there was no inevitable outcome that she could see, she said, eating her last chip, 'And how are your children?'

'They're fine,' he said, 'fine. Saul started grammar school. We were pleased about that. What about yours?'

'Oh, they're all right, too. I've had some dreadful nights with Laura recently. I must say I thought I was through with all that – I mean, the child's five now – but she says she can't sleep and has these dreadful nightmares, so she's been in my bed every night for the last fortnight. It's wearing me out. Then in the morning she just laughs. She doesn't kick; it's just that I can't sleep with anyone else in the bed.'

'What does Oliver say?' he asked, and she said, without thinking, 'Oh, I don't sleep with Oliver any more,' and wondered as she said it how she could have made such a mistake, and wondered how to get out of it. But fortunately at that instant his moussaka arrived, making it unnecessary to pursue the subject. Though once it had become unnecessary, she regretted the subject's disappearance; she thought of saying what was the truth itself – that she had slept with nobody since she had slept with him, that for three years she had slept alone, and that she was quite prepared to sleep alone forever. But she was not entirely sure that he would want to hear it, and she knew that such a remark, once made, could never be retracted, so she said nothing.

'It looks all right,' he said, staring at the moussaka. He took a mouthful and chewed it, and then he put his fork down and said, 'Oh, Lord, oh, Lord, what a Proustian experience. I can't believe it. I can't believe that I'm sitting here with you. It tastes of you, this stuff. Oh, God, it reminds me of you. You look so beautiful, you look so lovely, my darling. Oh, God, I loved you so much. Do you believe me – that I really loved you?'

'I haven't slept with anyone,' she said, 'since I last slept with you.'

'Oh, darling,' he said. And she could feel herself fainting and sighing away, drifting downward on that fatefully descending, eddying spiral, like Paolo and Francesca in hell, helpless, the mutually entwined drifting fall of all true lovers, unresisting. It was as though three years of solitude had been nothing but a pause, nothing but a long breath before this final acknowledgement of nature, damnation and destiny. She turned towards him and said, 'Oh, my darling, I love you. What can I do? I love you.' And he, with the same breath, said, 'I love you, I all the time love you, I want you,' and they kissed there, their faces already so close that they hardly had to move.

Like many romantics, they habitually connived with fate by remembering the names of restaurants and the streets they had once walked along as lovers. Those who forget forget, he said to her later, and those who do not forget will meet again.

(1968)

4

A Pyrrhic Victory

They grew more and more tired as they climbed the hill, and although it was past two o'clock and there was no reason why they should not sit down and eat their lunch, nobody suggested stopping. Anne was exhausted: her head ached with the sun, she felt both sick and hungry, and her feet and ankles were bleeding, scratched by the coarse, twiggy plants that bordered the narrow track. A cloud of insects followed her, biting from time to time. The passion flower that Charles had picked for her so gallantly from the tree outside the grocer's was wilting in her hot hand: she remembered how Hannah had laughed at him for picking it, and she discreetly let it drop. Charles, who was following, trod on it without noticing. He was carrying the lunch, and his hands were full of paper packages, so that every time she stumbled or scrambled up a steep patch she had to manage for herself, although he reached out chivalrously and ineffectually to help her. It made him look silly, to reach out and achieve nothing but a gesture. She wished he would not do it, she needed not to think him silly.

She wanted so much to sit down, and to make the others sit down, but she was afraid to suggest it in case they should laugh at her, or leave her there and go on without her. Once she had admitted she was tired, she would have to give up the climb, in order to preserve an appearance of free-will. She did not want to betray her weakness, and if she spoke, weakness of some kind would be forced upon her: either she would be the first to give in, or she would have to admit how much she needed their company by going on after confessing that she was exhausted. So she said nothing. She went on walking, and hoped that they would at least stop when they reached the top of the hill.

Johnny and Hannah were walking on yards ahead, showing no signs of fatigue: remembering the night before, she wondered how on earth they managed to walk so fast. They had all made themselves very sick on a horrid mixture of Vino Aleatico and Liebfraumilch, a mixture in which the crudity of contrast had struck even her innocent palate, as well as her stomach: she had spent the night leaning over the wash-bowl, trying hard to dissuade Charles from holding her hand, and she had gathered from Hannah that she and Johnny had suffered much the same in their room. And yet here they all were now, striding up hillsides as though they were in the best of health and condition. Did the others find this kind of behaviour natural? Was it only she herself, at seventeen and straight out of school, who reacted with such amazement, with such bewildered admiration? And who was it who had set this ridiculously high standard they were all so sternly reaching for?

She supposed that it must be Johnny. Hannah and Charles both had their lapses from the general level of high, gritty grace, they both had impulses which the other two, and indeed even she herself, in Charles's case, derided: Charles had his flower-plucking, hand-holding tendencies, and Hannah, for example, an occasional excess of literacy in unfamiliar languages, which the others found for some unrevealed but unsurprising reason ludicrous. And as for Anne herself, what was she but an airy mass of loopholes? So full of holes was she that there seemed at times to be no fabric: she had not been able to take anything without some inner protest, not the hitch-hiking by night, nor the allocation of bedrooms, nor the rash expenditure of money, nor the excessive mixing of excessive drink, not this high, insurmountable hill. Her whole self rebelled at everything they did, and yet somehow, with immense effort, she managed to keep her mouth shut and do it.

Her body kept telling her that she could not go on any longer, borne down by sickness, hunger and heat, but she did not listen, though at times she thought that the strain of continuing in all this foreign, unfamiliar landscape would make her simply drop down dead or unconscious in protest. It was an initiation, she knew that, into more than the facts of what she had for the first time done: this emotional state itself would be with her, on and off, forever, this sense that at any moment she would cease to bear it and cease by some stroke of simultaneous dissolution to exist. Throughout her life it would recur, as she would continue to put herself deliberately into situations which were foreign and intolerable, and as she would continue, wearily, without pleasure, but with determination, to tolerate them. These three people here, and the place itself, and the speed, and all those other people and places extending before her, she would accommodate them or die, and sometimes she felt that dying was the easier, the more likely of these alternatives.

It was Johnny, of course, who demanded the speed, who set the standards, who was himself the foreignness she fought against in person. He was the only one who had never exposed himself: he had got in first, he had been playing this wandering game for two whole years before they had met him, he was the real impregnably negative American thing itself. Everything he spoke of, dollars and railroads and bars and baseball, was so strange to her that her mind ached with the effort to contain it, and she knew that she would show white gleaming scars, cracked and seamed for life, after the stretching of this encounter. He had arrived at some point so far from anything she had ever known, he was so perfect an example of what (though she could not distinguish what) he clearly was: and she knew that at the very least she would have to go far enough after him to see, however indistinctly, the true nature of his features, which were at present dim with distance.

But in comparison with herself, the other two seemed to have arrived at that distant place as well. At least they were not left limp and breathless, she saw few traces in them of the battles she fought for every uphill, forward step. From wherever it was that they were, they viewed life with a distrust that was the first thing in them that had impressed her: they treated life as though it were a bad film, constantly on the watch for sentimental patches, for poor acting and cardboard sets. She had once foolishly remarked on the charm of a certain view: 'Oh look,' she had said, and all they had replied was, 'Look at what?' Their severity and their scorn appealed to her, for she too wanted above all not to be tricked, not to be taken in, not to admire as sap and foliage what was truly canvas, and that was why she kept on walking, with her dirty shirt sticking to her back and her skirt to her legs. She did not want to be the one to spoil the moment, to accept prematurely, to scare away that other, better thing that waited for them round the corner, shy, poised and ready to run.

She was almost at her last gasp when they reached the brow of the hill: she was turning over in her mind phrases that she knew she could not, simply could not say – innocent phrases: 'I feel sick'; 'Couldn't we stop and have lunch now?'; words that would not pass her lips no matter what the extremity. And then there they were at the top, and below them, miraculously, lay the sea. The steep slope crumbled away in hurried steps down to the rocks and the cool, profound green of the Mediterranean: she had not thought it was so close. With a sigh of reprieve she began the descent: here, at least, was some reason for stopping, for nobody, not even the strongest, could go on walking now unless, like Christ or the Gadarene Swine, they set out across the sea. She was reminded of those family quarrels about choosing picnic sites, and the relief that would descend when a place had been chosen that was acceptable to all.

She turned round to share her memory with Charles, who indulged her, but the sight of his stiff, effete white face changed her mind. He was a London child, he had doubtless never been on a picnic in his life, his parents were probably expensively and stylishly divorced. How had she got herself here, where she could not even open her mouth without feeling herself quite foolishly exposed?

She had protested enough about coming in the first place: she must have known what a shocking experience it would be. When Johnny had first said, 'Let's go to Elba,' she had had no intention of going, she had foreseen those cracks and scars. The others had refused as well, Hannah because she had to see someone the next morning in Florence, and Charles because he had confused the location of Elba with that of Corsica. And they had, of course, gone, after wasting a good four hours quarrelling on dusty streets corners behind Rome station – they had all known that they would go, from the moment that Johnny had opened his mouth. For who could resist such a prospect? Elba, an island not of imprisonment but of embarkation. With the bottom of the hill a few stony yards away her spirits suddenly rose: here they were, after all, and lunch could not now be far away. She began to feel triumphant that she had got there at all. There is no room for complaints amongst purists, and she was glad that she had survived the trial in silence, as pure outwardly as her stricter companions were doubtless pure within.

At the foot of the cliff there was a little bay, and there they stopped, having reached the impassable edge of the water. As if bowing to necessity, not indulging a weakness, they sat down round a small enclosed rock pool, near the open sea. Hannah slipped off her sandals and put her feet in the water with an intent expression on her face. Anne began to feel more and more of a failure for being hungry, and nobody mentioned eating. They talked, desultorily, about a man whose apartment they had borrowed in Florence. After an age Johnny suddenly said, 'I'm hungry, what the hell are we waiting for?' and immediately put them all in the wrong for not eating. 'I'm hungry too,' she said, but it was too late. 'Why on earth didn't you say so then?' said Charles, and there she was, caught out being complaisant again, caught out waiting for someone else to take the lead. She avoided their eyes, bending down to take off her shoes and she too put her hot feet in the water. It was cool and sharp, and the little scratches began, delicately and pleasurably, to sting. The lunch was at last unpacked: the bread had gone dry, the cheese was sweating in the sun, and the mortadella, which nobody liked anyway, was even coarser and more gristly than usual. Charles had difficulty in opening the sardine tin, and managed to cut himself: she was rather touched when he complained that it hurt, and even Hannah was too exhausted to sneer.

Anne wondered if the sea itself here was full of sardines: she leant against a rock, chewing her final tasteless Italian apple, and staring out across the even water. She felt so much better now that she had eaten, she could see now how beautiful it was, and there was no other word for it: she wanted to exclaim, to cry, to share the beauty of it, the surprise of sitting by the Mediterranean on a hot day in June, the unending surprise of the easy colourful world lying about her. She wanted more than anything to share it, to know by sharing it that it was so, and she remained silent, as the others were. She could not risk it. She was afraid of having missed the point, as though she were to come out of some film and reveal by a careless comment that some final irony and therefore the whole plot itself had eluded her. In the pool at her feet the rock was pink, and the seaweed was of a sun-charged, brilliant green that does not grow above water.

She sat and stared, at the weeds and stones. Hannah had taken off her jersey and was lying curled up with her head on it and her eyes shut. Charles was smoking, staring inland, at nothing. Johnny was folding up bits of wrapping paper from the bread. She felt alone: she let her expression lapse. The sea was swelling into the pond through a cleft, sucking over the encrusted weeds and shells, the whole vast heaving sea pushing an inquisitive finger into the hole before her. There were anemones, and little pink mottled fish lurking near the mottled stone. She thought of the visits she used to make with her family as a child to Scarborough, on the Yorkshire coast, where too there were rock pools, though dark and cold and grey compared with all this lavish colour. What she had liked then had been the waves breaking in great showers of spray on the rocks when the sea was rough: a wild, rough coast, but beautiful, and she would try to get out near those mountains of water, she would try to get wet. And at the age of twelve, caught for the first time in the effort to share and to assert, she had begun to write appalling Swinburnian poems. She remembered them with horror, wondering what they would think, these silent three, if they could ever have seen those scraps of flowery paper, what they would think now if they could read her mind and see imprinted there her flowery emotion for them and for this scene.

Johnny had finished folding up the wrapping paper. He lifted up a stone and put it underneath. She was surprised: it seemed an odd thing for him to do, as though she were to see him shutting gates on farms or wiping his feet on doormats: an action in an alien tradition. He caught her watching him, and looked up and said, 'What shall I do with the sardine tin?'

'I don't know,' she said.

Hannah opened her eyes and sat up at the sound of their voices: she could never stay in one position for long. Charles turned round to face them, and they all sat quietly for a moment. Some seabirds flew overhead, screaming. There was a silence, and Anne could have sworn, she could have staked her life, she could have hazarded her future on what they were and what they were watching and what they had got there with them, for it was authenticity itself, but that was not enough, oh no, not enough for her, she was one of those that had to know.

'Where's the sardine tin?' she said, and when Johnny handed it to her she held it for a moment, and then, as they idly watched, unsuspecting, she dropped it into the pool. It sank at once, and a dark oily smear spread over the surface of the water, pouring upwards from that wrenched metal lump. The fish fled, and the anemones shrank and closed in horror: she felt the three of them too withdraw and wince and shrink from what she had done, she felt with satisfaction the great depth of their shock. Charles even made a sound in protest, and Johnny reached out, too late, an arresting hand. But they said nothing: as she had said nothing, they said nothing. And what she was conscious of, as she sat there calmly smiling, was victory: like Napoleon she had conquered in that action continents, she had conquered Europe, this tideless foreign sea, she had conquered America, all those railroads and all that Bourbon, she had conquered England and that child in a cotton frock.

But of the nature of that victory she was never sure: she had thought to destroy, in one last unnatural effort, her admiration for that gaudy picture postcard set, but even as she sat there amongst the debris, imprisoned, exiled, yet victorious, she wondered whether she had not perhaps left herself, more clearly than ever, but in less painful isolation, with that moment, poised beautifully before the ugliness of its own ruin, poised there before the destruction of sharing and articulation and definition, which was as necessary, as painfully necessary to its existence as water, rocks, and sea, and fish, and faces.

(1968)

5

Crossing the Alps

Our destiny, our being's heart and home,
Is with infinitude, and only there;
With hope it is, hope that can never die,
Effort, and expectation, and desire,
And something evermore about to be.

Wordsworth, *The Prelude*, Book vi, 1.603–7
Cambridge and the Alps

He couldn't believe it at first. So much planning, so much foresight, such elaborate persuasions, such manoeuvres, all to be so idly undone. It wasn't possible: he wouldn't have believed it possible, had he not always, in his heart, expected the worst. But the slow relentless fulfilment of those worst expectations dismayed him unbelievably: as the size of the disaster bore down on him, he protested, he suffered, he moaned inside himself, he knew he could not take it, that he would never cease to resent it.

He knew that it was his own fault. That made it somewhat worse, of course. He should never have washed his hair. Or, at least, he should never have gone to bed with it so wet. It was the price of vanity and idleness. But the price was so high, so wickedly disproportionate to the offence, that he felt he would never trust providence again. Providence had seemed to smile upon them momentarily: but it had been a trick, and how viciously she had withdrawn her favours. If it had happened earlier, he would have taken it better: he would have welcomed disappointment like a familiar friend. But now, after so long, after such trials endured, such unprecedented successes – he moaned and shut his eyes. The irony of it, the irony of it. He almost wished himself dead, and surely would have had he not felt himself to be, anyway, dying.

To begin with, he had deceived himself. He had tried to pretend that it was not happening, that it would not happen. As he stood there waiting for her, waiting for her impossibly awaited arrival, he ignored the symptoms, telling himself that he did not feel so bad, that his throat was merely dry from anxiety, his head ached from the expectation of long-delayed relief, and that with her arrival he would feel quite well again, for she would cure him, miraculously, he would forget such suspicions immediately as soon as she emerged from the station. He watched the exit, nervously, and then looked back at the car. The road shimmered, gently, in the heat. It was so hot: just such a day as they had hoped for. Ridiculous, to feel ill, on such a day. He shivered. Perhaps she would not come: perhaps she had already been overtaken by disaster, perhaps she lay ill in bed or dying, in those places where he could not telephone, perhaps her child was ill, or her sister, perhaps the train had crashed. He looked at his watch. It was due in five minutes. He sneezed. Hay fever, he said to himself: a complaint from which he had never suffered in his life.

Then he began to wonder why he had not gone up to London to collect her. What extraordinarily tortuous process had led them to select such a spot for a rendezvous – as inconvenient for him, almost, as it must be for her? Perhaps she would forget to get off the train and would go hurtling on to Southampton, leaving him standing here forever. She would look for him in Southampton, but he would never find her, they would miss each other, they would never meet again. He

felt for the tickets in his pocket. She had forgotten her passport, perhaps. Incompetent, she was, finally, for all her energy
and hard work and self-sacrifice. She wasted most of it,
through incompetence. In fact, for all the weeks of forethought,
she had probably missed the train. She would be standing in
London still, weeping a little, giving up, ready to go home and
despair, telling herself that she should never have been so
wicked as to try, even so briefly, to escape. Without him there
to force her, she gave up too quickly. He feared her nature.
She lacked pertinacity. She would give up, in the end. She
would remain faithful to her dreadful obligations, but herself
she would give up, him she would give up, if he were not there
to bully and persuade. How could he get at her, as she stood
there at Waterloo Station, weeping a little, not knowing where
to go?

He heard the whistle of the approaching train. He felt
slightly sick, and sneezed again. He had arranged not to go
onto the platform – 'Don't come into the station,' she had said,
'please don't, I'll come and look for you, wait for me. I want
to worry,' she said, 'that you might not be there.' 'You know
I'll be there,' he said. 'Yes, I know, but I want that moment of
anxiety, when I look for you and think you might not be there.'
That moment of anxiety, were she there, she would be enduring now, for the train had stopped, and was emptying its
passengers onto the hot quivering asphalt. He looked away,
but could not, finally, keep his eyes from the exit: sophistica-
tion of torment had its limits, even for him. An elderly woman
came out, with some paper parcels from town, and then a
child, and then there she was, herself, unmistakable, carrying
her suitcase, handing over her ticket, not looking in his direction. Through the barrier, she put down her case, and
disembarrassed, looked up. Their eyes met, across the deserted
car park. She walked towards him, very slowly it seemed, and

he could not move. But when she reached him, he found himself smiling, and said to her, 'I got you here, after all.'

'Are you pleased to see me?' she said, reaching out a hand to touch his arm.

'I was afraid you might forget to come,' he said, and they both laughed: they could as soon have forgotten such an assignation as a certain date for death. But her laughter itself alarmed him: her features trembled in the act, and it alarmed him, he wished that the trembling (so necessary in some ways) could be done with for both of them, he had tried to arrange it so that they might both, for a little while at least, not need to suffer. He opened the car door for her, and said, 'Get in,' hoping that when he had shut her in there, in that confined space, she would feel safer and let go a little. But she sat there, rigid and intent, and as he drove off he started to brace himself – a little wearily, and how he hated himself for his reluctance – to do the inevitable, to ask the right questions, to comfort, to reassure, to appease. It took so long, sometimes: how could he admit his hope that she might this once, in honour of the occasion, cut it out? She had threatened him so often, saying, 'A day will come when you simply won't be able to stand it any more,' and he had denied it, endlessly, faithfully: but he knew she was right, there are limits to anyone's endurance, nobody fails to give in in the end. As she herself had decided, two months before, when she had tried to gas herself and the child. Tried ineffectively, of course: she had repented in time, and he had even seized upon the event, and the publicity of doctors and ambulances, to force her to accept that she must get away for a while from her dreadful sentence, but it had taken two months of hard work to persuade her. 'You're stupid,' he had said to her, shaking her, staring appalled at her blotched and swollen face: 'Stupid. You throw yourself into it so remorselessly, you forget that the only thing you

must do – for yourself, for the child himself – is to survive.'
'Survive for what?' she had said, dully, admitting for the first
time the pointlessness of her sacrifices: for the child was
doomed, he could not anyway survive with any prospect of
a reasonable future. And he had been obliged to voice to her
her own stubborn certainties, to reassert for her her own
tragic persistence: hearing from her the moribund, flat tones
of reason, and from himself the ridiculous, noble, elevated
statements of devotion. They had not come well from him,
he had thought, but in the end she had succumbed and had
leaned against him, as so often before, and had said: 'You,
you know what you are talking about, because what do you
do for me but look after me, but look after me without any
prospects of future, without any satisfaction or hope? I admire
you for it,' she said. 'I love you,' he said. 'It satisfies me, that
I love you, I get enough from it, you don't know what I get,
but it's more than I'd ever hoped for.'

'That, too, I get,' she said: speaking of the child. And she
had picked up again, from where she had put it down, the
usual burden: able, even, with her amazing capacity, to make
him feel wanted, to give him happiness, to make him forget,
as they talked and lay together and pursued their circum-
scribed excursions, the sad terms of their contract. They had
a good time together, in practice: never failing to enjoy one
another's company. He had thought that all they needed for
entire felicity was a few days away together, with light and
air, away from that depressing flat and child, away from her
depressing work, away from his own depressing wife. He
drove carefully along the wide summer road towards Southampton and freedom, and waited for her to start to repent,
so that he could embark on consolation.

But she did not repent. She sat there, and slowly, by his side,
she started to soften. She liked being there, he could tell it

from the way she lit herself a cigarette and began to smile at the passing hedges. She had arrived completely: whatever remorse she had felt about her departure and her elaborate abandoning of the child had already been endured and done with – done with on the train, perhaps, or even before. She had alighted with nothing more than an ordinary nervousness. It was made, he said to himself: a whole week, and the weather, and the journey, and the hotel bedrooms. He reached for her hand, and once more, he sneezed.

'You've got a cold,' she said critically.

'Hay fever,' he said nonchalantly.

'Rubbish, you're not a hay-fever type. It's not something you just get, you know.'

'You'll have to look after me,' he said, little foreseeing how much she would have to do so.

'I brought some pills, of various sorts. I'll cure you.'

'I spoke to your sister last night,' he said, now that conversation had been initiated, willing, even eager, to discuss the outside world and its difficult components.

'What did you do that for?'

'Oh, I don't know. I just wanted to make sure that everything was all right. What a strange woman she is.'

'How do you mean, strange?'

'Oh, I don't know. She takes it so calmly. My going off with you.'

'Well, it's nothing to her, is it?'

'No, I suppose not,' he said, and returned to his driving: remembering as he did so her sister's voice, so uncannily similar, so apparently unmoved by the unfamiliarity of a telephone call from him, so unimpressed by her own sister's joys and sorrows, so unexceptional even in her willingness to conspire with them. He had expected – he did not know what – an air of alarm, of participatory guilt, perhaps even a moment of shared affection for this woman who sat by his side. But he hadn't had it: all he'd had was a distracted, preoccupied, off-hand reassurance that she would do what was expected of her, keep their whereabouts quiet, look after the child and the nurse for the child, and not let that dreadful mother know where they had gone. She hadn't even sounded interested: looking back, he was offended that she hadn't sounded interested. Surely he and his affairs were obsessively interesting? He at least found them so.

On the boat, they did all right. He had by then a sore throat, but she gave him some aspirin and some seasickness pills and they even managed to get some sleep. When they woke up, they had breakfast, as the car had not yet been unloaded, and they looked at the map.

'We must be mad to go so far,' she said, looking at the distances they idly proposed to cross. 'It's quite nice here,' she said, looking out at Le Havre and the blue morning sea.

'We can't stay here, we've got to get off,' he said, for this too he had planned, knowing that any kind of inactivity would breed regrets.

'It might make you ill,' she said, though without conviction: she liked the idea of moving as much as he did. Such static lives they led, at their separate homes.

'I won't be ill,' he said.

But by the evening he was feeling, he had to admit it, like death. They had driven all day, it was true, not allowing themselves much time to rest, and the large car was tiring to drive: it felt heavier as the day wore on, and after nightfall it seemed to require a physical effort to propel it. He went on as long as he could, and she assured him that they had gone far enough to reach Yugoslavia the next day, as they had planned: so they stopped at the next town (always so much farther, the next town, than one thinks it will be) in a country he took to be

Switzerland. The hotel that she selected (he had given up enough, by then, to leave it to her) was large and German, and he revived slightly at the sight of the vast double bed and the thought of a meal: revived further after a couple of glasses of the duty-free whisky they had bought on the boat, and which he had until that point been too nervous to drink. They sat together on the bed, having kicked off their shoes, touching slightly at the shoulder, thinking of the night ahead, which was what they had come for: but when she spoke, smiling softly to soften the blow, encompassing with her infinite knowingness his slight surprise, what she said was, 'You know, darling, I think I ought to ring my sister.'

'Of course, of course,' he said, in his obliging and all-tolerant role. 'Of course, should I go or stay?'

'Stay, stay, of course,' she said, restraining him, and he sat there while she rang England to beg for reassurance. She tried to conceal from him the extent of her suppliance, having been unable to allow him to leave the room in case he suspected worse, and when he heard her speak, he knew (she was right in this) that at least worse was not happening, there were no tears, no moans, no evident regrets. He heard it all, he heard her out, so close that he could touch her – which, when she put down the receiver, he did. She turned to his touch, and her face seemed to respond to his enquiry with the full measure of its possible, indestructible appeal. 'Oh, they're all right,' she said, and laughed. 'Of course they're all right. God knows, a week of it won't kill them, will it?' She looked at him, and her eyes narrowed and fixed on him. 'And if it did,' she added, 'I wouldn't much care. Come on, let's go and eat before everything shuts up.'

So they went down to the restaurant, and sat and stared at the menu: he had always believed himself the equal of any language, at least on the menu level, but German, amazingly, defeated them both. They thought they recognized the word for eggs, and the word for meat, but as she said, lowering her typed list, raising her eyebrows at him: '*What* meat?' Dangerous stuff, meat, she said: not in any way a safe bet. Eggs were better, she advised him: she chose eggs, but he, always rather ashamed of his interest in food (particularly when accompanying her Spartan tastes, for his wife at least in this, if not in other things, was more indulgent), rashly ordered a steak tartare. Neither meal, one would have thought, could have required much preparation, and they had expected to be able to eat it quickly and get to bed; but, alas, it did not arrive for three-quarters of an hour, allowing him time to reflect that he had, quite certainly, a temperature, that his throat was getting worse and worse, and that she, for all her apparent fidelity, must, after so long an affair, be sick of the sight of him, and was not waiting, as he fondly imagined, with an anxiety equal to his own, to feel his arms around her yet again. Characteristically, the last of these fears, being the only one from which any amusement could be extracted, was the only one that he voiced, and they filled the time quite agreeably by discussing whether or not she still loved him, whether he even admitted that she had ever loved him, what she had loved him for, and when she had started (supposing that she had) to do so; they embarked upon the theme of how kind they would have been to each other if circumstances had given them half a chance (a safe topic, for the alignment of circumstances against them was so formidable that they would never be expected to take on commitments more serious than those of the heart), and as they were explaining to one another their infinite resources the food, at last, arrived. The highly artistic arrangement of the steak tartare explained in part, he said, the delay: a good five minutes at least it would have taken, she replied, to lay out those enticing little piles of pepper and salt and onion, but what of the remaining forty? She winced at the sight of his raw egg.

When they finally got to bed, he was tired and aching in every bone. He collapsed and lay flat. She got in after him, having spent more time than usual (she was the least vain of women, punitively careless of her appearance) in combing her hair, and washing her face: and he knew what she was going to say.

'You're too tired,' she said, getting in beside him, sitting high up on the round scroll of pillow, looking down at his limp form. 'You're too tired, my darling, go to sleep, shall I read to you? I bought a good book for my holiday, look, I'll read you a bit of it, shall I?' And she produced her book: it was about old people and kinship patterns in a perishing London working-class community. 'It's very interesting,' she said, smiling at him, mocking him slightly, 'really very interesting. I'll read you a page or two and you'll be asleep in no time, even in this ridiculous bed.'

She gestured, with one bare foot, at the eiderdown arrangement under which they were expected to sleep. 'Poor *darling*,' she said, with sudden conviction: and he knew as suddenly (such frail knowledge and how dare one ever presume or act upon it?) that it was herself she was pitying, that she was missing him there, cold and away from him, high and perched up, not daring to flatten herself to his level, fearing to expose and make party to the situation both himself and herself. The certainty that she was missing him made him feel so much better that he grabbed at her gesturing ankle, and she let it rest upon his chest, then gradually pulled herself towards him, and then it was all right: though afterwards, as she lay there breathless, soaked in his quite unnaturally cold sweat, she did murmur, 'Oh, God, I'm so sorry, I shouldn't have let you do it, I meant not to let you, it's probably killed you and then I'll be so sorry, but don't you see, I couldn't help it? I couldn't help it, I couldn't help it, you see.'

'Why should you *try* to help it, when I want you so badly?' he said, trying to wipe his face on the eiderdown, wishing there were some more conventional sheet available: but his heart was pounding, his chest creaking, his throat ravaged, and he recognized that, of course, though one would still do it if one had to die instantly afterwards, one would neverthe-less, instantly afterwards, much prefer not to die.

'Regretting it?' she asked him, as he arranged her for sleep: but even as he protested, he knew that in another year he would have admitted it, he would have merely answered, 'Yes.' And who knows, she then might merely have held on to him a little tighter, or possibly, not impossibly, laughed. He had faith in such developments. One had to have faith; without it, what should one do? They, those two, he and she, they had nothing else.

When he woke in the morning, he could hardly open his eyes, and he could not speak. She was awake first: she always was, the rigorous routine of home never allowed her to sleep late. For too many years now she had risen early to get the child off to the Centre, the beds made and herself off to work. He lay there with his eyes shut, listening to her brush her teeth. He felt so dreadful that he half wished they were back in London, back in the comfortable, boring, frustrating grind of the average week, smiling at one another in the canteen, shar-ing a cigarette at the end of a corridor when they met by chance, parting at the doorway as they returned to their respec-tive obligations. At least they had known where they were, and a certain melancholy gaiety had become so natural to them that he knew they had both enjoyed it: they had enjoyed their meetings and their partings, their resentments, their odd outcries of despair. He felt too ill to deal with the notion of a holiday. He groaned and turned restlessly, and she said to him, 'How are you, darling? Wishing us safe back at home?' He moaned again. 'If we weren't here,' she said, approaching him – as he was dimly aware through the shut hot red lids of his eyes – 'if we were back there, you'd just be looking in at the office to make sure I was there. And I would be. I always am.'

'I feel ill,' he said, 'and it can't be after ten, can it?'

'I've been up for hours,' she said, 'I couldn't sleep.'

Then she brought him a glass of water and he drank it, but still felt no better: she suggested, feebly and unpersuasively, that he stay in bed for the day, but fully acknowledged his horror when he looked frantically round the hotel room and said, 'What, *here*?' She even smiled.

So he pulled himself together and they got up and paid their bill and left. Salzburg for lunch, they had idly arranged, two weeks ago, sitting over their conspiratorial lunch, looking at an infinitesimal map of Europe that he had on the back of one of his Common Market notebooks: and they got there for lunch, but it wasn't an early one. They had eggs, again, again defeated by the menu, and wondered what to do with him. He felt in a way better, but rather ominously better: he felt lightheaded and slightly unreal, and his limbs felt vague and weightless. He poured beer over his throat as a kind of penance, and she suddenly said, very clearly and distinctly, as though speaking to him from a great distance, through thin mountain air (which it was, perhaps), 'I know what you need, you need some strong drink.'

'What about the driving?' he said, shrinking from the thought of all the as-yet-uncovered miles.

'I'll drive,' she said.

'But you don't drive,' he protested, hoarsely.

'Oh, yes I do,' she said, and when he looked at her (what a waste of looking this illness was, he seemed to have been contemplating nothing but the inside of his own head for the last day and night), he saw that she was positively gay, with a kind of defiant satisfaction, as though, despite her undoubted solicitude, she were enjoying this disaster.

'I used to drive quite well,' she said. 'I like it. I'll drive, and we'll buy you some codeine and you'll feel better in no time.'

'The car's too heavy for you,' he said.

'I could drive for a while anyway, but first of all, we'll buy some things to make you better. You stay here, and wait till I come back.'

'Don't leave me,' he said. 'I'll come with you.'

So they went together, through the sunny streets of that famous place, looking for whatever the Austrians used as chemists; the chemist would not sell them codeine without a prescription, so they had to make do with some throat mixture and some more aspirins. She led him back to the car, and with a sense of hopeless submission and abandon he allowed himself, for the first time ever, to be put in the passenger's seat. She didn't start too well: she reversed smartly into a yellow stone wall, swore, pulled away, set off on the left-hand side of the road, couldn't find the indicator, and then was away. He opened his bottle of whisky, sat back and gave up. He shut his eyes, and must have fallen asleep, because when he opened them they were driving through acres of flowers and dark-green trees, and there were Alps rising again on the horizon. She was singing to herself: Mozart, inevitably. A passing tribute.

'Hello, darling,' he said, and she stopped singing to pay him attention.

'Lovely, isn't it?' she said. 'Lovely. But I don't like the look of those mountains. Are you going to enjoy being driven through those mountains?'

'I've given up,' he said. 'I might as well die here as anywhere, don't you think?'

'Have another drink,' she said, and accelerated towards the snowy backdrop.

'I'm having such a lovely time,' she said to him, after a while, as the road began to ascend, sharply and dangerously. 'What about you?'

He held tight to the whisky, knowing he could not refuse her a drink if she asked for one: and after a little while she did.

'What I need is a little drink,' she said, as pine trees and icy torrents fell away from the edge of the car into nothingness.

'Of course,' he said, and handed it over. Trust, that was what it was called: mutual trust. He shrank down into his seat until she seemed larger than he was: she seemed to have taken on some extra quality that he could not quite name, and he conceded it to her entirely, slumped as he was, and feverish. He knew that he had a temperature: perhaps he would soon start to have hallucinations. Dusk was falling, and he was also hungry: but how could he, who was supposed to be ill, suggest that they might have something to eat? And even if they stopped, she would only allow him something horrible, like another egg, or a sandwich. He was in her hands.

It was so strange a sensation, after all these many months – years almost – when he had told himself that he had been looking after her, that as he lay back there in his unnatural condition he began to look back over the time they had known each other, and wonder whether it had been as he supposed, or whether it had been, as it now was, quite otherwise. She had seemed so desperate in that first real conversation they had ever had, initiated in a Ministry lift when she had been, in fact, crying: he, who had covertly desired her for months without realizing it, suddenly knew what he was after in his abrupt delight at the sight of this God-sent weakness. Later, when she told him the reason for her tears, he had flinched a little, not having expected quite such flights of tragedy, despite the brief rumours that, through mutual friends, had already reached him: the dotty mother, the cruelly defective child, the cruelly defected husband. 'It wasn't his fault,' she had said of this last character, blinking and indeed laughing as she drank up her gin, 'I mean really, who could have stuck it? And it was so clear that I preferred the child to him, and what man could ever have taken his wife preferring a child like *that*? A nice child maybe, that would be natural, but God, you should see mine . . .' And later, he had seen it: and so much of his love for her had overflowed and surrounded her by this time that he too had regarded it with a kind of love. He had taken the part of reason, from time to time, suggesting clinics and suitable schools, advising indulgence, but he so admired her obstinacy and knew she recognized his attempts as merely verbal, noises of encouragement intended to magnify and support her right decisions. Heroic, he thought her: and he could not deny that his entry into her life had been of the utmost simplicity, so avid had she been for company and human touching. The rewards of the touching he had foreseen, and he was not disappointed.

He had met the husband too, and discovered that, as he had suspected, they had been at school together. He had thought the name familiar. And looking back on him now, as they moved through the baffling darkness, he recalled him with an uneasy clarity: a horribly cheerful man, Derek, extroverted and yet by no means stupid, easy to get on with, in fact almost irresistibly good company, and not at all the kind of person to contemplate a lifetime of clouds and sorrows. He had walked out of it almost immediately, and in that pub where they met he had said gaily, speaking of his own wife, 'Oh, Christ, Daniel, she doesn't mind, she likes it, what she couldn't stand was my not liking it. I wish you all the best with her,' he said, 'she'll get on well with you, you've both got a taste for gloom. Look at that woman you married.' And how could Daniel reply that he did not find Derek's wife gloomy, that, on the contrary, she seemed to him of a remarkable resilience? But perhaps it was true that she liked a situation of sorrow. Perhaps she was so happy now, driving along really quite competently, because she was able to prove herself against the odds? And himself there, incapable and suffering, like a sick child. Perhaps she felt at home. It was not at all what he had intended. He had intended a holiday.

A little farther on, just as he had dozed off, having decided that she intended to drive all night, she pulled the car up abruptly by the side of the road and got out. She wandered off out of the range of his vision, and he decided that he too should take advantage of the stop, but could hardly find the strength to move. Finally, he did so: then stood by the car waiting for her to return. They were entirely surrounded by the vast presence of mountains: huge, they towered above the dwarfed car and fell away below it, at a gradient so steep that one wondered how the trees could maintain their incredible, defiant, perpendicular grip. It was alarmingly silent: a bird cried, and there was the faint but very distant sighing of a waterfall. He could hear no movement from her, not a sound or a rustle, and as his eyes grew accustomed to the light he saw her standing at the far end of the lay-by, leaning on the low wall and looking downward. He went towards her, and stood by her, and touched her cheek, which was cold from the night air.

'You shouldn't be out in the cold,' she said, softly, not turning to him. 'You're ill.'

'I'm better,' he said, and indeed he felt so very strange that it was hard to tell if he were better or worse. Certainly, whatever he had was less locally painful.

'Where are we?' he said, after a while, and she turned to him and said, 'We're going downward, now. We're through the mountains, really. We can sleep in Yugoslavia. We said we would.'

'It's so quiet, here,' he said. 'Listen.'

They listened to the silence, and then she said, 'I can't understand it, can you, people being comforted by nature? What use is all this to me? It's nothingness, without people.' And he agreed, but as he meekly got back into the passenger's seat, he thought for the first time in his life (and delirious, possibly, through illness or alcohol) that there was more to it than that, and that those vast moving shapes and abrupt inclines and icy summits were, after all, emblems of conditions, in the grip of which, in her frail human presence, he too moved.

They reached Yugoslavia. She had a moment of exaltation and triumph at the frontier, leaping out of the car, talking gaily in lousy Italian to the frontier people, leaving him sitting there stupefied while she went off to buy him a dry ham sandwich and a bottle of slivovitz: animated, gay, swinging her hair about like a person in a film, laughing. 'Poor, poor darling,' she said, as she sank down by him again, sinking her teeth into her hunk of bread, 'I bet you're too ill even to *think* you love me, aren't you?' And, incredibly, she laughed.

'Why on earth are you so cheerful?' he managed to mutter, as the dry crumbs lacerated his infinitely delicate throat.

'I don't know,' she said, switching on the engine. 'A sense of achievement, perhaps? Or because I've got you so helpless at last. Come on, we're off to Ljubljana.'

He had completely forgotten where Ljubljana was, so he did not protest: he had no notion of the time, nor of the distances they had covered or were to cover. From time to time, as he lay there, half asleep, a feeble spasm of resentment would shake him: all that waiting for this. The excursion of a lifetime, achieved through a sequence of miraculous coincidences (his wife going off to Canada for the week with all the children, who could possibly have foreseen or counted on that?), and all he could do with it was to shrivel up with an aching head and a painful body and wish that she would let him lie down in a comfortable bed. He didn't even fancy the whisky any more: dutifully, like a good patient, he unscrewed the top of the slivovitz, sniffed it, and tried a sip. It was quite nice, nicer than he had remembered from his last experience with it years before: dry and fruitlike and tasting very strongly of the pale yellow colour that it was. Why not purple, he thought to himself, as he swallowed another mouthful, why is it not purple like plums are, and that was his last conscious thought before he woke up in Ljubljana and found that she was trying to lift him out of the car, assisted by someone who looked like a hotel porter. She and the man in uniform were laughing: at him, no doubt, and angrily he staggered to his feet. 'Darling,' she said, as he swayed a little, clutching at the open car door, 'we're here.' And there, indeed, they were, as in some nightmare or vision: vast glass doors and arcades swam before his eyes, for she seemed to have driven the car more or less into the hotel. There was a deadly silence, as there had been in the mountains, and he knew that it must be very late. She pushed open the doors and he staggered, crumpled, after her, and was pushed into a lift. When they arrived at the bedroom he could see that she had already been up there and arranged everything, for her nightdress was laid out on the bed: she had done it all, she, who was incapable of lighting herself a cigarette in a slight draught. And she had done it all, moreover, while he was asleep in the car: she had left him there, in much the same way as he and his wife had been accustomed to leave small sleeping children while they had lunch in country restaurants. She and the porter seemed on excellent terms, speaking English and Italian and French to one another: they were probably mocking him, but his ears were buzzing and humming so loudly that he could not hear. He sat down on the bed, and finally the porter went away; and when she turned to him from the door, which she had shut and locked, he felt suddenly angry, as though he had been made a fool of behind his back, or derided in his sleep.

'Where in God's name are we?' he said, looking around him with irritation: the hotel was modern and streamlined, and the bed and chairs were upholstered in a kind of black cushioned leather, of the sort that had always figured largely in his erotic fantasies.

'In Ljubljana, of course,' she said: she was calmly getting undressed for bed.

'You must be mad,' he said. 'Why ever didn't you stop before?'

'Because we planned it this way,' she said. 'How are you feeling, now? Better?'

'I feel dreadful,' he said, and she was smiling down at him so benignly that he felt himself on the verge of tears.

'You'd better get some sleep,' she said, and started to untie his shoes. He let her take them off, and as she knelt there he was possessed by such a lucid sorrow that he reached out for her and held on to her; she put her head on his knees, and he stroked her hair.

'Darling,' he said, 'I'm so sorry, I'm so sorry, it's so hopeless, we haven't a chance, we've never had a chance. We're so kind to each other, but it's hopeless, it's entirely hopeless, we might as well give up. What good does it do, to be so careful, to be so kind and careful?'

He made her cry: she started to cry, and he stroked her hair.

'I don't mind, I don't mind,' she said into his knees.

'The thing is,' he said, seeing it quite clearly at last, 'that if

I had you, I'd ruin you. You know I would, don't you? Or if you had me? There isn't a hope of people doing anything better with one another. Not a hope.'

'That's not so,' she said. 'But if it were, it wouldn't matter.'

'Of course it would matter,' he said, aching. 'We've told ourselves for so long that we – if we were given the chance, we . . .'

But he couldn't say all the things that they would have been able to have, and to be, and to do: love, harmony, absence of pain and cruelty, absence of absence.

'But darling,' she said, and he could feel her shaking with some new kind of emotion, 'don't you see, my love, that we simply haven't a *chance* of being given a chance? It's wonderful, really. It's miraculous. Even now – ' and she looked up at him, with great rings under her eyes smeared grey with fatigue – 'even now, when we did have a bit of a chance, you've gone and got this horrible illness, so we'll never know what it would have been like if you hadn't. We'll never have to worry about it, we can just carry on being kind, and making promises. It's amazing, really. There'll never be any reason to know that we couldn't do it.'

'Couldn't do what?' he said, though he knew what she meant: he simply wanted to see if she would say it.

'I don't know,' she said, embarrassed by the simplicity of the sentiment, rising to her feet and pulling back the covers of the bed. 'I don't know. Be happy, I suppose I meant.'

'I am happy,' he said, watching her as she arranged her things by the bedside: her glass of water, her book on old people, her pack of cigarettes, her bottle of pills.

'Do you know,' she said, conversationally, as he got into bed by her, 'this is the most enormous place, this hotel, and this modern bit is just stuck on the front of it, it's not like this at all really, there are acres and acres more of it, very old and faded and peeling, with nineteenth-century murals and dirty mosaic corridors and Art Nouveau windows and God knows what else. They've just stuck this black leather bit on for people like you and me. Foreign tourists. You must come and look at the rest of it in the morning. It's rather frightening, the contrast. But magic. You'll like it.'

'I'll come and see it,' he said, 'if I'm not dead by then.'

'Do you want me to read to you, or are you going to sleep?' she said: she had actually opened her book at the bookmark.

'You're amazing,' he said.

'Yes, I am, aren't I,' she said, complacently, smiling without looking at him. 'And I'll tell you another thing. You'll never ruin me, because you'll never have the time to set about it properly. It takes time to ruin another person.'

'That's all right, then,' he said, and shut his eyes, as she started to read her book: images moved through his mind in confusion, pine trees, road signs, passing cars, hillsides, and he could never decide whether he and she were people who had the stature to cope with the disasters that had befallen them, and why it was that she had been asked to deal with that child, and how gloriously it had hardened her nature (perhaps it was stature that he had glimpsed as he sat by her looming above him in the car – she had forgotten to ring London, he would remind her in the morning to ring London), while all that he had to bear (all, why all?) was a chill caught from going to bed with his hair wet and a frigid hysterical wife: but perhaps, after all, it was ridiculous to measure in this way, because both tragedy and love are not human possessions, they are not allocated, and they fill the air, they are the backdrop like the pine trees, and there is nobody alive who does not live in these perpetually ebbing and flowing conditions, so that her sorrows were in a real sense his, and everyone's, and he was not coldly caring for them or using them or manipulating them as he had sometimes feared, any more than she was him, because they were all a part of the same thing, joined as this black leather was to those faded frescoes; a mystic sense of the unity of all sorrow filled him as he lay there, delirious with influenza and alcohol, and if this was so then how could he abuse, or ruin her?

In the morning, he could hardly remember what had gone through his mind the night before, but he remembered, solicitously, to remind her to ring London to see how things were: and she thanked him, although she had, of course, remembered herself.

And oddly enough, long after they had returned to England, years after, he had only to think of pine trees and Alpine landscapes to be reminded of something half realized, a revelation of comfort too dim to articulate, a revelation that had lost its words and its fine edges and its meaning, but not its images. He thought of pine trees, and he thought of her, and the memory (why should he not choose, even for himself, a word of some dignity?) – the memory sustained him.

(1969)

6

The Gifts of War

Timeo Danaos et dona ferentes.

Aeneid, Book II, I.49

When she woke in the morning, she could tell at once, as soon as she reached consciousness, that she had some reason to feel pleased with herself, some rare cause for satisfaction. She lay there quietly for a time, enjoying the unfamiliar sensation, not bothering to place it, grateful for its vague comfortable warmth. It protected her from the disagreeable noise of her husband's snores, from the thought of getting breakfast, from the coldness of the linoleum when she finally dragged herself out of bed. She had to wake Kevin: he always overslept these days, and he took so long to get dressed and get his breakfast, she was surprised he wasn't always late for school. She never thought of making him go to bed earlier; she hadn't the heart to stop him watching the telly, and anyway she enjoyed his company, she liked having him around in the evenings, laughing in his silly seven-year-old way at jokes he didn't understand – jokes she didn't always understand herself, and which she couldn't explain when he asked her to. 'You don't know *anything*, Mum,' he would groan, but she didn't mind his condemnations: she didn't expect to know anything; it amused her to see him behaving like a man already, affecting superiority, harmlessly, helplessly, in an ignorance that was as yet so much greater than her own – though she would have died rather than have allowed him to suspect her amusement, her permissiveness. She grumbled at him constantly, even while wanting to keep him there: she snapped at his endless questions, she snubbed him, she repressed him, she provoked him. And she did not suffer from doing this, because she knew that they could not hurt each other: he was a child, he wasn't a proper man yet, he couldn't inflict true pain, any more than she could truly repress him, and his teasing, obligatory conventional schoolboy complaints about her cooking and her stupidity seemed to exorcize, in a way, those other crueller onslaughts. It was as though she said to herself: if my little boy doesn't mean it when he shouts at me, perhaps my husband doesn't either: perhaps there's no more serious offence in my bruises and my greying hair than there is in those harmless childish moans. In the child, she found a way of accepting, without too much submission, her lot.

She loved the child: she loved him with so much passion that a little of it spilled over generously onto the man who had misused her: in forgiving the child his dirty blazer and shirts and his dinner-covered tie, she forgave the man for his Friday nights and the childish vomit on the stairs and the bedroom floor. It never occurred to her that a grown man might resent more than hatred such second-hand forgiveness. She never thought of the man's emotions: she thought of her own, and her feelings for the child redeemed her from bitterness, and shed some light on the dark industrial terraces and the waste lands of the city's rubble. Her single-minded commitment was a wonder of the neighbourhood: she's a sour piece, the neighbours said, she keeps herself to herself a bit too much, but you've got to hand it to her, she's been a wonderful mother to that boy, she's had a hard life, but she's been a wonderful mother to that boy. And she, tightening her woolly headscarf over her aching ears as she walked down the cold steep windy street to join the queue at the post office or the butcher's, would stiffen proudly, her hard lips secretly smiling as she claimed and accepted and nodded to her role, her place, her social dignity.

This morning, as she woke Kevin, he reminded her instantly of her cause for satisfaction, bringing to the surface the pleasant knowledge that had underlain her wakening.

'Hi, Mum,' he said, as he opened his eyes to her, 'how old am I today?'

'Seven, of course,' she said, staring dourly at him, pretending to conceal her instant knowledge of the question's meaning, assuming scorn and dismissal. 'Come on, get up, child, you're going to be late as usual.'

'And how old am I tomorrow, Mum?' he asked, watching her like a hawk, waiting for that delayed, inevitable break.

'Come on, come on,' she said crossly, affecting impatience, stripping the blankets off him, watching him writhe in the cold air, small and bony in his striped pyjamas.

'Oh, go on, Mum,' he said.

'What d'you mean, "go on",' she said, 'don't be so cheeky, come on, get a move on, you'll get no breakfast if you don't get a move on.'

'Just think, Mum,' he said, 'how old am I tomorrow?'

'I don't know what you're talking about,' she said, ripping his pyjama jacket off him, wondering how long to give the game, secure in her sense of her own timing.

'Yes you do, yes you do,' he yelled, his nerve beginning, very slightly, to falter. 'You know what day it is tomorrow.'

'Why, my goodness me,' she said, judging that the moment had come, 'I'd quite forgotten. Eight tomorrow. My goodness me.'

And she watched him grin and wriggle, too big now for embraces, his affection clumsy and knobbly: she avoided the touch of him these days, pushing him irritably away when he leaned on her chair-arm, twitching when he banged into her in the corridor or the kitchen, pulling her skirt or overall away from him when he tugged at it for attention, regretting some-times the soft and round docile baby that he had once been, and yet proud at the same time of his gawky growing, happier, more familiar with the hostilities between them (a better cover for love) than she had been with the tender wide smiles of adoring infancy.

'What you got me for my birthday?' he asked, as he strug-gled out of his pyjama trousers: and she turned at the door and looked back at him, and said, 'What d'you mean, what've I got you? I've not got you anything. Only good boys get presents.'

'I *am* good,' he said, 'I've been ever so good all week.'

'Not that I noticed, you weren't,' she said, knowing that too prompt an acquiescence would ruin the dangerous pleasure of doubtful anticipation.

'Go on, tell me,' he said, and she could tell from his whining plea that he was almost sure that she had got what he wanted, almost sure but not quite sure, that he was, in fact, in the grip of an exactly manipulated degree of uncertainty, a torment of hope that would last him for a whole twenty-four hours, until the next birthday morning.

'I'm telling you,' she said, her hand on the door, staring at him sternly, 'I'm telling you, I've not got you anything.' And then, magically, delightfully, she allowed herself and him that lovely moment of grace: 'I've not got you anything – *yet*,' she said: portentous, conspiratorial, yet very very faintly threatening.

'You're going to get it today,' he shrieked, unable to restrain himself, unable to keep the rules: and as though annoyed by his exuberance she marched smartly out of the small back room, and down the narrow stairs to the kitchen, shouting at him in an excessive parade of rigour, 'Come on, get moving, get your things on, you'll be late for school, you're always late': and she stood over him while he ate his flakes, watching each spoonful disappear, heaving a great sigh of resigned fury when he spilled on the oilcloth, catching his guilty glance as he wiped it with his sleeve, not letting him off, unwilling, unable to relax into a suspect tenderness.

He went out the back way to school: she saw him through the yard and stood in the doorway watching him disappear, as she always watched him, down the narrow alley separating the two rows of back-to-back cottages, along the ancient industrial cobbles, relics of another age: as he reached the Stephensons' door she called out to him, 'Eight tomorrow, then,' and smiled, and waved, and he smiled back, excited, affectionate, over the ten yards' gap, grinning, his grey knee socks pulled smartly up, his short cropped hair already standing earnestly on end, resisting the violent flattening of the brush with which she thumped him each morning: he reminded her of a bird, she didn't know why, she couldn't have said why, a bird, vulnerable, clumsy, tenacious, touching. Then Bill Stephenson emerged from his back door and joined him, and they went down the alley together, excluding her, leaving her behind, kicking at pebbles and fag packets with their scuffed much-polished shoes.

She went back through the yard and into the house, and made a pot of tea, and took it up to the man in bed. She dumped it down on the corner of the dressing-table beside him, her lips tight, as though she dared not loosen them: her face had only one expression, and she used it to conceal the two major emotions of her life, resentment and love. They were so violently opposed, these passions, that she could not move from one to the other: she lacked flexibility; so she inhabited a grim inexpressive no-man's-land between them, feeling in some way that she thus achieved a kind of justice.

'I'm going up town today,' she said, as the man on the bed rolled over and stared at her.

He wheezed and stared.

'I'm going to get our Kevin his birthday present,' she said, her voice cold and neutral, offering justice and no more.

'What'll I do about me dinner?' he said.

'I'll be back,' she said. 'And if I'm not, you can get your own. It won't kill you.'

He mumbled and coughed, and she left the room. When she got downstairs, she began, at last, to enter upon the day's true enjoyment: slowly she took possession of it, this day that she had waited for, and which could not now be taken from her. She'd left herself a cup of tea on the table, but before she sat down to drink it she got her zip plastic purse from behind the clock on the dresser, and opened it, and got the money out. There it was, all of it: thirty shillings, three ten-bob notes, folded tightly up in a brown envelope: twenty-nine and eleven, she needed, and a penny over. Thirty shillings, saved, unspoken for, to spend. She'd wondered, from time to time, if she ought to use it to buy him something useful, but she knew now that she wasn't going to: she was going to get him what he wanted – a grotesque, unjustifiable luxury, a pointless gift. It never occurred to her that the pleasure she took in doing things for Kevin was anything other than selfish: she felt vaguely guilty about it, she would have started furtively, like a miser, had anyone knocked on the door and interrupted her contemplation, she would bitterly have denied the intensity of her anticipation.

And when she put her overcoat on, and tied on her head-square, and set off down the road, she tried to appear to the neighbours as though she wasn't going anywhere in particular:

she nodded calmly, she stopped to gape at Mrs Phillips' new baby (all frilled up, poor mite, in ribbons and pink crochet, a dreadful sight, poor little innocent, like something off an iced cake, people should know better than to do such things to their own children); she even called in at the shop for a quarter of tea as a cover for her excursion, so reluctant was she to let anyone know that she was going into town, thus unusually, on a Wednesday morning. And as she walked down the steep hillside, where the abandoned tram-lines still ran, to the next fare stage of the bus, she could not have said whether she was making the extra walk to save two pence, or whether she was more deviously concealing her destination until the last moment from both herself and the neighbourhood.

Because she hardly ever went into town these days. In the old days she had come this way quite often, going down the hill on the tram with her girl friends, with nothing better in mind than a bit of window-shopping and a bit of a laugh and a cup of tea: penniless then as now, but still hopeful, still endowed with the touching faith that if by some miracle she could buy a pair of nylons or a particular blue lace blouse or a new brand of lipstick, then deliverance would be granted to her in the form of money, marriage, romance, the visiting prince who would glimpse her in the crowd, glorified by that seductive blouse, and carry her off to a better world. She could remember so well how hopeful they had been: even Betty Jones, fat, monstrous, ludicrous Betty Jones had cherished such rosy illusions, had gazed with them in longing at garments many sizes too small and far too expensive, somehow convinced that if she could by chance or good fortune acquire one all her flesh would melt away and reveal the lovely girl within. Time had taught Betty Jones: she shuffled now in shoes cracked and splitting beneath her own weight. Time had taught them all. The visiting prince, whom need and desire had once truly transfigured in her eyes, now lay there at home in bed, stubbly, disgusting, ill, malingering, unkind: she remembered the girl who had seen such other things in him with a contemptuous yet pitying wonder. What fools they all had been, to laugh, to giggle and point and whisper, to spend their small wages to deck themselves for such a sacrifice. When she saw the young girls today, of the age that she had been then, still pointing and giggling with the same knowing ignorance, she was filled with a bitterness so acute that her teeth set against it, and the set lines of her face stiffened to resist and endure and conceal it. Sometimes she was possessed by a rash desire to warn them, to lean forward and tap on their shoulders, to see their astonished vacant faces, topped with their mad over-perfumed mounds of sticky hair, turn upon her in alarm and disbelief. What do you think you're playing at, she would say to them, what do you think you're at? Where do you think it leads you, what do you think you're asking for? And they would blink at her, uncomprehending, like condemned cattle, the sacrificial virgins, not yet made restless by the smell of blood. I could tell you a thing or two, she wanted to say, I could tell you enough to wipe those silly grins off your faces: but she said nothing, and she could not have said that it was envy or a true charitable pity that most possessed and disturbed her when she saw such innocents.

What withheld her most from envy, pure and straight and voracious, was a sense of her own salvation. Because, amazingly, she had been saved, against all probability: her life, which had seemed after that bridal day of white nylon net and roses to sink deeply and almost instantly into a mire of penury and beer and butchery, had been so redeemed for her by her child that she could afford to smile with a kind of superior wisdom, a higher order of knowledge, at those who had not known her trials and her comforts. They would never attain, the silly teenagers, her own level of consolation; they would never know what it was like to find in an object which had at first seemed painful, ugly, bloody and binding, which had at first appeared to her as a yet more lasting sentence, a death-blow to the panic notions of despair and flight – to find in such a thing love, and identity, and human warmth. When she thought of this – which she did, often, though not clearly, having little else to think of – she felt as though she alone, or she one of the elected few, had been permitted to glimpse something of the very nature of the harsh, mysterious pro-cesses of human survival; and she could induce in herself a state of recognition that was almost visionary. It was all she had: and being isolated by pride from more neighbourly and everyday and diminishing attempts at commiseration, she knew it. She fed off it: her maternal role, her joy, her sorrow. She gazed out of the bus window now, as the bus approached the town centre and the shops, and as she thought of the gift she was going to buy him, her eyes lit on the bombed sites, and the rubble and decay of decades, and the exposed walls where dirty fading wallpapers had flapped in the wind for years, and she saw where the willowherb grew, green and purple, fields of it amongst the brick, on such thin soil, on the dust of broken bricks and stones, growing so tall in tenacious aspiration out of such shallow infertile ground. It was signif-icant: she knew, as she looked at it, that it was significant. She herself had grown out of this landscape, she had nourished herself and her child upon it. She knew what it meant.

Frances Janet Ashton Hall also knew what it meant, for she too had been born and bred there; although, being younger, she had not lived there for so long, and, having been born into a different class of society, she knew that she was not sentenced to it for life, and was indeed upon the verge of escape, for the next autumn she was to embark upon a degree in economics at a southern university. Nevertheless, she knew what it meant. She was a post-war child, but it was not for nothing that she had witnessed since infancy the red and smoking skies of the steelworks (making arms for the Arabs, for the South Africans, for all those wicked countries) – it was not for nothing that she had seen the deep scars in the city's centre, not all disguised quite comfortably as car parks. In fact, she could even claim the distinction of having lost a relative in the air raids: her great-aunt Susan, who had refused to allow herself to be evacuated to the Lake District, had perished from a stray bomb in the midst of a highly residential suburban area. Frances was not yet old enough to speculate upon the effect that this tale, oft-repeated, and with lurid details, had had upon the development of her sensibility; naturally she ascribed her ardent pacifism and her strong political convictions to her own innate radical virtue, and when she did look for ulterior motives for her faith she was far more likely to relate them to her recent passion for a new-found friend, one Michael Swaines, than to any childhood neurosis.

She admired Michael. She also liked him for reasons that had nothing to do with admiration, and being an intelligent and scrupulous girl she would spend fruitless, anxious and enjoyable hours trying to disentangle and isolate her various emotions, and to assess their respective values. Being very young, she set a high value on disinterest: standing now, for his sake, on a windy street corner in a conspicuous position outside the biggest department store in town, carrying a banner and wearing (no less) a sandwich board, proclaiming the necessity for Peace in Vietnam, and calling for the banning of all armaments, nuclear or otherwise, she was carrying on a highly articulate dialogue with her own conscience, by means of which she was attempting to discover whether she was truly standing there for Michael's sake alone, or whether she would have stood there anyway, for the sake of the cause itself. What, she asked herself, if she had been solicited to make a fool of herself in this way merely by that disagreeable Nicholas, son of the Head of the Adult Education Centre? Would she have been prepared to oblige? No, she certainly would not, she would have laughed the idea of sandwich-boards to scorn, and would have found all sorts of convincing arguments against the kind of public display that she was now engaged in. But, on the other hand, this did not exactly invalidate her actions, for she *did* believe, with Michael, that demonstrations were necessary and useful: it was just that her natural reluctance to expose herself would have conquered her, had not Michael himself set about persuading her. So she was doing the right thing but for the wrong reason, like that man in *Murder in the Cathedral*. And perhaps it was for a *very* wrong reason, because she could not deny that she even found a sort of corrupt pleasure in doing things she didn't like doing – accosting strangers, shaking collection-boxes, being stared at – when she knew that it was being appreciated by other people: a kind of yearning for disgrace and martyrdom. Like stripping in public. Though not, surely, *quite* the same, because stripping didn't do any good, whereas telling people about the dangers of total war was a useful occupation. So doing the right thing for the wrong reason could at least be said to be better than doing the wrong thing for the wrong reason, couldn't it? Though her parents, of course, said it was the wrong thing anyway, and that one shouldn't molest innocent shoppers: Oh Lord, she thought with sudden gloom, perhaps my *only* reason for doing this is to annoy my parents: and bravely, to distract herself from the dreadful suspicion, she stepped forward and asked a scraggy thin woman in an old red velvet coat what she thought of the American policy in Vietnam.

'What's that?' said the woman, crossly, annoyed at being stopped in mid-stride, and when Frances repeated her question she gazed at her as though she were an idiot and walked on without replying. Frances, who was becoming used to such responses, was not as hurt as she had been at the beginning of the morning: she was even beginning to think it was quite funny. She wondered if she might knock off for a bit and go and look for Michael: he had gone into the store, to try to persuade the manager of the toy department not to sell toy machine-guns and toy bombs and toy battleships. She thought she would go and join him; and when a horrid man in a cloth cap spat on the pavement very near her left shoe and muttered something about bloody students bugger off ruining the city for decent folk, she made her mind up. So she ditched her sandwich-board and rolled her banner up, and set off through the swing doors into the cosy warmth: although it was Easter the weather was bitterly cold, spring seemed to reach them two months later than anywhere else in England. It was a pity, she thought, that there weren't any more Easter marches: she would have liked marching, it would have been more sociable; but Michael believed in isolated pockets of resistance. Really, what he meant was, he didn't like things that he wasn't organizing himself. She didn't blame him for that, he was a marvellous organizer, it was amazing the amount of enthusiasm he'd got up in the Students' Union for what was after all rather a dud project: no, not dud, she hadn't meant that, what she meant was that it was no fun, and anyone with a lower sense of social responsibility than herself couldn't have been expected to find it very interesting. Very nice green stockings on the stocking counter, she wondered if she could afford a pair. This thing that Michael had about children and violence, it really was very odd: he had a brother who was writing a thesis on violence on the television and she supposed it must have affected him. She admired his faith. Although at the same time she couldn't help remembering a short story by Saki that she had read years ago, called 'The Toys of Peace', which had been about the impossibility of making children play with anything but soldiers, or something to that effect.

When she reached the toy department, she located Michael immediately, because she could hear his voice raised in altercation. In fact, as she approached, she could see that quite a scene was going on, and if Michael hadn't looked quite so impressive when he was making a scene she would have lost nerve and fled: but as it was she approached, discreetly, and hovered on the outskirts of the centre of activity. Michael was arguing with a man in a black suit, some kind of manager figure she guessed (though what managers were or did she had no idea) and a woman in an overall: the man, she could see, was beginning to lose his patience, and was saying things like:

'Now look here, young man, we're not here to tell our customers what they ought to do, we're here to sell them what they want,' and Michael was producing his usual arguments about responsibility and education and having to make a start somewhere and why not here and now; he'd already flashed around his leaflets on violence and delinquency, and was now offering his catalogue of harmless constructive wooden playthings.

'Look,' he was saying, 'look how much more attractive these wooden animals are, I'm sure you'd find they'd sell just as well, and they're far more durable' – whereat the woman in an overall sniffed and said since when had salesmen dressed themselves up as university students, if he wanted to sell them toys he ought to do it in the proper way; an interjection which Michael ignored, as he proceeded to pick up off the counter in front of him a peculiarly nasty piece of clockwork, a kind of car-cum-aeroplane thing with real bullets and knives in the wheels and hidden bomb-carriers and God knows what, she rather thought it was a model from some television puppet programme, it was called the Desperado Destruction Machine. 'I mean to say, look at this horrible thing,' Michael said to the manager, pressing a knob and nearly slicing off his own finger as an extra bit of machinery jumped out at him, 'whatever do you think can happen to the minds of children who play with things like this?'

'That's a very nice model,' said the manager, managing to sound personally grieved and hurt, 'it's a very nice model, and you've no idea how popular it's been for the price. It's not a cheap foreign thing, that, you know, it's a really well-made toy. Look – ' and he grabbed it back off Michael and pulled another lever, to display the ejector-seat mechanism. The driver figure was promptly ejected with such violence that he shot right across the room, and Michael, who was quite well brought up really, dashed off to retrieve it: and by the time he got back the situation had been increasingly complicated by the arrival of a real live customer who had turned up to buy that very object. Though if it really was as popular as the manager had said, perhaps that wasn't such a coincidence. Anyway, this customer seemed very set on purchasing one, and the overalled woman detached herself from Michael's scene and started to demonstrate one for her, trying to pretend as she did so that there was no scene in progress and that nothing had been going on at all: the manager too tried to hush Michael up by engaging him in conversation and back-ing him away from the counter and the transaction, but Michael wasn't so easy to silence: he continued to argue in a loud voice, and stood his ground. Frances wished that he would abandon this clearly pointless attempt, and all the more as he had by now noticed her presence, and she knew that at any moment he would appeal for her support. And finally the worst happened, as she had known it might: he turned to the woman who was trying to buy the Desperado Destruction Machine, and started to appeal to her, asking her if she wouldn't like to buy something less dangerous and destructive. The woman seemed confused at first, and when he asked her for whom she was buying it, she said that it was for her little boy's birthday, and she hadn't realized it was a dangerous toy, it was just something he'd set his heart on, he'd break his heart if he didn't get it, he'd seen it on the telly and he wanted one just like that: whereupon the manager, who had quite lost his grip, intervened and started to explain to her that there was nothing dangerous about the toy at all, on the contrary it was a well-made pure British product, with no lead paint or sharp edges, and that if Michael didn't shut up he'd call the police: whereupon Michael said that there was no law to stop customers discussing products in shops with one another, and he was himself a bona-fide customer, because look, he'd got a newly purchased pair of socks in his pocket in a Will Baines bag. The woman continued to look confused, so Frances thought that she herself ought to intervene to support Michael, who had momentarily run out of aggression: and she said to the woman, in what she thought was a very friendly and reasonable tone, that nobody was trying to stop her buying her little boy a birthday present, they just wanted to point out that with all the violence in the world today anyway it was silly to add to it by encouraging children to play at killing and exterminating and things like that, and hadn't everyone seen enough bombing, particularly here (one of Michael's favourite points, this), and why didn't she buy her boy something constructive like Meccano or a farmyard set: and as she was saying all this she glanced from

time to time at the woman's face, and there was something
in it, she later acknowledged, that should have warned her.
She stood there, the woman, her woollen headscarf so tight
round her head that it seemed to clamp her jaws together into
a violently imposed silence; her face unnaturally drawn,
prematurely aged; her thickly veined hands clutching a zip
plastic purse and that stupid piece of clockwork machinery:
and as she listened to Frances's voice droning quietly and
soothingly and placatingly away her face began to gather a
glimmering of expression, from some depths of reaction too
obscure to guess at: and as Frances finally ran down to a
polite and only very faintly hopeful enquiring standstill, she
opened her mouth and spoke. She said only one word, and
it was a word that Frances had never heard before, though
she had seen it in print in a once-banned book; and by some
flash of insight, crossing the immeasurable gap of quality that
separated their two lives, she knew that the woman herself
had never before allowed it to pass her lips, that to her too
it was a shocking syllable, portentous, unforgettable, not a
familiar word casually dropped into the dividing spaces. Then
the woman, having spoken, started to cry: incredibly, horribly,
she started to cry. She dropped the clockwork toy onto the
floor, and it fell so heavily that she could almost have been
said to have thrown it down, and she stood there, staring at
it, as the tears rolled down her face. Then she looked at them,
and walked off. Nobody followed her: they stood there and
let her go. They did not know how to follow her, nor what
appeasement to offer for her unknown wound. So they did
nothing. But Frances knew that in their innocence they had
done something dreadful to her, in the light of which those
long-since ended air raids and even distant Vietnam itself
were an irrelevance, a triviality: but she did not know what
it was, she could not know. At their feet, the Destruction

Machine buzzed and whirred its way to a broken immobility, achieving a mild sensation in its death-throes by shooting a large spring coil out of its complex guts; she and Michael, after lengthy apologies, had to pay for it before they were allowed to leave the store.

(1970)

7

A Success Story

This is a story about a woman. It couldn't have been told a few years ago: perhaps even five years ago it couldn't have been told. Perhaps it can't really be told now. Perhaps I shouldn't write it, perhaps it's a bad move to write it. But it's worth risking. Just to see.

This woman was a playwright. She was one of the few successful women playwrights, and she had had a hard time on the way up, for she came from a poor background, from a part of the country hostile to the arts, from a family which had never been to the theatre in its life. She wasn't really working class: more lower middle class, which made her success all the more remarkable, as her plays didn't have shock value, they were quite complicated and delicate. But they worked: they were something new. She made her way up: first of all she was assistant stagehand at her local repertory, then she worked in the office at a larger provincial theatre as she didn't really have much interest in life behind the scenes – and all the while she was writing her plays. The first one was put on by the rep she was working in, and it was very much noticed. Kathie (that was her name – Kathie Jones) used to say modestly that it was noticed because she was a woman, and women playwrights were a rarity, and there was some-thing in what she said. But her modesty couldn't explain why she went on writing, professionally, had her plays transferred to the West End, had them filmed, and did really very nicely. She was good at the job, and that was why she succeeded. She was also good, somewhat to her own surprise, at all the things that went along with the job, and which had kept women out of the job for so long: she was good at explaining herself, at arguing with megalomaniac directors, at coolly sticking to her own ideas, at adapting when things really couldn't be made to work. She had good judgement, she was calm and professional, she could stand up for herself.

She was not, of course, world famous, let us not give the impression that she was an international name. No, she was a success in her own country, in her own medium. Some of the gossip columns thought her worth mentioning, some of them didn't. Not that there was much to mention: she was a quiet, hardworking girl, with her own friends, her own circle of close friends – some of them writers, one or two friends from the early days at grammar school in the Midlands, one or two journalists. She was considered rather exclusive by some, and she was. She didn't much care for a gay social life, partly because she hadn't time, partly because she hadn't been brought up to it and didn't quite know how to cope. She lived with a man who was a journalist, and who travelled a great deal: he was always going off to Brazil and Vietnam and up Everest. He was an exceptionally good-natured man, and they got on well together. Sometimes she was sorry when he went away, but she was always so busy that she didn't miss him much, and anyway it was so interesting when he came back. He, for his part, loved her, and had confidence in her.

So really, one could say that her life had worked out very nicely. She had a job she liked, a reputation, a good relationship, some good friends, a respectable though fluctuating income. At the time of this story, she was in her early thirties, and had written five successful plays and several film scripts.

She had a play running at a lucrative little theatre in the West End, and was amusing herself by working on a television adaptation of a play by Strindberg. Her man was away: he was in Hungary, but he would be back soon, he would be back at the end of the week. At the moment at which we close in upon her, she was just putting the phone down after speaking to him: they had exchanged news, she had told him what was in his post which she always opened for him, he had said that he loved her and was looking forward to coming back and kissing her all over but particularly between her stockings and her suspenders, if she would please wear such antiquated garments on his return to greet him. Then he told her to enjoy her evening; she was just about to go out to a rather grand party. So she was smiling, as she put down the telephone.

She was quite a nice-looking woman. This we have not mentioned till this point, because it ought not to be of any importance. Or ought it? Well, we shall see. Anyway, she wasn't bad-looking, though she was nothing special. She had rather a long, large-featured face, with a large nose: she had big hands and large bones. Some people thought her beautiful, but others thought she was really plain. You know the type. As a child, she had been plain, as her mother had never tired of saying, and consequently she had no confidence in her appearance at all. Nowadays she didn't care much, she was happy anyway, and as long as her lover continued to take an interest in the serious things of life, like her legs, then she wasn't much interested in looking in the mirror. In fact, she hardly ever did, except to brush her hair, and she wore the same clothes most of the time, until they wore out. But tonight was different. She would have to have a look at herself, at least. So when she'd put the phone down she went into the bathroom to have a look.

Tonight was rather a special, grand sort of party, not the

usual kind of thing, so she'd put on her best dress, a long green-blue dress that she'd once thought suited her rather old-fashioned looks. She wasn't so sure, now, she wasn't at all sure what she looked like these days, the older she got the more variable she seemed to be. Not that it mattered much, one way or the other. But one might as well wear one's best dress, once in a while. She'd bought it for one of her own first nights, years ago, and hadn't worn it much since. She didn't go to her own first nights any more, or anyone else's for that matter. It had cost a lot of money, for those days. (Not that she spent much money on clothes now – in fact she spent less.) Staring at herself, hitching it a bit at the shoulder, she wondered whether she'd put it on because she was still, whatever she told herself, slightly nervous about the kind of do she was going to. Surely not. Surely not, these days. Why should she care?

The party she was going to was being given by one of the grandest (socially speaking) theatrical entrepreneurs in London. And there she was going to meet the hero of her childhood dreams. It was all quite romantic. His name was Howard Jago (quite the right sort of name, but people like that have that kind of name) and he was one of the biggest American writers of his generation. He had written plays that made her heart bleed when she was sixteen. They still, oddly enough, moved her profoundly.

She admired him more than she admired any other living writer. He hadn't kept up with the play writing – she knew well enough that playwrights, compared with other writers, have a short working life – but he was now doing screenplays, and also a certain amount of political journalism. He had published a couple of novels, which she had liked immensely: he seemed indefatigable.

When she was a child, she had wanted more than anything

to meet him. She had even written him a fan letter telling him so. He did not reply. Probably it never reached him.

She had had several opportunities to meet him before, as he was quite often in Europe, and was published by her publishers. But she had always declined.

Why had she declined? Was she afraid of being bored or disappointed? Afraid of not being disappointed? Was she afraid that he might not have heard of her (when, by the rules of the game, he should have done) or might find her boring? Combing her hair, now, looking at herself in the mirror, she wondered. Perhaps she had simply been too busy, on other occasions: or Dan had been at home and had not wanted to go. He didn't care for grand parties, and neither as a rule did she. They preferred to get very drunk quietly at home amongst friends: that was their favourite form of social life.

She couldn't work out why she hadn't wanted to meet him before: nor why, now, she had decided that she would.

She put him out of her mind, as she went downstairs and found herself a taxi. There would be plenty of other people there that she would know.

And so indeed there were. She knew nearly everybody, by sight or in person. She thought with some relief, as she looked round the massive house in Belgravia, and its glittering inhabitants – film stars in outré garments, diplomats, writers, cabinet ministers, actors, actresses – she thought that at least she didn't have to feel nervous any more. In a way that took some of the thrill away, but it was much pleasanter to be comfortable than thrilled. Being thrilled had always been so exhausting, and such a letdown in the end. Nowadays, she sought and found more lasting pleasures. Nevertheless, she had been very different once. Ambitious, she must have been, or she wouldn't have found herself here at all, would she? And, as she talked to a friend and kept an eye open for Howard

Jago, she said to herself, if I'd known twenty years ago that I would ever find myself here, in a room like this, with people looking like this, I *would* have been delighted. A pity, really, that one couldn't have had that particular thrill then – the thrill of knowing. It wasn't worth much now.

The house was enormous. Tapestries hung on the walls and statues stood in corners. The paintings were by Francis Bacon and Bonnard and Matthew Smith and Braque.

After a while, she saw her host approaching her. He was leading Howard Jago in her direction: Howard Jago was doing his rounds. He looked as she had imagined him: wild, heavy, irregular, a bit larger than life-size, the kind of man who looks even bigger than he looks on the television. (She had caught a glimpse or two of him on the television.)

'And this,' said her host, 'is one of the people you particularly asked to meet. This is Kathie Jones.'

Kathie smiled, politely. Jago shook her hand.

'I enjoyed your play the other night,' said Jago, politely.

He looked as though he was being careful. He looked as though he might be a little drunk.

'That's very kind of you,' said Kathie. 'I must tell you how very much I have always admired your work.'

'I've admired it . . .' and she was going to say, since I was a child, which would have been true, but had to stop herself because it might have been a rude reflection on his age, and went on with '. . . I've admired it ever since I first found it.'

They looked at each other, with assessment, and smiled, civilly. Kathie couldn't think of anything else to say. She had remembered, suddenly, exactly why she hadn't wanted to meet him: she hadn't wanted to meet him because she knew he was a womanizer, she knew it from a friend of hers, an actress, who'd had a bad time with him in New York. He can't help it, her friend had said, he's a real sod, he hates women, you know, but he just has to get off with them, he can't let them alone . . .

The memory paralysed her. She wondered why she hadn't thought of it earlier. It was obvious, anyway, from his work, that he had a thing about women, that he didn't like them and had to have them. He was a great enough writer for it not to matter to her: it was a measure of his greatness, for she did care about such things considerably.

She thought with a sudden nice physical recollection of Dan, who liked women, and loved her in particular, to her great delight.

She stood there, and smiled, and said nothing. Or rather, she said, 'And how long are you in London this time, Mr Jago?'

And he replied, with equal banality. It's all right, she was saying to herself, it's safe. It doesn't matter. (What did she mean by that?)

And as she listened to him, she saw approaching a film actress, a lady of considerable glamour, approaching with some purpose. 'Howard, Howard, *there* you are, I *lost* you,' she wailed, throwing her arm around his neck, possessively, her bosom heaving, her necklace sparkling: she started to stroke his greying hair, passionately, as she turned to greet Kathie. 'Why hello, *Kathie*,' she said, 'what a surprise, I haven't seen you in *years*. Howard went to see your play, was he telling you? . . . Oh look, Howard, there's Martin – ' and she marched him off: but Kathie Jones had already turned away. Well rid of him, she thought herself. He was drunk: he swayed slightly as Georgina grabbed him. Georgina was well away. She was a young lady with a will of iron. She was quite amusing on some occasions. Kathie wished them joy, and turned to look for a sympathetic friend, thinking as she went that the poor sixteen-year-old child she had been would have been shocked, shocked beyond anything, to have missed the opportunity to ask him, to hear him speak, even, of what he felt about, perhaps, the freedom of the will (one of his themes) and evolution (yet another). She smiled to herself, and went and talked to some publishers. They were much more interesting than Howard Jago had had a chance to be.

It was a couple of hours before he came back to her. She had been enjoying herself. There was plenty to drink, and some very good buffet food, and some people she knew well and some she hadn't seen for ages: she had been drinking quite steadily, and was sitting on a settee with an actress and her husband and another couple she'd never met before, laughing, very loudly, all of them, choking almost, over some anecdote about a play of hers, when he came back. He was looking more morose than before, and more obviously drunk. As he approached, Kathie made space for him on the settee by her, as he clearly intended to sit: they were still laughing over the story, as he sat. 'Hello again,' she said, turning to him, secure now, expecting nothing, willing to include him in the circle. 'Do you know Jenny, and Bob . . .'

'Yes, yes,' he said crossly, 'I know everyone, I've met everyone in this place. I want to get out.'

'Why don't you go, then?' asked Kathie, politely, slightly at a loss: and even as she spoke, she saw Georgina bearing down on them. Jago saw her too, and flinched: he rose to his feet, pulling Kathie to hers.

'Come on,' he said, 'let's get out of here.' She was thrilled. She had never heard anyone talk like that except in a movie. And Howard Jago turned his back on Georgina, with calculated offence, and marched Kathie across the room, gripping her elbow, again in a way that she had only seen in the movies.

He paused, as they reached the bar, having shaken off their pursuer.

'You're not alone, are you?' he then said, turning to her

with an amazing predictable heavy old-world gallantry. 'It's not possible that the best-looking and most intelligent woman in the room could have come here alone, is it?'

'Yes, I'm alone,' said Kathie.

'Where's your man, then?'

'He's in Hungary,' said Kathie.

'I've had enough of this party,' said Howard Jago. 'Let's get out of it, for Christ's sake.'

'I don't know . . .' said Kathie. 'I should say goodbye . . .'

'There's no need to say goodbye,' he said. 'Come on. Let's get out.'

She hesitated.

He took her arm.

She went.

They went downstairs and looked for a taxi: they found one easily, as it was that kind of district. They got into it. Then he said, again as though in a play or a film written by some playwright infinitely inferior to either of them, 'Where shall we go, to my place or yours?'

'Yours,' she said. 'But only for a little while. I have to get home. I've a script conference in the morning.' She was lying.

'Jesus,' he said, looking at her legs, actually moving the skirt of her dress so that he could look at her legs, 'you've got a beautiful pair of legs.'

'They're nothing special,' she said, which was true.

They arrived at his hotel, just off Bond Street. They got out, and went into the hotel, and up to his room. He asked the night porter to bring them a drink.

The room was large and expensive. Kathie sat in a chair. So did he. They drank the drink, and talked about the party, and about the people at it – their host, and Georgina, and various other playwrights, and the actress he had made so unhappy in New York the year before. Kathie knew exactly what she was doing: nothing on earth would induce her to get into that bed. She made it clear, as one does make it clear. They laughed a lot, and rang for some more drinks and a sandwich, and talked a lot of nonsense. She felt him move away. He had sense, after all. And when she said she ought to go, he looked at her, and said, 'Ah, I'm too old for you, you know.'

But he can't have said this with much conviction, or she wouldn't have responded with the awful line she then delivered (which she had said, years before, to an Italian actor in Rome) – 'You shouldn't try,' she said, smiling falsely, 'to seduce innocent girls from the country.'

He laughed, also falsely. She kissed him: they parted.

She went down and got a taxi and was in bed and asleep in half an hour.

And that is the end of the story. They were to meet again, over the years, at similar parties, and he was to remark again upon her legs and her looks. They never had any serious conversation. But that isn't part of the story.

The point is: what did she think about this episode? She emerges not too badly from it, anyone would agree. She behaved coolly but not censoriously: she said some silly things, but who doesn't in such a silly situation? She had no regrets on her own behalf, though a few on behalf of that sixteen-year-old girl who had somehow just missed the opportunity of a lifetime. She had grown up so differently from what she had imagined. And she had some regrets about her image of the man. It was spoiled, she had to admit it (not quite forever, because oddly enough some years later she went to see one of his early plays and felt such waves of admiration flowing through her, drowning her resentments, as though his old self were still speaking, and she listening, in some other world without ages). But for years and years, she thought she was never going to be able to take his work seriously again, and when she described the evening to Dan, she was so rude about him and his boorish chauvinist masculine behaviour that Dan, who usually sided with her and was as indignant as she was about such matters, actually began to feel quite sorry for Howard Jago, and to take his part. *Poor* Mr Jago, he would say, fondly, whenever his name came up, *poor* Mr Jago, he would say, lying safely between Kathie's legs, *what* a disappointing evening, I feel quite sorry for him, picking you, my love.

But that isn't all. It ought to be all, but it isn't. For Kathie, when she told the story to Dan, was lying. She tried to lie when she told it to herself, but she didn't quite succeed. She was an honest woman, and she knew perfectly well that she had received more of a thrill through being picked up by Howard Jago at a party, even picked up as she had been, casually, to annoy another woman – she had received more of a thrill from this than she would have got from any discussion, however profound, of his work and hers. She would trade the whole of his work, willingly, and all the lasting pleasure it had given, for that silly remark he had made about her legs. She would rather he fancied her, however casually, than talked to her. She would rather he liked her face than her plays.

It's an awful thing to say, but she thought of his face, looking at her, heavy, drunk, sexy, battered, knowing, and wanting her, however idly: and it gave her a permanent satisfaction, that she'd been able to do that to him, that she'd been able to make a man like him look at her in that way. It was better than words, better than friendship.

It's an awful thing to say, but that's how some women are. Even nice, sensible, fulfilled, happy women like Kathie Jones. She would try to excuse herself, sometimes: she would say, I'm only like this because I was a plain child, I need reassurance. But she couldn't fool herself. Really, she knew that she was just a woman, and that's how some women are.

Some people are like that. Some men are like that, too. Howard Jago was exactly like that. People like admiration more than anything. Whatever can one do about it? Perhaps one shouldn't say this kind of thing. One ought not to have said such things, even five years ago, about a woman like Kathie Jones. The opposite case, for political reasons, had to be stated. (This is only a story, and Howard Jago didn't really hate women, any more than Kathie hated men.) But Kathie Jones is all right now. The situation is different, the case is made. We can say what we like about her now, because she's all right. I think.

(1972)

8

A Day in the Life of a Smiling Woman

There was once this woman. She was in her thirties. She was quite famous, in a way. She hadn't really meant to be famous: it had just happened to her, without very much effort on her part. Sometimes she thought about it, a little bewildered, and said to herself, This is me, Jenny Jamieson, and everybody knows it's me.

Her husband was quite famous, too, but only to people who knew what he was doing. He was famous in his own world. He was the editor of a weekly, and so he had quite a pull with certain kinds of people. It was through his pull, really, that Jenny had got her job. She was getting bored, the little child was at nursery school and the big ones at big school, so he had looked about for her and asked a few friends and found her a nice little job at a television station. But he hadn't quite bargained for how she would catch on. Everybody had always thought Jenny was pretty – in fact, she'd been a very recognizable type for years, had Jenny: pretty, a little restless, driven into the odd moment of malice by boredom, loving her children, cooking dinners, flirting a little (or possibly more) with her husband's friends and old lovers. She deserved a little job. But when she got going, when she got on the screen, she was transformed. She became, very quickly, beautiful. It took a few weeks, while she experimented with hairstyles and clothes and facial expressions.

And suddenly, she was a beauty, and total strangers talked of her with yearning. And that wasn't all, either. She was also extremely efficient. Now, she always had been efficient; she'd always been able to get all the courses of a four-course meal onto the table, perfectly cooked, at the right moment. She was never late to collect children from school, she never forgot their dinner money or their swimming things, she never ran out of sugar or lavatory paper or sellotape. So people shouldn't have been surprised at the way she settled down to work.

She was never late. She never forgot appointments. She never forgot her briefing. She began quietly, interviewing people about cultural events in a spot in an arts programme, and she always managed to say the right things to everyone; she never offended and yet never made people dull. She was intelligent and quick, she had sympathy for everyone she talked to, and all the time she looked so splendid, sitting there shining and twinkling. Everyone admired her, nobody disliked her. In no time at all, she had her own programme, and she was able to do whatever she fancied on it. She used to invite the strangest people to be interviewed, and she would chat to them, seriously, earnestly, cheerfully. She told everybody that she loved her job, that she was so lucky, that it fitted in so well with the children and her husband, that she didn't have to be out too much. It's a perfect compromise, she would say, smiling. She didn't take herself very seriously – it's just an entertainment, she would say. I've been lucky, she would say. All I do is have the chats I'd love to have at home, and I get paid to do it. Lovely!

Her husband did not like this state of affairs at all. He became extremely bad-tempered, never came home if he could avoid it and yet would never commit himself to being out, because he did not want to make Jenny's life any easier. He wanted to make it as difficult as possible. So he would arrive unexpectedly and depart unexpectedly. He stopped bringing his friends home. He made endless unpleasant remarks and innuendoes about Jenny's colleagues in the television world, as though he had forgotten that he had introduced her to them in the first place. Sometimes he would wake up in the middle of the night and hit her. He would accuse her of neglecting him and the children. She was not quite sure how this had all happened. It didn't seem to have much to do with her, and yet she supposed it must be her fault. At night, when it was dark, she used to think it was her fault, but in the morning she would get up and go on smiling.

Then, one night, she came back from work, as she usually did on Wednesday evenings, late, tired. She noticed, as she parked the car outside the house, that the downstairs lights were still on, and she was sorry, because she did not feel like talking. She was too tired. She would have quite liked to talk about her programme, because it had been interesting – she had been talking to a South African banned politician about the problems of political education – but her husband never watched the programme these days. She found her key, opened the front door. Her head ached. She was upset, she had to admit it, about South Africa. Sometimes she thought she ought to go and do something about these things that upset her. But what? She pushed open the living-room door, and there was her husband, lying on the settee. He was listening to a record and reading.

She smiled. 'Hello,' she said.

He did not answer. She took off her coat and hung it over the back of a chair. She was going to make herself a milk drink, as she usually did, and go straight to bed. But just for the moment, she was too tired to move. She had had a long day, so she stood there, resting, thinking of the walk to the kitchen and how comfortable it would be to get into bed. She was just about to ask her husband if he would like a drink too – though he never did, he didn't like milk and coffee kept him awake – when a strange thing happened. Her husband put down his book and looked up at her, with an expression of real hatred, and said, 'I suppose you're standing there waiting for me to offer to make you a drink, aren't you?'

Now, the truth was that he had hardly ever made her a drink, in the evening after work, so she could not possibly have been expecting such a thing. He had done so perhaps three times in the last six months. The thought of his offering to get up and make her a drink had never crossed her mind. So she answered, politely. 'No, I was just going to ask you if you would like one.' And then an even stranger thing happened. For no sooner were the words out of her mouth than a rage so violent possessed her, as though an electric current had been driven through her, that she began to shake and scream. She screamed at him for some time, and he lay there morosely, watching her, as though satisfied that he had by accident pressed the right button.

Then she calmed down and went and made her drink and went to bed. But as she lay down, she felt as though she had had some kind of shock treatment, that she had suffered brain damage and that she would never be the same again. Let us not exaggerate. This was not the first time that this kind of thing had nearly happened to her. But this time it had happened, and the difference between its nearly happening and its happening was enormous. She was a different woman. She went to bed a different woman.

In the morning, she woke up, as usual, at about half-past seven, and thought of the day ahead. Every day, she got up regularly at a quarter to eight, and gave the children their breakfast. Various people, including her husband, suggested from time to time that she should engage somebody to help her with these things, but she always said that she preferred to do them herself, she liked to be with the children and she did not like other people to see her at that hour in the morning. Also, she would say, smiling disbelievingly, I'm afraid I might get lazy. If I give myself half an excuse, I might get lazy and stay in bed.

On this particular morning, it did cross her mind that she might stay in bed all day. I really do not see the point of carrying on, she thought, as she lay there and remembered what had happened to her the night before. I cannot possibly win, she thought. Whatever I do, I will lose, that is certain. I might as well stay in bed.

But no, she thought, it is more honourable to fight to the death.

So she got out of bed.

She had not often thought in these terms before. Rather, she used to say to herself, If death were announced, I would continue, like a saint, to sweep the floor. She had not thought, much, of winning or losing or battlefields.

She had her bath, as she always did, and while she was in the bath her eldest child brought her the post and the papers and opened her letters for her. She read *The Times* while she got dressed and looked at the *Guardian* while she brushed her hair. Then, before going down to breakfast, she read the lists of things to be done that lay by her bedside table. There were several lists, old and new, and it was never safe to read the newest one only. Some of the words on the lists were about shopping: haricot beans, it said at one point; Polish sausage, at another; then vitamin pills; shoelaces for Mark; raw carrots (?); Clive Jenkins; look up octroi. It would be hard to tell whether these notes were a sign of extreme organization or of panic. She could not tell herself. Carried over from list to list was a message that said *Hospital Thursday*. This seemed to indicate either that she was so worried about going to the hospital that she kept repeating the message to herself, neurotically, night after night, or that she was so little aware of it that she thought she might forget. But today was the day, so she would not forget.

She went downstairs and made breakfast. Two children wanted bacon sandwiches, and one said she would eat only a slice of leftover melon. She made herself a cup of coffee, and while they ate, she emptied the dishwasher and started to restack it, and took the dry clothes out of the airing cupboard and sorted them into piles to put away in drawers. Then she encouraged the children to put on their coats and shoes, and took them out, and put them in the car and drove them to school. They were all, by now, at the same school, which made life easier, as she would cheerfully remark. She remembered to remind them, as they ran off, that she would not be there to collect them, as she had an appointment, but that Faith would collect them and give them tea and supper. Then she went home and remembered to put a pound note in an envelope in the cupboard for Faith, in case she left before she herself got home in the evening. She would have done this, if her husband were home, but as usual he had not said whether he would be home or not, so she had to provide for every possibility, and one of these was that Faith would want to find a pound note in the cupboard.

Then she made the beds, and put the dry washing away, and stacked the breakfast things and ran down to the shops (which were luckily near) to buy tea and supper for the children, because although Faith was perfectly capable of doing this in theory, in practice she always did something silly, and anyway the women in the shops always shortchanged her with Jenny's money because she wasn't English, and Jenny did not consider herself quite rich enough to be shortchanged every day, though sometimes she let it go. Then, when these things were done (it was now half-past nine), she went up to her bedroom to change, because she couldn't possibly spend the whole day in the jersey and skirt she was wearing, because she had to go and give the prizes at a School Speech Day that evening and wouldn't have time to come home to change in between all the other things she had to do. She was due at a committee meeting at ten-thirty; she would make it all right, but only if she made her mind up quickly about what to wear.

She had quite a lot of clothes, as her job demanded that she should, but none of them looked very good this morning. They had buttons missing, or needed cleaning, or were too avant-garde for a Speech Day. She could not find anything suitable. Racked by indecision, sweat standing up in soft beads on her upper lip and running down her arms and thighs, she stood there in front of the wardrobe and thought, Is this it? Is this where I stop?

But no, because she finally decided that her long grey dress, although slightly too smart, would please the children at the school, if not the headmistress, and, after all, they would expect her to look a little colourful or they would not have invited her. So she put it on. It was a little too smart for a committee meeting, too, but the committee wouldn't mind. She put it on, and then her boots, so she wouldn't have to change her stockings, which had holes. She did not wear tights. She considered them unhygienic. And then she got her briefcase, and put in it her minutes for the meeting, and some old notes for her speech, and her appointment card for the hospital, and the correspondence with the head-mistress of the school, and a book by the man she was supposed to meet for lunch. And then, thinking that she had got everything, she said goodbye to her husband, who had watched some of her preparations from bed and some from his desk, which stood in the bedroom. And off she went towards the bus stop.

She did not take her car into town. She did not like driving in London. How very sensible you are, people would say, and Jenny Jamieson would say yes, it is sensible, and she would chat about the antisocial inconveniences of driving in the West End, and from time to time, she would think, If they knew how very very frightened I am of the traffic, would they continue to think me sensible?

She arrived at the committee meeting in good time, as usual, and took her place, but as she nodded and smiled at her fellow committee members, she was obliged to recognize that something rather unpleasant had happened, connected no doubt with the shock she had sustained the evening before. The unpleasant thing was that she did not like the look of these people any more. She had never liked them very much, that was not why she had attended the meeting: she attended because she considered it her duty. It was a committee that had been set up to enquire into the reorganization of training schemes for aspiring television producers, directors and interviewers, and it also considered applications and suggestions from some such aspirants. Jenny considered she ought to sit on this committee, because her own entry into the world they desired had been so irregular, and she thought that she, a lucky person, ought to try to be fair to those people who had not had her contacts. Not everybody, after all, had the good fortune of being married to Fred Jamieson. But her colleagues on the committee did not seem to have been moved by such motives.

The longer she knew them, the more convinced she had become that they were simply there in order to give an appearance of respectability and democracy to a system that functioned perfectly well, that continued to function and which they had no intention of altering. It was a system of nepotism, as she knew from her own experience. Whatever polite recommendations they might make, younger sons and friends of friends and clever young people from fashionable universities would continue to be favoured. She had accepted this, in a way, and had thought her presence useful, even if only because she occasionally managed to make out a case for some course of action or some individual who would otherwise have been considered negligible. She had understood why the others behaved as they did: most of them were older than herself, they had been brought up in a world of patronage, they had done well on it, they were kind, well-meaning, urbane, amusing, cynical, rather timid people, they could not be expected to rock any boat, let alone the one in which they were sitting. She had respected these things in them, she had understood. And now, suddenly, looking round the polished table at their faces – at thin grey beaky Maurice, at tiny old James Hanney, at brisk young smoothy Chris Bailey, at two-faced Tom (son of one of the powers), at all the rest of them – she found that she disliked them fairly intensely.

This is odd, she said to herself, looking down at her minutes. This is very odd.

And she thought, What has happened to me is that some little bit of mechanism in me has broken. There used to be, till yesterday, a little knob that one twisted until these people came into focus as nice, harmless, well-meaning people. And it's broken, it won't twist any more.

She tried and tried, she fiddled and fiddled inside her head to make it work, but it wouldn't work. They stayed as they were, perfectly clear, not a bit blurred by her inability to reduce them to their usual shapes. Horrible, they were.

The mechanism had broken because it had been expected to do too much work. She had been straining it for years.

She didn't think she could bear the look of things without it.

She kept very quiet during the meeting, because she did not know how to express herself in this new situation. She could hardly remember the kind of things that she used to say, that she would have said if she hadn't been so filled with horror and disgust. Once or twice a diplomatic phrase occurred to her, she realized how she could have thrown in a small spanner or suggested a different approach, but it didn't seem worth bothering. And what frightened her most was that she had always known, intellectually, that it wasn't worth bothering, that her contributions were negligible; and yet she had continued to make them, because she *felt* that it was worth doing, she *felt* that she should. And now she didn't feel it. So it was simply herself that she had been indulging all this time. So there was no point in appealing any more to what she ought to do. It had never been a question of that. The actual situation, unillumined by her own good will and her own desire to make the best of things, was beyond hope.

Making the best of things, she thought, as the meeting ended, is a terrible thing to do. They must become worse before they become better, as Karl Marx said.

She did not smile very much as she left the meeting. She put on a preoccupied look instead, which absolved her from the obligation.

She was due for lunch, at one, in a French restaurant in Soho. She was to entertain a clergyman, due for interview. He had outspoken views on violence in Africa and the need for the churches to offer their support. She was hoping for conviction from him, for she herself veered towards pacifism, weakly. She was not looking forward to the lunch. There had been a day when lunches had been her delight: newly released from the burden of cooking unwanted meals for infants, and herself brooding morosely over a boiled egg or a piece of cheese, she had embarked on large meals and wine and shellfish and cigarettes and coffee and chat, with great pleasure. But the pleasure had faded, and now she feared to fall asleep in the afternoons. She was so tired, these days.

Her secretary had booked the table. The clergyman, said her secretary, had seemed delighted at the prospect of lunch. And as Jenny's programme paid its interviewees badly, in her now sophisticated view, lunch was considered a justifiable expense. She looked at her watch, as she got out of the taxi. Five to one, it was. She was due at the hospital at three, she must make sure she was not late, Africa or no Africa.

She was drinking a glass of tonic when the clergyman arrived. She always ordered tonic if she got there first, because it looked like gin and didn't put other people off drinking. Other people did hate to be discouraged from drinking, she had found. The clergyman, deceived, ordered a Campari. He was expecting her to twinkle and glitter and glow like something on a Christmas tree: she could see the expectation in his eyes, as he looked at her over the menu. And she thought, Dare I disappoint him? And then she thought, sickened, as she decided on a salad: I treat people like children, and I treat my children like adults.

She thought of her children, with unaccountable yearning. The yearning was mixed, vaguely mixed, with the thought of the hospital. Jenny Jamieson loved her children with a grand passion. Sometimes, looking at them, she thought she would faint with love.

The clergyman ordered soup and *poulet grandmère*. She joined him with the *poulet*. They talked about Mozambique and Angola and Rhodesia and the leadership of the Zulus.

They talked about the World Council of Churches. She was able to watch him enjoy the familiar shock of the thoroughness with which she had done her homework. She had a good memory for dates and facts and had found it extremely useful: it commanded instant respect. She knew that he knew more of the realities than she did – he had been there, after all, he had lived with them – but he was not as good at dates. She had been a good examinee and was now a good examiner.

But she did not like the clergyman. She had wanted to like him, as he had wanted to like her. But they did not like each other. She did not like him, really, because he had agreed to eat lunch with her and appear on her programme. She thought of Groucho Marx this time, not Karl, and his remark that he did not want to belong to any club that admitted him as a member. What were they doing there, both of them, sitting eating an expensive meal, when an agreement had just been made that decided that Africans in Rhodesia could not vote until they had £900 income a year? The average income for an African in Rhodesia was £156 p.a., or so she had read in her morning's paper.

It occurred to her that the clergyman did not like her for much the same reason. It was not possible for them to like each other, sitting in such a place.

The allowances we have to make, she thought, are just too much for us.

In another mood she might have essayed an ironic hint, a smile, to indicate that she had recognized that this was so, to do him the credit of thinking that he too might have known it. But why should they be let off?

She continued to think, however, that she might feel differently about the whole matter on Wednesday week, when the clergyman was to appear on her programme. So she asked questions and made notes of answers, as they ate their chicken and declined pudding and drank black coffee. Then the clergy-man had to go, and she had just time to arrive comfortably, by taxi, at the hospital.

She was rather surprised to find herself at the hospital, as she had been rather surprised to find herself at her doctor's the month before. She was an exceptionally healthy woman, was Jenny Jamieson, and so afraid of hypochondria (an afflic-tion she truly despised) that she never allowed herself to think about her health. She ignored her body. It was not a subject that could be contemplated with much pleasure, for although beautiful now, momentarily, she expected daily the decay of beauty and did not allow herself to dwell too much on pleas-ure or on fear. She was a sensible woman. Probably you begin to see by now how sensible she was. But nevertheless, although sensible, on this occasion, she had allowed a splendid igno-rance to go on a little too long. For several months now, she had been bleeding when she ought not to have been and had been too busy even to worry about it. Occasionally, she would say to herself, Oh, God (wiping the sheets on the bed, throw-ing away another pair of paper knickers), oh, God, I must do something about that. And then the phone would ring, or a child would call, or the post would arrive, or it would be time to go to the studio, and she would forget. So she didn't get round to going to the doctor until one morning, when the company rang her up and said that, unexpectedly, they wouldn't be wanting her after all, as her guest had been held up by an air strike in Florida. So she had a morning off, and instead of sitting down with the paper and a cup of coffee to enjoy it, she instantly, and, as it seemed, entirely arbitrarily, began to worry about the bleeding, and went up to the doctor's and sat in his surgery waiting to see him for an hour and a half. She rather thought (being a healthy person) that he would say not to be so silly, when she described her symptoms. She expected him to say that it was nothing at all. But he didn't. Instead, he listened gravely and attentively, and didn't smile once (though she smiled enough for two) and told her she ought to go and see a gynaecologist. 'Oh, all right,' she said. And so here she found herself, in a gynaecological hospital, waiting patiently for her turn.

She waited for hours. Thank God she had known it would take hours. She kept thinking how demoralizing it would have been, if one hadn't known. Luckily one was not as young and nervous as one used to be.

The surgeon was a short, nice old man. He dug around inside her with his fingers until she cried out. Does that hurt, he said. No, no, she said. Because it did not hurt. It frightened her, it did not hurt her.

She was still expecting him to smile, as she sat up on the white paper sheet in her beige petticoat, and to tell her that there was nothing there.

And he did smile. But what he said was, 'You'd better come in for a little operation.'

She didn't listen very attentively to his answers to her sensible questions, though she forced herself (as though on the screen) to ask them all. She asked about malignant growths, and cervical smears, and polyps and ulcers, but she wasn't listening. She remembered, faintly, a dreadful interview with a cabinet minister, when she had been so crumpled up with bellyache that she had hardly been able to hear a word the man was saying. The surgeon seemed to be trying to reassure her: he patted her on the knee. He did not recognize her: probably he was too busy carving women up to watch the television. She had no illusions about the extent of her notoriety. And anyway, women in their petticoats look much the same. She loved him, for patting her knee through the hospital sheet.

'You go to the appointments lady, my dear,' he said. 'See when they can fit you in.' There would be a bed free in three weeks' time.

I know what beauty is, she thought, as she walked through the front door of the hospital, dreading already her return: beauty is the love that shone through my face. And it is dying, it has been murdered, and they will see nothing but their own ugliness. Beauty is love, she thought.

She was so dazed by her encounter with the surgeon that she wandered, idly, for half an hour or so. She walked up and down the streets off Oxford Street, looking in pornographic bookshop windows.

She was terrified. She was ill, she was dying. She was looking her last on the *Loves of Lesbos*, the *ABC of Flagellation*. I have wasted my life, she thought. Oh, God, she thought, direct me, please.

On the train, she sat down quietly and began to work out the implications of death. Her life, luckily, she had heavily insured, some years before. It had seemed a good idea at the time, and she had never regretted it. Her husband, though competent in some ways, was feckless: he was also much hated, as editors often are, and if ever he lost his power to control others, others would not waste time in trying to ruin him. She had thought to herself, some years ago, as soon as she began to earn good money, I should insure myself, for the children's sake. Well, she had done it, she had not merely thought about it, she had done it. That was the kind of woman she was. So she need not worry about their material future.

But what of their need for her?

She loved them. She had made herself indispensable. That had been her aim.

Would they weep for her?

The rain fell, outside, on the dark countryside. Two men, commuters, were playing cards, as they did every night. She envied their will to brighten their lot. Inside, she was weeping away, she was weeping blood. Whatever should she say to the girls, at the other end of this journey?

A friend of hers, recently, had killed herself. Jenny, with mechanical kindness, had comforted husband and mistress and child, in so much as it was in her to do so. It was the woman who had been her friend, after all, and she was dead. The child did not seem to notice much. So much sympathy had been lavished upon the survivors. But the woman, Jenny's friend, was dead forever. She was beyond sympathy and love and fear. She was no more. What rage must have possessed her, at the moment of extinction, to know what tenderness would accrue to others from her death, while she lay rotting.

Jenny had a vision of herself dead, and her survivors basking in the warm sun of condolence. So much pleasanter for them than her presence, it would be. They did not much care for her presence, these days.

Though that, of course, was not true of the children. No, they would grieve for her, if she died, as she would, forever, for them, if they were to die.

And as she sat there, she knew that this was it, this was the reckoning. She would have to think about those things that she so much ignored. She would have to contemplate, now, here, her own not-being: would she die under the knife, would she expire in the hands of an incompetent anaesthetist, would she fade slowly from malignant growths, the months running down into weeks, the weeks into days? She had heard recently of a friend's friend who had died at home: in the morning she had had breakfast, had played cards with her child, had chatted to her friend. Then she had fallen, as it seemed, asleep.

But she had been dead, there in her bed, and no gentle shaking, no offers of the already-prepared lunch, had been able to wake her. What a mystery, how devious was death, to creep so wickedly in so many quiet ways. Death was certain: her luck had run out. Death sat with her there in the carriage, but what questions could she put to this unwanted guest? She must decide, here, on the five fifty-eight, about the existence of God, and the power of human love, and the nature of chance.

She had not neglected these subjects entirely. But she had postponed judgement. Now she would have to decide. Time had run out.

She had always, until this moment, politely supposed that God must exist. At least, she had given him the benefit of the doubt – as she had given it to Fred Jamieson. But it did strike her now, again with a sudden electric sense of shock, that her own premature and sudden death would disprove the existence of God entirely, and that her faith in him had rested only on her belief that he would fulfil his obligations as she would fulfil hers. And if he failed (as the very existence of the hospital suggested he might), then he could not exist at all. How could a God exist who would be so careless of his contracts as to allow her to die and break her own contracts to her own infants?

Her children would be ruined by her death. No corrupt adult reassurances, no promises of treats, would buy them off. Any confidence in fate would be ruined by her removal. She had loved them so, and it was her love that would undo them. Her friend who had killed herself had not loved her child, so the child had survived. It was her own love that would undo them.

The apathy of God, the random blows of fate and the force for good and ill of human love: these things, combined, constituted a world so bitter, so dark, so tragic, that she felt her heart weep and die like her body.

They would cry for her and there would be no comfort. She would be dead and gone and powerless, and thus they would know the dreadful truth.

She was parting herself from God, she was leaving and turning her face from him. Only in leaving him did she realize how much she would have liked him to be there: as she would have liked her husband to like her. But it was not to be. God was too weak, too feeble, she had looked after him too nicely for too long. She had felt sorry for him because of his non-existence. If I give him a chance to behave better, she had thought to herself for years, vaguely, maternally, he might learn how to do it: he might learn better from me and show his face to me.

But he couldn't show her his face because he didn't have one. That was why she hadn't seen it so far. She felt sorry for him, as one for a friend caught out making an empty boast. She didn't want to question him too closely about his reasons for having lied to so many for so long: she didn't want to make a fool of him. She was very careful, was Jenny Jamieson: she never made a fool of people on the box, and she was very delicate about doing it even in her own head. She always regretted it when people insisted on condemning themselves out of their own mouths, and she would do her best to prevent them. So now, too, she thought (or could imagine) that she would soon find some means of concealing from God her own violent and utter loss of faith in him: she would find some way of humouring him along. There was no point in getting angry about the matter: he was too weak to withstand anger.

The train stopped at a station, started again, continued on its way.

What grieved her most was the thought that her children would never know about the intensity of her love, the depth of her concern. It was impossible to convey to them the nature of her emotion. To a lover, one could explain such things: lovers, ripped asunder by death, at least know that the other, on the point of death, had thought of the terms of love. For a lover, death need not be a rejection and an abandoning. But for a child, it could not be anything else: no child could know how much he was loved, his mind could never encompass the massive adult passion.

She thought, I will write them a letter. In this letter, I will explain how much I loved them, and how sorry I was to abandon and forsake them, and I will give the letter to my solicitor, and he will lock it away in a safe and give them each their copy when they are eighteen.

But she knew that she would not write such a letter. For the writing of it would seal her own death warrant and date it, and it was as yet undated. She could not afford to run a risk of making certain what was at the moment at least open to hope. So she would die, in three weeks' time, in a year's time, and the letter would be unwritten and they would never know. She died and left us, they would say, because she didn't care enough for us, she didn't care enough to live.

She imagined their faces, their nightmares, their sick and endless deforming resentments, their lonely wakenings, their empty arms, their boarding schools, their substitute consolations.

And this was the price of love.

It did not seem tolerable, it did not seem possible.

She would go out like a light, she would be switched off forever. There would be nothing to grieve with, no ghost to hover anxiously over their heads. She would be forced to default, coerced by death into breaking her contract. She had contracted herself to her children, for the period of their infancy: she would have to break the contract and she would have no excuse.

The bitterness of it filled her and possessed her, but she was beginning to breathe again, because she knew, now, what it was that she feared. She had faced it, and it was nearly time to get off the train; she could think about it again later. She would store it away, for future consideration. And meanwhile, she would have to think of something to say to the girls. She opened her bag, and took out an old envelope and began to scribble herself some notes for a speech.

The headmistress met her on the station. She had been met by many such people, on many such stations, and had always, at the time, thought to herself how nice they were, these people. It was only afterwards, in retrospect, that she would come to admit to herself that some of them were quite frightful. She wondered, now, as she walked up to the waiting woman in her fur coat, if one of the consequences of her last day of life would be that the dislike would always, now, set in instantly, that the judgement would always, now, be made at once, because there was so little time left for other ways of doing things. The thought crossed her mind, in the instant as she approached, paused, checked that it was the right person with the right look of recognition, and extended her cold hand: and it was so – she knew at once that she did not like this woman at all, that she could have no time for her at all. Afterwards, she thought, if I had not conceived such a motion, it would not have been so: as part of her was to believe, despite the evidence, for the rest of her life, that if she had not gone to the doctor that morning, the thing inside her would not have existed at all. She should never have condoned its existence.

As they drove back to the school, the headmistress in the

fur coat talked about town councillors and local education authority people and how one had to give them sherry. She then started to complain bitterly about the fact that her school had been turned into a comprehensive. As Jenny Jamieson had accepted the invitation because the school was a comprehensive, she was not well inclined towards this line of conversation. Nor did she think much of Miss Trueman's reasons for despising town councillors and aldermen, nor of her tact in uttering them. She had often received surprises of the same kind and could never decide whether those who spoke to her in such a vein simply mistook her own moderately fashionable and public political views and prejudices – or whether they were utterly indifferent to them and would have uttered them stubbornly, tactlessly, regardless of the nature of the audience.

So she did not have much to say in reply to the small talk of the headmistress, Miss Trueman. However, upon arriving at the school, she managed to make the usual obligatory remarks about the charm of its location, the modernity of its buildings, its handsome array of Speech Day flowers.

They were to have sherry before the ceremony. Jenny Jamieson went to the headmistress's lavatory and discovered to her alarm that she was losing rather a lot of blood: doubtless the surgeon had prodded whatever was producing the blood rather hard and had disturbed it considerably. She had nothing to stop it with: she had not brought anything, had not thought of it. She disliked the headmistress too much to ask her if she had any Tampax. Anyway, she thought, she is probably too old to need such things, this woman. She had a moment of panic, standing there in the centrally heated lavatory. But she decided to ignore the blood. After all, she said to herself, it takes an awful lot of blood to show. One can feel quite soaked sometimes and when one looks at one's clothes it hasn't even got through one layer, let alone to the surface.

Nevertheless, she declined a glass of sherry. She was not feeling too well, and the room was far too hot. She had a glass of water instead, as there were no soft drinks. So much for gracious living, she thought, as she watched Miss True-man deftly condescending to the town councillors and the staff, and endured a succession of people who said how wise she was not to drink before speaking and how glad they were that they didn't have to speak themselves. She felt rather dizzy and was extremely aware of the place where the surgeon had poked her.

There were some tropical fish in a tank on a bookshelf. They had some babies, protected by an inner glass tank. They would have eaten their own babies otherwise, the mothers. She commented on the fish and admired them, for want of better things to say, and a woman to whom she had been introduced started to tell a story about her own children's goldfish and how they kept dying.

Jenny Jamieson did not like this conversation because her own fish had died the year before, and she had been extremely unhappy on the day of their death, when they had floated around keeling over, the two of them, at a sad angle, as though they had lost their sense of watery balance. She had disliked the sense of death in the room, but had been unable to save or kill them and had not moved them out of the room because it would have seemed to her to be graceless, heartless, to make them die in a strange place. Let them die here, she had thought, and had endured their passing. Then she had gently buried them at the end of the garden under the lower branches of the cotoneaster.

But what was this woman saying to her now, interrupting her own memories of funeral? She was saying, in a harsh and brutal nasal voice, laughing as she said it, 'And I told the kids I'd buried them. I'd buried them in the garden, I said, but of course I hadn't. I'd put them in the obvious place . . .' And one or two other people laughed, but Jenny had missed her cue, she didn't know what the other woman was saying. She knew her face had looked momentarily blank and baffled, and she started to speak, to say that where else should one bury them but in the garden, when the other woman said, heartily, 'You know, I flushed them away, well, I mean to say, wouldn't you?' and Jenny worked out that this woman had actually put her children's goldfish down the lavatory and then said that she had buried them in the garden. She did not know which was more unnatural, the woman's insensitivity, or her own sensitivity, which made her so slow to recognize the meaning of words, the end of life, the obvious places to put dead bodies. She had flushed their little gold bodies down into the sewers, and what was wrong with that? Jenny Jamieson shivered and trembled: heaps of corpses filled her vision. She had buried her fish gently, reluctantly, sorrowfully: they had been in her charge and they had died. Her solicitude had been more than godly, for God left dead dogs on beaches and crushed rabbits on the brows of roads. Gold spectacles, gold fillings, mounds of pilfering and salvage. But flesh is not for salvage: it is not even flotsam or jetsam. It is waste.

And now it was time to go into the School Hall, and there was the platform, and the school orchestra, and the serried ranks of parents and children, and the returning sixth-formers who had left the year before, all dolled up, free of Miss Trueman's surveillance, all come back to give the old thing a slap in the eye. And there were the prizes, dozens and dozens of them, all to be handed out with a cheerful smile; she would smile till the muscles of her face grew rigid and stiff. And here was a child presenting her with a bouquet; it smelled sickly, of cemeteries and death; it was already decaying through its cellophane in the intense and human heat. And now the headmistress was about to deliver her report.

Jenny Jamieson sat back on her chair. There was no need to listen to the report. She thought again of the surgeon's fingers and the white hospital sheet. She thought of the goldfish, wavering and keeling over, slowly gasping, unprotesting, dying in silence, rejected by their element, floating hopelessly upward. She was losing a lot of blood now; she could feel it seeping from her. Her knickers were quite wet. She was glad that she had put on her grey dress: it was of a thick material, though unfortunately it was pale enough to show, if marked. But it would absorb a good deal before it marked.

Miss Trueman talked of the difficulty of adapting to new ways, and the problem of the less gifted, and the marvellous way the school had coped with the upheavals of the last few years, and how it was now a happy unity, where each could find her place, with work fitting to her talents – 'for we all have talents,' said Miss Trueman, 'though we may not all take our A levels.'

The school was rigidly streamed and had managed to segregate all its new nonacademic intake very thoroughly.

'Our A-level results,' said Miss Trueman, 'are still as high as ever, we are proud to say.'

Jenny Jamieson thought, I will never let anyone inside me again. Too often, now, I have politely opened my legs. It shall not happen again. Too many meals I have politely cooked, too many times have I apologized.

'Unfortunately,' said Miss Trueman, 'Mrs Hyams has had to retire this year through ill health, but I am sure we all join in sending her our very good wishes . . .'

Jenny Jamieson looked at the mothers and fathers, and at the girls. Blank and bored and docile they looked. They sat in rows, very quietly, and let Miss Trueman (Harrogate and Somerville) look down upon them.

She thought, again, of her own children, and the bland confidence with which she had assumed that she herself would one day sit in such a hall, as a parent, and listen to others make dull and foolish speeches and hand out prizes to her own three. How much she had expected of life. She had expected to see them grow up, to see their long legs and their adult faces and their children. It was impossible that an accident, like death, could separate them from her. And yet it was possible: such things happened, daily.

She felt her spirit tremble, as it prepared to launch itself across this dizzy gulf: had it the power? Would its wings carry it to the other shore or would she fall, here, now, forever, into the darkness?

And she thought to herself: those who do not love, die, and they are forgotten, and it is of no account. But those who love as I have loved cannot perish. The body may perish, but my love could not cease to exist: it does not need me, I am dispensable, I may drop away in that hospital like an old husk, but I am not needed, the years I put in are enough (Freud would say, Klein would say, those mighty saints and heralds) – it is enough, I am released from existence, I am freed, for my love is stronger than the grave.

Her spirit, breathless, reached the other side. With immense excitement, with discovery, with revelation, she said to herself: My love is stronger than the grave.

Later she was to say to herself, All revelations are banal. But even so, it is as hard to receive them as it is to gaze at the sun, which is, after all, a commonplace and daily sight.

Still later she was to say to herself, That was the moment at which it was decided that I should not die, for that was the moment at which I accepted death.

But at the time, she sat there neatly, listening to Miss True-man, who was by now reciting her own biography: 'How fortunate we are,' she was saying, 'to have with us this evening Mrs Jamieson, who is so well known to all of us. How privileged we are,' said Miss Trueman, with a most subtle and magnificent note of superiority in her privileged tones, 'to have with us a woman who has distinguished herself . . .'

Some of us, of course, thought Jenny Jamieson, are so constructed that we have to end up smiling. She thought this then, even while she was still trembling with the intensity of her conviction. She was quick.

And she rose to her feet and smiled and began her speech on cue. And whether it was a shame or a dignity, she could not tell, she did it well, this kind of thing. But, as has been said already, she did most things well. Even her spiritual crises she endured well. And came up smiling. And stood there smiling, speaking of new opportunities for girls these days and how important it was to think in terms of having careers as well as husbands, 'for the two, these days,' said Jenny Jamieson, smiling confidently (shining, confident, a beautiful example), 'for the two these days, can be so easily combined. We are so fortunate these days,' said Jenny Jamieson, 'and we must take every advantage of our opportunities.'

It would be hard to say what she herself thought of this ending. The force of her nature was very strong. She could not act without conviction. So she manufactured conviction. That is one way of looking at it. There are other ways.

What is true is that while she was standing there, and smiling, and speaking with such good cheer about the future of womankind, blood was seeping out of her, and trickling down her thigh, under her stocking and into her boot. There was an awful lot of it. Thank God, she said to herself, as she spoke to others of other things, thank God I put a long dress and boots on, so it doesn't show.

For twenty minutes, she spoke and bled.

Looking back, she was to think of this day as both a joke and a victory, but at whose expense, and over whom, she could not have said.

(1973)

9

Homework

I hope I don't give the impression that I'm complaining about her behaviour. On the contrary, I know she has always been very good to me, very generous with her time, very friendly and sympathetic – and I can't really expect it, there's absolutely no reason why she should see me at all. She's a very busy woman, I know – I'm always telling her that I realize how busy she is, and that she mustn't let me put her out, that the minute I start boring her with my little worries she must just tell me to pack up and go. And she never does – to do her justice she never does, and even on this last occasion (and I was a little upset) – well, I quite understood how she felt. No, she has always been very generous to me. I always make it perfectly clear to her that all she has to do if she wants to put me off is just give me a ring. I'm always in, I say. You're the busy one, not me, I'm nobody, I always say: just you give me a ring if you can't manage Tuesday, we can easily fix another day. I'm *always* free. But she never does.

So you can imagine how uneasy it made me, to see her treat Damie so badly. It's so unlike her, she's such a patient, generous, understanding person, and that poor little boy – well, he's not so little now, he must be about twelve, I suppose – but he certainly does get the rough end of her tongue. And the other day – I was really shocked. I wanted to say something, but I didn't know how to, and it was hardly my place.

I got there as usual, at about half-past five. She always says, come round as soon as you like – I used to get there at about half-past six, in time for supper, but lately I've got into the habit of arriving an hour or so earlier, so we can chat over tea. Once I got there about five, and she was on the telephone, and she stayed on it for hours and hardly looked at me once while she was talking – so, I've been careful not to get there before half-past, recently. Once, I got to her street so early I had to walk round and round the block to fill in the time, and I met her on one of the rounds; she was rushing down to the butcher, forgotten to buy the mince for supper – funny, how it's usually mince when I go, I can't imagine they have mince every evening – and she said, 'Whatever are you doing?' and I said, 'Oh, just walking round the block, I didn't want to bother you by getting there too early – ' and she said not to be silly, to come along in at once, so I did. But I still don't really like to get there much before half-past five, if I can help it. It doesn't seem fair on her: she always seems to have so much left to do when she gets back from work. Of course, she says she doesn't mind me being there while she's getting supper ready: she likes to have someone to talk to, she says. I always offer to help her, but she says she's not very good at being helped, she'd rather do things herself.

Anyway, on this particular evening I got there at about twenty past five: she was just clearing away the tea things. I thought she looked a bit tired, and I told her so, but she said it wasn't anything in particular: she'd had a late night the night before (she tells *me* that she has to be in bed by eleven) and then a long day at the studio: they started work at eight, for some reason. She didn't tell me much about the programme, so I gathered it wasn't going too well, and tactfully kept off the subject. She asked me how I was getting on with Mary (that's the woman I share a flat with), and how my father was, and I told her about them. (My father's in an Old People's Home: I see him at weekends.) I told her about them, while she started chopping up onions and things to go in the mince. (I wish she wouldn't put green pepper in: I've noticed that everyone fishes it out except her.) While I was trying to explain about Mary and how she couldn't go on an Easter holiday with me after all although she'd said she would be free, the phone went three times: two business calls, and one call that she put down *very* sharply, I thought. 'Now look,' she said, in this very odd tone, 'now look, you'll have to ring again later. And mind you do. I'll be very very annoyed with you if you don't ring later.' It didn't sound like her at all: I could tell she was irritable, from her voice. I'm glad she doesn't use that tone to me. But I suppose it is annoying, the phone going all the time, and the children running in and out. 'Oh, buzz off, Kate,' she kept saying to the little girl, who kept coming in to show her things she was making (origami, it was) – 'oh, buzz off, Kate, go and watch telly, I'm trying to talk to Meg, can't you see?' She really was a bit sharp, but nothing like as sharp as she was to Damie later. Anyway, I don't think Kate is as sensitive as Damie, she just went whistling back to the television, which they seem to watch all day and night, or at least when I'm there.

I was just explaining about the fact that Mary had already talked me into paying a deposit for the cottage for Easter when there was another interruption: the front-door bell, this time, and she gave such a start that she chopped her finger on the chopping knife. '*I'll* answer it,' I said, and set off down the corridor, but she wouldn't have that: no, she had to answer it herself, and off she went, dripping blood and sucking her finger. I couldn't quite see who it was: it was a man, I think, delivering something, but she'd put it down by the time she reached the kitchen. She didn't tell me who it was. Then we had ten minutes to ourselves before the phone went again: I knew who it was this time, it was her ex-husband, Tony. She always puts on that special brisk tone when she speaks to him. I know it conceals a lot of pain, but you certainly wouldn't guess it, unless you knew her well, like I do. Obviously he wanted to discuss something to do with one of the children: I could almost hear what he was saying, he's got such a loud voice. They talked for a few minutes, with her trying to put him off: I started to read the paper to show I wasn't listening, and after a while she said firmly, 'Now look, Tony, I can't talk now, Meg's here,' and he rang off almost at once. I smiled at her as she came back to the chopping block, feeling quite pleased to have fulfilled the humble little function of having helped to get rid of him, but she didn't look too pleased.

Still, I must say she was very nice about Mary. She even offered to lend me the deposit money until I could get it back from the travel agency, if I was hard up. I declined, of course. I don't like borrowing money, even from someone like her who's got plenty of it. And she agreed with me that Mary had behaved very thoughtlessly – people are *so* inconsiderate, we agreed, they never think of the other person's feelings, they never even notice when they are causing inconvenience. Yes, it's amazing how insensitive people can be, she said, when Damie burst in again (I forgot to say, he'd already been in several times) – anyway, he burst in for about the fifth time, this time with some question about his history homework. Now if it had been me, I know I'd have tried to pay the poor boy a little attention, but she snapped at him in a terrible voice, 'Oh, for Christ's sake, Damie, bugger off, can't you, can't you see I'm trying to talk to Meg?' To do the child justice, he hardly batted an eyelid. He just pottered off again with his textbook. But one never ought to speak to a child like that, even if one *is* a working mother. Particularly if, like her, you're always trying to put over the image of yourself as a kind of super-woman.

Anyway, by this time she was looking a little flustered, and what with one thing and another she still hadn't got the shepherd's pie in the oven, and it was getting on for half-past six. I asked again if I could help, but she said there wasn't anything I could do, unless I wanted to go and get myself and her a drink, from the other room. So I said I would, to humour her, really, because I'm not much of a drinker. (She is, though. I've sometimes been astonished by the amount she puts away. I've seen her get through well over a quarter of a bottle of gin in the evening.) So I went off into the other room to the table where she keeps the drinks: I knew she'd have gin and water (mother's ruin) because she always does, but I thought I'd have a Dubonnet and bitter lemon. There was some Dubonnet left in a very dusty bottle, probably the same bottle that I had some from last time (I don't think she likes it) but I couldn't see any bitter lemon, so I went back into the kitchen and asked her if she'd got any anywhere else. She said she might have got some in the cellar, and I said I'd go down and look for it, but she said better not, I'd never find it, and anyway it was very dark and cobwebby down there and the light was broken. So I said not to bother, I was quite happy to have the Dubonnet by itself or with tonic or soda. But she'd already set off down into the cellar, and I could hear her stumbling around down there. 'Don't worry,' I shouted, 'I don't want to be a nuisance, I'll be perfectly happy with sherry instead' – but I was too late. I heard her swear as she fell over something – she does use bad language, but perhaps everybody does these days – and then she came up with a very old-looking bottle of bitter lemon. 'Honestly,' I said, 'I'd have been *perfectly* happy with something else.' 'Oh, that's all right,' she said, and at last got around to getting the pie in the oven. At this rate, I thought, looking at my watch, we'll be lucky if we eat before half-past seven. And I hadn't had anything except a Mars Bar and a ham sandwich since lunch.

One would have thought things would quieten down a little then, and I did hope they would, because I was really looking forward to asking her what she thought about what Dr Scott had said about trying to reduce my Tranquillex prescription: he thinks that's what's been making me put on so much weight lately. Apparently it's a common side effect. Also, of course, I wanted a chance to hear about her programme. But things didn't turn out that way. No sooner had we sat down at the kitchen table (she poured herself out an enormous tumblerful of gin, at least it looked enormous to *me* but perhaps there was a lot of water in it) – no sooner had we sat down (she was putting a plug on a table lamp that the cat had knocked over and fused, I've often noticed how incapable she is of just sitting down and doing nothing) – no sooner had we sat down, than the twins burst in, dressed in some funny-looking uniform, saying they'd just got back from the Woodcraft Folk meeting. To tell you the truth, I'd hardly noticed they weren't there, the house was already so noisy without them. They really are the sweetest children, and very happy, amazing when you think how little time their mother has for them – anyway, then we had to listen to a long rigmarole about what they'd been up to at the Woodcraft Folk, which they said was a kind of guer-rilla warfare training for Marxist boy scouts – very funny, I suppose, though I don't think I'd like eight-year-olds of mine to be quite so precocious. Then they saw that we were having a drink, and began to demand bottles of Coke and crisps and peanuts and something called Corn Crackers. And she found she hadn't any Coke, so she sent them off to the off-licence to buy some, and a packet of Corn Crackers each for all the kids, and one for me. (They were quite nice, actually.)

But what with one thing and another, we'd hardly had time to exchange more than two sentences quietly together before the pie was ready and it was supper time. And those two sentences weren't very satisfactory: she said she couldn't possibly advise me about the Tranquillex, not being a qualified doctor, but that if I wanted to lose weight, perhaps I ought to join Weight Watchers. In other words, she missed the point entirely.

The pie was quite nice, and to do her justice I did notice that Damie at least had stopped fishing the green pepper out, so perhaps one can force anyone to like anything in the end. As usual, there wasn't any dessert, only fruit and cheese. She says she hates making puddings, and anyway, she says, they do one no good. Quite right, I suppose.

It was half-past eight by the time we had finished, and then, thank goodness, the twins went off to put themselves to bed, and Kate went to watch television, and Damie went off to finish his homework, and I helped with the washing up. At least she thought I was good enough to help with that. So we did have some time to talk. She asked me more about how I was getting on with Mary – really getting on, not just this business about the cottage – and was really sympathetic, as she used to be when I first met her, and not just listening with half an ear, as she is so often these days. And also, she asked me some more about Dr Scott, and asked if I'd ever thought of having any psychiatric treatment, and told me some story about a friend of hers who was getting remarkable results. I said, how ever could I afford it, we weren't all as rich as her and her friends, and that anyway I didn't really have much faith in that kind of thing, and she agreed, and put the coffee on, and poured herself another gin. (I didn't know people drank gin *after* dinner. I said I didn't want anything more to drink.)

We had coffee in the kitchen, to avoid disturbing the children in the other room. Damie always does his homework in front of the blaring telly, and how he manages to do so well at school is a mystery to me. Modern children *are* a mystery. She told me a story about a man at work who kept trying to take her out to dinner, and then the phone went – again – it was her sister this time, and they went on for hours, some problem about her sister's baby's nursery school which they both seemed to find extremely amusing, though I couldn't see the joke myself. When she rang off, finally, the phone went again the moment she put it down, and I think it must have been the caller who had annoyed her so much earlier, because she snapped back very abruptly with that same funny note – 'Oh, it's you is it, yes, I know I told you to ring again later, but it's not later enough, it's still early – ' and then there was a longish silence, while she listened to the other person, and I couldn't hear a word, because unlike her ex-husband Tony the other person was speaking very softly. And then, she said, in a softer tone, but still, I thought, very irritable, 'Oh. Oh, yes, I see. Well, that's different, isn't it? Yes, eleven should be all right. About eleven. See you soon.' (Hear from you soon, I suppose she meant.) 'Till later, then,' she said, and rang off.

She seemed in a slightly better temper, oddly enough, after this call, and started to tell me about her ex-husband's new girlfriend, and how well the two of them were getting on, and how she hoped that he would make up his mind to marry her. She puts a brave face on things, I'll say that for her. And, as the atmosphere was a little more peaceful, I thought I'd tell her about Mary's husband and how tiresome he's being over the allowance he's supposed to pay. But just as I embarked on it, Kate came in to say goodnight, and Damie came in with his homework. He wanted her to help him. It was physics, and she said she'd never been any good at physics, and he said that didn't matter, it was supposed to be just common sense at this stage (they do the Nuffield course, I think), to which she said that she'd never had any common sense either; but she agreed to have a look at it, and I could see her getting cross all over again when she found she couldn't understand it. So I asked her if I could have a look (not that I'm any good at physics either, but two heads are better than one) but she rather childishly said No, she wanted to be able to understand it herself, and that if a child of twelve was supposed to be able to do it surely she could too.

It would have been all right, I suppose, if Damie hadn't leant over the table while he was trying to explain something in the textbook to her, and knocked over the table lamp that she'd just been fixing. And then I really don't know what happened to her. She flew into such a rage, I've never seen anything like it. She picked the lamp up and hurled it at the wall, then she threw the physics textbook at Damie's head and started hurling abuse at the poor boy – such terrible language too, I hope he didn't understand it – and then she picked up her coffee cup and threw that after him, as he retreated down the corridor. I can't tell you how astonished I was. I was really amazed. And this was the capable woman we're all supposed to think is such a model of efficiency and calm. Poor Damie, I didn't know what to do, I could hear him crying in the other room. I didn't know what to say to her either: I said something about how she must be feeling tired after such a long day and not to blame herself too much, but she'd buried her head in her hands and wouldn't answer. I said I'd make her another cup of coffee, but she still said nothing. So I just sat there for a while, then I said, 'Shall I go and see how Damie is?' and she muttered that it would be better to leave him alone, and if I didn't mind very much she thought she'd go to bed, perhaps she wasn't feeling too good after all.

So I could hardly stay on after that, could I? I picked up the lamp and put the bits of coffee cup in the bin. It was still only half-past nine, and usually I don't leave till eleven, but there didn't seem much point in staying. She didn't seem to want to fix another day to see me: give me a ring, she kept saying. I wonder if she'd had too much to drink.

Anyway, I felt I had to go. I put my head round the sitting-room door on my way out, and Damie seemed all right again: he was getting on with the homework as though nothing much had happened. When I got out, though, instead of walking straight to the tube, I walked round the block, thinking I'd look in through the sitting-room window on my way back. I was still feeling anxious about Damie, of course. (She never draws the curtains: the whole street can see in.)

And would you believe it, when I got back round the block and looked in, there were she and Damie, sitting on the settee together, hugging each other and laughing their heads off. Laughing, they were. I can't think what at. There didn't seem to be anything to laugh at, to me.

So I went and caught the tube home.

You know, sometimes I think she's a little unbalanced. I wouldn't like to suggest it myself, but I really do think she could do with some kind of treatment.

(1975)

10

The Merry Widow

When Philip died, his friends and colleagues assumed that Elsa would cancel the holiday. Elsa knew that this would be their assumption. But she had no intention of cancelling. She was determined upon the holiday. During Philip's unexpectedly sudden last hours, and in the succeeding weeks of funeral and condolence and letters from banks and solicitors, it began to take an increasingly powerful hold upon her imagination. If she were honest with herself, which she tried to be, she had not been looking forward to the holiday while Philip was alive: it would have been yet another dutifully endured, frustrating, saddening attempt at reviving past pleasures, overshadowed by Philip's increasing ill health and ill temper. But without Philip, the prospect brightened. Elsa knew that she would have to conceal her growing anticipation, for it was surely not seemly for so recent a widow to look forward so eagerly to something as mundane as a summer holiday – although it was not, she reasoned with herself, as though she were contemplating an extravagant escapade. Their plans had been modest enough – no Swans tour of the Greek isles, no luxury hotel, not even a little family pension with check tablecloths and local wine in the Dordogne, but a fortnight in a rented cottage in Dorset. A quiet fortnight in late June. An unambitious arrangement, appropriate for such a couple as Philip and Elsa, Elsa and Philip.

Perhaps, she thought, as she threw away old socks and parcelled suits for Oxfam and the Salvation Army, as she cancelled subscriptions to scholarly periodicals, perhaps she should try to imply to these well-meaning acquaintances that she felt a spiritual *need* to go to Dorset, a need for solitude, for privacy, a need to recover in tranquillity and new surroundings from the shock (however expected a shock) of Philip's death? And indeed, such an implication would not be so far from the truth, except for the fact that the emotion she expected to experience in Dorset was not grief, but joy. She needed to be alone, to conceal from prying eyes her relief, her delight in her new freedom and, yes, her joy.

This was unseemly, but it was so. She had been absolutely fed up to the back teeth with Philip, she said to herself, gritting those teeth tightly as she wrote to increase the standing order for oil delivery, as she rang the plumber to arrange to have a shower attachment fitted to the bathroom tap. Why on earth shouldn't she have a shower attachment, at her age, with her pension and savings? Her jaw ached with retrospective anger. How mean he had become, how querulous, how determined to thwart every pleasure, to interfere with every friendship. Thanks to Philip, she had no friends left, and that was why she was looking forward with a voluptuous, sensuous, almost feverish longing to the delights of solitude. To get away, away from all these ruined relationships, these false smiles, these old tweed suits and pigeonholes full of papers – to be alone, not to have to pretend, to sleep and wake alone, unobserved.

It had not been Philip's fault, she told others, that he had become 'difficult'. It had been the fault of the illness. It had been bad luck, to be struck down like that when not yet sixty, bad luck to have such constant nagging pain, bad luck to be denied one's usual physical exercise and pleasures, one's usual diet. But of course in her heart she thought it *was* Philip's fault. Illness had merely accentuated his selfishness, his discreet malice, his fondness for putting other people in their place. Illness gave him excuses for behaving badly – but he had *always* behaved badly. He had seized upon illness as a gift, had embraced it as his natural state. When younger, he had made efforts to control his tongue, his witticisms at the expense of others, his desire to prove the rest of the world ignorant, foolish, ill mannered. Illness had removed the controls, had given him licence. He had seemed to enjoy humiliating her in public, complaining about her behind her back, undermining her when they sat alone together watching television. It had reached the stage where she could not express the slightest interest in any television programme without his launching an attack on her taste, her interests, her habits of mind. If she watched the news, she was news-obsessed, media-obsessed, brainwashed into submission by the news-madness of the programme planners; if she watched tennis or athletics or show-jumping, he would lecture her on the evils of competitive sport; if she watched wildlife documentaries, he would mock her for taking an interest in badgers and butterflies when she ought to be attending to the problems of the inner cities; if she watched a comedy series, he would call her escapist, and the comedy would be attacked as cosy middle-class fantasy or as a glorification of working-class subculture. Whatever she watched was wrong, and if she watched nothing – why, she was a television snob, unable to share the simple pleasures of Everyman. Night after night, at an oblique angle, through the small screen, he had abused her. It was not television he hated, it was her.

There was no television in Dorset. Apologetically, the owners of the little Mill House had explained that the valley was too deep for good reception, the picture quality too poor to make it worth providing a set. Good, Philip had said, but he had not meant it. If he had lived, if he had been alive to go on this Dorset holiday, he would undoubtedly have found some devious way to complain about its absence. Her lack of conversation, perhaps, would have been trundled out: better a mindless television programme, he would have declared, than your small talk, your silences.

Dead he was, now, and there would be no complaints. No television, and no complaints. There would be silence.

The evening before her departure, Elsa Palmer sat alone in the drawing-room with a tray of bread and cheese and pickle, and tomato salad, and milk chocolate digestive biscuits, and a pile of road maps, and her bird book, and her butterfly book, and her flower book, and her Pevsner. The television was on, but she was not watching it. She ate a bit of cheese, and wrote down road numbers in an orderly way. A10, A30, A354. There didn't seem to be any very obvious way of getting to Dorset from Cambridge, but that made the exercise of plotting a route all the more entertaining. She would pass through towns she did not know, get stuck in high streets she had never seen, drive past hedgerows banked with unfamiliar flowers. Alone, with her car radio. If she took a wrong turning, nobody would reprimand her. If she chose to listen to Radio 2, nobody would know. She could stop for a cup of coffee, she could eat a sandwich from her knee and drop crumbs on her skirt. And, at the end of the journey, there would be the Mill House, where nothing would remind her of Philip. She would lose herself in the deep Dorset countryside, so different from these appalling, over-farmed, open East Anglian wastes. There would be a whole fortnight of walkings and wanderings, of scrambling up coastal paths and rambling through woods, of collecting specimens and identifying them

from her books in the long, light, solitary evenings. Unobserved, uncriticized.

Philip, of late, had taken increasingly strongly against her
passion for identifications. 'What's in a name?' he would say,
when she tried to remember a variety of sweet pea, or to spot
a distant little brown bird at the end of the garden. As he
always beat her down in argument by sheer persistence (and
anyway, was it fair to argue with an ill man?) she had never
been able to defend her own pleasure in looking things up
in reference books. It had seemed a harmless pleasure, until
Philip attacked it. Harmless, innocent, and proper for the
wife of a university lecturer. An interest in flowers and butterflies. What could be wrong with that? By some sleight of
reasoning he had made it seem sinister, joyless, life-denying.
He had made her feel it to be a weakness, a symptom of a
character defect. She would never work out quite how he
had managed it.

The Lulworth Skipper. A local little butterfly, that haunts
Lulworth Cove. She looked at its portrait and smiled approv-
ingly. Yes, she would walk along the Dorset Coast Path, with
the Ordnance Survey map in her pocket, and go to Lulworth,
and search for the Lulworth Skipper. And if she did not find
it, nobody would know she had been defeated. Her pleasure
would be her own, her disappointment her own.

Marriage has warped me, thought Elsa Palmer the next day,
as she dawdled through Biggleswade. Marriage is unnatural,
thought Elsa Palmer, as she stopped at the red light of some
roadworks in Aylesbury.

Marriage and maternity. She thought of her children, her
grandchildren. They had all attended the funeral, dutifully.
She had found herself bored by them, irritated with them.
After years and years of cravenly soliciting their favours, of

begging them to telephone more often, of blackmailing them into coming for Christmas (or, lately, into inviting herself and Philip for Christmas), she now, suddenly, had found herself bored, had admitted herself to be bored. Stuart was a slob, Harriet was a pedantic chip off the old block (and always ill, my God, what stories of migraines and backaches, and she was only twenty-nine) and even young Ben had been incredibly tedious about his new car. And the grandchildren – whining, sniffing, poking their noses, kicking the furniture, squabbling, with their awful London accents and their incessant demands for sweets. Spoiled brats, the lot of them. Elsa smiled, comfortably, to herself, as she sailed through the landscape, divinely, enchantingly, rapturously alone. The weather responded to her mood; the sun shone, huge white clouds drifted high, vast shadows fell on the broad trees and the green-gold trees. An Indian summer, in June.

She had cautioned herself against disappointment at her journey's end; could the mill really be as charming as it appeared in its photographs? Was there some undisclosed flaw, some blot in the immediate landscape, some pylon or pig farm on its doorstep? Maybe, maybe: but some charm it must surely have, and the description of the little river flowing through the house and the garden, dividing the front garden from the little paddock at the back, could not be wholly fictitious. There were trout in the stream, she was assured. She pictured herself reclining in a deckchair, lying on a rug on the grass, reading a book, sipping a drink, looking up every now and then to gaze at the trout in the shallows, the waving weed. Inexpressibly soothing, she found this image of herself.

And the mill, when finally she arrived in the late afternoon, was no disappointment. It was smaller than it looked in the photographs, but houses always are, and it was right on the

road, but the road was a small road, a country road, a delight-
ful road, and she liked the way the garden gate opened onto
a flinty courtyard where she parked her car. Rustic, unpreten-
tious. A little lawn, with a wooden table; creepers growing up
the house; a nesting blackbird watching anxiously, boldly,
curiously; and beyond the lawn, the little river, the River Cerne
itself, which flowed right through what was to be, for a whole
fortnight, her own little property. The border was paved, and
next to the idle mill wheel was a low stone wall, warm from
the day's sun. She sat on it, and saw the promised trout flicker.
It was all that she had hoped. There was a little bridge over
the river, leading to the tree-shaded, thickly hedged paddock,
part also of her property. You can sit there, the owners had
assured her, quite out of sight of the road. If you don't like to
sit down on the lawn at the front, they had said, it's quite
private, through the back.

Quite private. She savoured the concept of privacy. She
would save her exploration of it until she had collected the
key and been shown round, until she had unpacked and made
herself at home.

The interior of the house, as displayed to her by Mrs Miller
from the village, was perhaps a little too rustic-smart: she
was introduced to a shining wooden kitchen table and benches
with diamond-shaped holes carved in them, a lot of glossy
bright brown woodwork, an open light wooden staircase up
to an upper floor and a semi-galleried sitting-room, a brass
horseshoe and a brass kettle, and a disconcerting fox's mask
grinning down from a wall. It was all newly decorated, spick
and span. But the millstone was still there, and the ancient
machinery of the mill could still be seen in the back rooms
of the house, and through the heart of the house flowed the
noisy, companionable sound of water. Elsa liked it all very
much. She even liked the varnished wood and the fox's mask.

Philip would have hated them, would have been full of witticisms about them, but she liked them very much. They were not to her taste, but she felt instantly at home with them. 'It's lovely,' she said, brightly, to Mrs Miller, hoping Mrs Miller would take herself off as soon as she had explained the intricacies of the electricity meter and revealed the contents of the kitchen cupboards. 'Oh, I'm sure I'll find everything I need,' she said, noting that milk, bread and butter had been provided. She was touched by the thoughtfulness of her absent landlords.

Mrs Miller vanished, promptly, tactfully. Elsa Palmer was alone. She wandered from room to room, examining the objects that make themselves at home in holiday cottages – an earthenware jug of dried flowers, a songbook open on the piano, a Visitors' Book, an umbrella-stand, a children's tricycle under the stairs, a stone hot-water bottle, a clock in a glass case, a print of a hunting scene. They made her feel amazingly irresponsible. She felt that for the first time for years she had no housekeeping cares in the world. She could live on Kit Kat or KiteKat and no one would comment. She could starve, and no one would care. Contemplating this freedom, she unpacked her clothes and laid them neatly in empty, paper-lined, mothballed, impersonal drawers, and made up the double bed in the low-ceilinged bedroom, and went downstairs. It was early evening. She could hear the sound of the mill stream. She unpacked her groceries: eggs, cheese, long-life milk, tins of tuna fish, onions, potatoes, a little fruit. A bottle of gin, a bottle of white wine, a few bottles of tonic.

With a sense of bravado, she poured herself a gin and tonic. Philip had always poured the drinks; in his lifetime she would no more have thought of pouring one for herself than she would have expected Philip to make an Irish stew. The thought of Philip struggling with an Irish stew struck her as irresistibly comic; she smiled to herself. Now Philip was dead, she could laugh at him at last. She adorned her gin and tonic with ice cubes and a slice of lemon. A merry widow.

The evening sun was mellow. It was one of the longest days of the year. She wandered out into the flinty courtyard and over to the little lawn. She sat on the low stone wall and sipped her drink. She watched a flock of long-tailed finches fluttering in a small tree. Tomorrow, if they returned, she would sit here and identify them. She thought they would return.

The weeds swayed and poured in the stream. Water crow-foot blossomed above the surface, its roots trailing. Trout rippled, stationary yet supple and subtle, motionless yet full of movement.

She sat and gazed as water and time flowed by. Then she rose and wandered over the little hidden wooden bridge to inspect the unseen paddock on the far side. As she crossed the bridge, a startled moorhen dislodged itself with great noise and splashing and she saw some chicks scrambling clumsily upstream. And there was the paddock – a long, triangular plot of land, planted with fruit trees, bordered on one side by a fence, on another by the stream and on the third by a high, irregular, ancient row of mixed tree and hedge, at the bottom of which ran another little tributary. The paddock, she discovered, was a sort of island. The music of the water was soft and reassuring. The grass was deep, knee-high. The stream was fringed with all sorts of wild flowers, growing in rich profusion and disorder – forget-me-not, valerian, comfrey, buttercup and many other species that she could not at once distinguish. A wild garden, overgrown, secret, mysterious. Nobody could overlook her here.

She sipped her gin and tonic and wandered through the long grasses in the cool of the evening. A deep, healing peace possessed her. She stood on the little triangular point of her island, where the two streams met, and stood on a tree root at the end of her promontory, gazing at a view that could not have altered much in a thousand years. A field of wheat glowed golden to her left, rising steeply to a dark purple wood. Long shadows fell. A small, steep view. The small scale of her little kingdom was peculiarly comforting. A few hundred yards of modest wilderness. She would sit here, perhaps, in the afternoons. Perhaps she would sleep a little, on a rug, under a fruit tree, in the sun, listening to the sound of water. Pleasant plans formed themselves in her imagination as she wandered slowly back and over the little bridge, plucking as she went a spray of blue forget-me-not. She would look it up, after her supper, in the flower book. How impatient Philip would have been with such a plan! It's *obviously* a forget-me-not, *anyone* can see it's a forget-me-not, Philip would have said, and anyway, who cares what it is? But he would have put it more wittily than that, more hurtfully than that, in words that, thank God, she did not have to invent for him. For he was not here, would never be there again.

Later, reading her flower book, examining the plant more closely, she discovered that it wasn't a forget-me-not at all. Its leaves were all wrong, and it was too tall. It was probably a borage, hairy borage – and after a while, she settled for green alkanet. *Anchusa sempervirens*. 'Small clusters of flat white-eyed bright blue flowers, rather like a forget-me-not or speedwell . . .' Yes, that was it. *Rather like*. Rather like, but not identical. Similar, but not the same. This distinction delighted her. She would forget it, she knew, but for the moment it delighted her. She was not very good at flowers, and forgot most of the names she so painstakingly established. At her age she found it difficult to retain new information, almost impossible to enlarge her store of certainties from the hundred names she had learned, half a century ago, as a brownie in the Yorkshire Dales. But the inability did not diminish her pleasure, it increased it. Philip had never been able to understand this. The safety, the comfort of the familiar well-thumbed pages; the safety, the comfort of the familiar process of doubt, comparison, temporary certainty. Yes, there it was. Green alkanet.

Her dreams that night were violent and free. Horses raced through dark fields, waterfalls plunged over crags, clouds heaped ominously in a black sky. But when she woke, the morning was serene and blue and filled with birdsong. She made herself a mug of coffee and sat outside, watching the odd car pass, the village bus, an old woman walking a dog. She planned her day. She would walk the mile and a half into the village, do a little shopping, visit the church, buy a newspaper, wander back, read her novel, eat a little lunch, then go and lie on a rug on the long grass in the paddock. The next day, she would be more ambitious perhaps, she would go for a real walk, a mapped walk. But today, she would be quiet. The luxury of knowing that nothing and no one could interfere with her prospect made her feel momentarily a little tearful. Had she really been so unhappy for so long? She saw the little long-tailed finches fluttering in the tree. They had returned to charm her.

Philip, she reflected, as she sat on the wall reading, would not have approved her choice of novel. She was reading a Margery Allingham omnibus, nostalgically, pointlessly. Philip had despised detective stories. He had mocked her pleasure in them. And indeed they *were* a bit silly, but that was the point of them. Yes, that was the point. After lunch, she took Margery Allingham into the paddock, with a rug and her sunhat, and lay under an apple tree. Impossible to explain, to the young, the satisfaction of sleeping in the afternoon. How can you *enjoy* being asleep, her children used to ask her. Now they too, parents themselves, were glad of a siesta, of an afternoon nap. Elsa lay very still. She could hear the moorhen with its chicks. She lifted her eyes from the page and saw a little brown water rat swimming upstream. A fringe of tall plants and weeds shimmered and blurred before her eyes. Sedges, reeds, cresses . . . yes, later she would look them all up. She nodded, drooped. She fell asleep.

After an hour she woke, from dreams of grass and gardens, to find her dream continuing. She was possessed by a great peace. She lay there, gazing at the sky. She could feel her afflictions, her irritations, her impatiences leaving her. They loosened their little hooks and drifted off. She would be redeemed, restored, forgiven.

The day passed smoothly into the evening, and gin and tonic, and the identification of long-tailed finches, and a reading of Pevsner. She marked churches she might or might not visit, and smiled at Pevsner's use of the phrase 'life-size angels'. Who was to know the life size of an angel? Had it not once been thought that millions of them might dance on the point of a pin? Might not an angel be as tall as an oak tree, as vast and powerful as a leviathan?

She slept like an angel, and woke to another blue uninterrupted day of laziness. She decided not to make a long excursion. She would spend another whole day in the delights of her new terrain. She repeated her walk to the village of the previous morning, she returned to a little lunch, she took herself off again to the paddock with her rug and her Margery Allingham. Already she had established the charm of routine, of familiarity. She felt as though she had been here forever. She read, nodded, dozed, and fell asleep.

When she woke, half an hour later, she knew at once that

she was no longer alone. She sat up hastily, guiltily, rearranging her hat, straightening her cotton skirt over her bare knees, reaching for her glasses, trying to look as though she had never dozed off in an afternoon in her life. Where was the intruder? Who had aroused her? Discreetly, but with mounting panic, she surveyed her triangle of paddock – and yes, there, at the far end, she could see another human being. An old man, with a scythe. She relaxed, slightly; a rustic old character, a gardener of some sort, annoying and embarrassing to have been caught asleep by him, but harmless enough, surely? Yes, quite harmless. What was he up to? She shaded her eyes against the afternoon sun.

He appeared to be cutting the long grass. The long grass of her own paddock.

Oh dear, thought Elsa Palmer to herself. What a shame. She wanted him to stop, to go away at once. But what right had she to stop him? He must belong to the Mill House, he was clearly fulfilling his horticultural obligations to his absentee employers.

Slowly, as she sat and watched him, the full extent of the disaster began to sink in. Not only was her solitude invaded, not only had she been observed asleep by a total stranger, but this total stranger was even now in the act of cutting back the very foliage, the very grasses that had so pleased her. She watched him at work. He scythed and sawed. He raked and bundled. Could he see her watching him? It made her feel uncomfortable, to watch this old man at work, in the afternoon, on a hot day, as she sat idling with Margery Allingham on a rug. She would have to get up and go. Her paddock was ruined, at least for this afternoon. Furtively she assembled her possessions and began to creep away back to the house. But he spotted her. From the corner of the triangle, a hundred yards and more away, he spotted her. He saluted her with an axe and called to her. 'Nice day,' he called. 'Not disturbing you, am I?'

'No, no, of course not,' she called back, faintly, edging away, edging back towards the little wooden bridge. Stealthily she retreated. He had managed to hack only a few square yards; it was heavy going, it would take him days, weeks to finish off the whole plot . . .

Days, weeks. That evening, trapped in her front garden, on her forecourt, she saw him cross her bridge, within yards of her, several times, with his implements, with his wheelbarrows full of rubbish. She had not dared to pour herself a gin and tonic; it did not seem right. Appalled, she watched him, resisting her impulse to hide inside her own house. On his final journey, he paused with his barrow. 'Hot work,' he said, mopping his brow. He was a terrible old man, gnarled, brown, toothless, with wild white hair. 'Yes, hot work,' she faintly agreed. What was she meant to do? Offer him a drink? Ask him in? Make him a pot of tea? He stood, resting on his barrow, staring at her.

'Not in your way, am I?' he asked.

She shook her head.

'On your own, are you?' he asked. She nodded, then shook her head. 'A peaceful spot,' he said.

'Yes,' she said.

'I'll be back in the morning,' he said. But, for the moment, did not move. Elsa stood, transfixed. They stared at one another. Then he sighed, bent down to tweak out a weed from the gravel, and moved slowly, menacingly on.

Elsa was shattered. She retired into her house and poured herself a drink, more for medicine than pleasure. Could she trust him to have gone? What if he had forgotten something? She lurked indoors for twenty minutes, miserably. Then, timidly, ventured out. She crept back across the bridge to inspect the damage he had done at the far end of the paddock. Well, he was a good workman. He had made an impression on nature; he had hacked and tidied to much effect. Cut wood glared white, severed roots in the river bank bled, great swathes of grass and flowers and sedge lay piled in a heap. He had made a devastation. And at this rate, it would take him a week, a fortnight, to work his way round. To level the lot. If that was his intention, which it must be. I'll be back in the morning, he had said. Distractedly plucking at sedges, she tried to comfort herself. She could go for walks, she could amuse herself further afield, she could lie firmly in her deckchair on the little front lawn. She had a right. She had paid. It was her holiday.

Pond sedge. *Carex acutiformis*. Or great pond sedge, *Carex riparia*? She gazed at the flower book, as night fell. It did not seem to matter much what kind of sedge it was. Carnation sedge, pale sedge, drooping sedge. As Philip would have said, who cared? Elsa drooped. She drooped with disappointment.

Over the next week the disappointment intensified. Her worst fears were fulfilled. Day by day, the terrible old man returned with his implements, to hack and spoil and chop. She had to take herself out, in order not to see the ruination of her little kingdom. She went for long walks, along white chalky ridges, through orchid-spotted shadows, through scrubby little woods, past fields of pigs, up Roman camps, along the banks of other rivers, as her own river was steadily and relentlessly stripped and denuded. Every evening she crept out to inspect the damage. The growing green diminished, retreated, shrank. She dreaded the sight of the old man with the scythe. She dreaded the intensity of her own dread. Her peace of mind was utterly destroyed. She cried, in the evenings, and wished she had a television set to keep her company. At night she dreamed of Philip. In her dreams he was always angry, he shouted at her and mocked her, he was annoyed beyond the grave.

I am going mad, she told herself, as the second week began, as she watched the old man once more cross the little bridge, after the respite of Sunday. I must have been mad already, to let so small a thing unbalance me. And I thought I was recovering. I thought I could soon be free. But I shall never be free, when so small a thing can destroy me.

She felt cut to the root. The sap bled out. She would be left a dry low stalk.

I might as well die, she said to herself, as she tried to make herself look again at her flower book, at her Pevsner, at her old companions. No others would she ever have, and these had now failed her.

Worst of all were the old man's attempts at conversation. He liked to engage her, despite her obvious reluctance, and she, as though mesmerized, could not bring herself to avoid him. It was the banality of these conversational gambits that delayed her recognition of his identity, his identification. They misled her. For he was an old bore, ready to comment on the weather, the lateness of the bus, the cricket. Elsa Palmer had no interest in cricket, did not wish to waste time conversing with an old man about cricket, but found herself doing so nevertheless. For ten minutes at a time she would listen to him as he rambled on about names that meant nothing to her, about matches of yesteryear. Why was she so servile, so subdued? What was this extremity of fear that gripped her as she listened?

He was hacking away her own life, this man with a scythe. Bundling it up, drying it out for the everlasting bonfire. But she did not let herself think this. Not yet.

It was on the last evening of his hacking and mowing that Elsa Palmer defeated the old man. She had been anticipating his departure with mixed feelings, for when he had finished the paddock would be flat and he would be victorious. He would have triumphed over Nature, he would depart triumphant, this old man of the river bank.

She saw him collect his implements for the last time, saw him pause with his wheelbarrow for the last time. Finished, now, for the year, he said. A good job done. Feebly, she complimented him, thinking of the poor shaven discoloured pale grass, the amputated stumps of the hedgerow. For the last time they discussed the weather and the cricket. He bade her goodbye, wished her a pleasant holiday. She watched him trundle his barrow through the gate, and across the road, and on, up the hillside, to the farm. He receded. He had gone.

And I, thought Elsa, am still alive.

She leaned on the gate and breathed deeply. She gathered her courage. She summoned all her strength.

I am still alive, thought Elsa Palmer. Philip is dead, but I, I have survived the Grim Reaper.

And it came to her as she stood there in the early evening light that the old man was not Death, as she had feared, but Time. Old Father Time. *He* is the one with the scythe. She had feared that the old man was Death calling for her, as he had called for Philip, but no, he was only Time, Time friendly, Time continuing, Time healing. What had he said, of the paddock? 'Finished for the year,' he had said. But already, even now at this instant, it was beginning to grow again, and next June it would be as dense, as tangled, as profuse as ever, awaiting his timely, friendly scythe. Not Death, but Time. Similar, but not identical. She had named him, she had identified him, she had recognized him, and he had gone harmlessly away, leaving her in possession of herself, of her place, of her life. She breathed deeply. The sap began to flow. She felt it flow in her veins. The frozen water began to flow again under the bridge. The trout darted upstream. Yes, Old Father Time, *he* is the one with the scythe. Death is that other one. Death is the skeleton. Already, the grass was beginning to grow, the forget-me-nots and green alkanets were recovering.

Rejoicing, she went indoors, to her flower book. It glowed in the lamplight, it lived again. She settled down, began to turn the pages. Yes, there they were, forget-me-not, green alkanet – and what about brooklime? Was it a borage or a speedwell? She gazed at the colour plates, reprieved, entranced. Widespread and common in wet places. She turned the pages of her book, naming names. Time had spared her, Time had trundled his scythe away. Philip had been quite wrong, wrong all along. Elsa smiled to herself in satisfaction. Philip was dead because he had failed to recognize his adversary. Death had taken him by surprise, death unnamed, unrecognized, unlabelled. Lack of recognition had killed Philip. Whereas I, said Elsa, I have conversed with and been spared by the Grim Reaper.

She turned the pages, lovingly. *Carex acutiformis, Carex riparia.* Tomorrow she would get to grips with the sedges. There were still plenty left, at the far end of the paddock, in the difficult corner by the overhanging alder. Tomorrow she would go and pick some specimens. And maybe, when she went back to Cambridge, she would enrol for that autumn course on Italian Renaissance Art and Architecture. She didn't really know much about iconography, but she could see that it had its interest. Well, so did everything, of course. Everything was interesting.

She began to wish she had not been so mean, so unfriendly. She really ought to have offered that old man a cup of tea.

(1989)

11

The Dower House at Kellynch:
A Somerset Romance

It is not always easy to distinguish attachment to person from attachment to property. I know it is widely held that Elizabeth was joking when she declared that she fell in love with Darcy when first she saw Pemberley. I used to think so myself. Now I am not so sure. Let me tell you my story, and you may make your own judgement. I have yet to make mine.

They call it the Dower House, but really it is nothing of the sort. It once fulfilled the function of a dower house, some time in the last century, the period at which the façade looking down over the pleasure gardens had been refurbished. One of the always more or less unfortunate Lady Elliots (or had it been a Lady Bridgewater?) was said to have been secluded there, and the improvements had been made for her benefit. The terrace with its Gothic alcoves, the urns and the sundial, the rounded finials on the roof had been added at this time, but it was no more a dower house than nearby Uppercross Cottage was a cottage. Both were renovated farmhouses. Uppercross Cottage, incidentally, is now known as The Elms, after the unfortunate whim of an early twentieth-century owner who decided the word cottage was inappropriate for so substantial a residence. The elms are all dead, of Dutch elm disease, but the name remains. It is a happy house and well maintained. It belongs to an architect from Taunton. His children and grandchildren play table tennis on the verandah in the summer evenings.

The Dower House is neither happy nor well maintained. But it is beautiful.

I fell in love with it at first sight. I was taken there by my friend Rose with whom I was staying at her farm on Exmoor. I did not know Somerset well, and we had spent a pleasant few days, walking, swimming in the icy River Barle, looking at churches and country houses. Rose was working on the illustrations for a book of European pond and river plants, and we collected specimens. On the whole we kept our own company, talking over our own affairs – I was still giddy with relief at having not long left my cad of a husband, she was involved with a philandering philosopher – but one evening she arranged for us to go over to Kellynch for dinner.

As we left the chalky uplands and descended into the red deeps, driving through increasingly narrow, high-banked purple-flowering lanes of foxglove and rosebay, Rose told me its history. Ever since some early Elliot had been obliged to let the Hall, at the beginning of the last century, the property had been hedged with difficulties. There had been a scandalous liaison round the time of Waterloo, which had scattered illegitimate children through the country, followed – or perhaps accompanied – by a marriage which had promised well, the bride being a Bridgewater and wealthy. But it had ended in long drawn out disaster. The Bridgewaters figured well in Debretts but not in other organs of record. They were, not to beat about the bush, said Rose, barmy. The duties and dignities of a resident landowner had appealed neither to Elliots nor to Bridgewaters. But they had hung on there, as the estate fell to pieces. During the Second World War Kellynch Hall had been requisitioned as an Officers Training Centre and it had never recovered. It was now a Field Study Centre.

She herself occasionally taught a course of botanical drawing there.

Yes, she said, slowing to avoid a pheasant, accelerating to overtake a tractor, there had been dramas. There had been suicides and incarcerations. The men drank and the women wept. The cold blood of the Elliots had mingled disastrously with the black blood of the Bridgewaters. One bride had thrown herself from an upper storey of Kellynch Hall on her wedding night: she had been caught in the arms of the great magnolia tree and had lingered on, an invalid. A daughter had taken her brother's shotgun and blown out her brains on Dunkery Beacon. A son had drowned himself in the pond. When the pond was drained, in the 1920s, said Rose, it was found to contain a deposit of bottles of claret both empty and full: old Squire William, the one who had sold off Parsonage Farm and the woods beyond Barton, had been in the habit of wandering down there of an evening, sometimes drunk, sometimes in a frenzy of remorse. In either state he had thrown bottles. The tench had thrived on them: never had such vast fish been seen. There was one stuffed on show in the Hall.

With such legends she entertained me as we drove westward. The present owner of the estate, Bill Elliot, with whom we were to dine, was now in his late thirties. His father, Thomas Elliot, had been a military man and had fought in the desert with Montgomery of Alamein, but the peace had disagreed with him and he had come home to drink himself to death, dying of cirrhosis of the liver in his sixties. Bill had inherited a property that was mortgaged, entailed and ill starred. Oppressed by this legacy, he had made a brief stay of execution by hiring the house, parkland and pleasure gardens to a film company for a costume movie. This venture had turned out well, for his dowerless sister Henrietta had insisted on appearing as an extra in the hunting sequence, had taken a nasty fall and had been wooed on her sickbed in Taunton Hospital by one of the film's more portly and substantial stars, who had married her. Did I know Binkie? Maybe I had seen him as a bishop in the latest Trollope series? He was really rather good.

But one cannot live off one windfall. And so Kellynch Hall had been let to the Field Study Centre on a 99-Year Maintaining and Repairing Lease. The Elliots had washed their hands of it. Bill was now camping out in the Dower House. I would like him, she hoped.

I wondered. As I struggled with the heavy metal latch of a broken-down five-barred gate – for it seemed we were to drive down a cart track to Kellynch – I struggled also with my feelings about the English land and its owners. I come, though I trust you cannot detect this, from the lower middle classes, to whom property is important – but by property we mean the freehold of a suburban house with a garden where you can hang out the washing, not farms and tenancies and arable acres. The Elliots of old would not have acknowledged the existence of my category of person. To them we did not signify. And now it was they who hung on by a thread. Kellynch Lodge, which had once belonged to the Russells, was owned by an absentee Canadian newspaper proprietor, and the Vicarage by a designer of computer software. Trade and the middle classes had triumphed.

Even Rose, who had done her best to declassify herself, sometimes annoyed me. She worked for her living, after a somewhat haphazard manner, but she carried with her the assumptions of a gentlewoman. She assumed I knew things I did not know, people I did not know. She lives in a world which I know largely through literature. I am the second-hand person, the ventriloquist. She is the real thing.

I relatched the gate with difficulty, got back into the car, and we edged carefully down what I now realized was not a cart track but an avenue of oaks leading towards Kellynch Hall. This had been the grand approach, and the trees, though some were stag-crested, were grand still: but they had returned so much to nature that the formality of their planting, ordained by some Elliot four centuries ago, was not at once apparent. They had been reabsorbed into the landscape, as had the great sweet chestnuts of the park boundary. Soft lumps of honey fungus sprouted from the old wood. The gold of a field of barley rose to our right. There was a hint of autumn fullness in the August air.

We descended, past the Big House, down the curved drive, through what had been the stable courtyard, to the Dower House. The melancholy deepened and tears stood in my eyes. I had never seen anywhere so beautiful in my life. Pink peeling walls, grey-yellow lichen-encrusted stone, single white roses, white doves. It had reached the moment before decay that is perfection.

Bill Elliot, too, was in his own way perfect. Decay had hardly touched him, though perhaps his hair was very slightly receding. He was extremely good looking – the Elliots are famed for their good looks. He was of no more than middle height, with the blue eyes, fair tanned skin, fine blond hair, regular features and open yet quizzical look of the beleaguered late twentieth-century English country gentleman. He was wearing a pair of moss-stained trousers rolled up to the knee and a limp blue shirt lacking most of its buttons. He put himself out to charm me, and I was charmed. I felt that it was a privilege to meet him. It was fortunate for me that he was not my type, I told myself.

It was a memorable evening. Bill's estranged wife Penny, who now lived with a trout farmer at Winthrop, had come over to join us. She had not brought the trout farmer. There was one other couple, a doctor who worked in Bristol and her husband, an ornamental blacksmith. Bill did the cooking, on an old-fashioned temperamental solid-fuel kitchen range which I was to get to know all too well. He made us a risotto, with a mixture of field mushrooms and slices of sulphurous yellow growth called Chicken-of-the-Woods. He said he would show me where it grew. It was delicious. We ate Somerset cheese, and salad, and blackberries and cream.

The Dower House was derelict. Patterned curtains hung tattered and drooping from bare rails, broken-springed chairs sprouted feathers, and feathers drifted under the kitchen door from a vast woodshed full of nesting doves. The wiring dated from between the wars. I had not seen such Bakelite plugs, such furred and twisted flex since my childhood.

We talked of the difficulties of the landed gentry as we sat around the scarred paint-stained seventeenth-century kitchen table. What should one do? Turn the stately homes into venues for pop concerts, into miniature zoos, into hotels? The Big House at Uppercross was now an expensive retirement home. The National Trust would not accept properties as gifts unless they were heavily endowed. I knew of these problems, but I had never met anyone who faced them in person. I had never felt much sympathy with them. But there was something touching about Bill Elliot, rinsing out a glass and drying it on a tea towel covered with garish pictures advertising Lyme Regis and its dinosaurs.

I said I had never been to Lyme. We wandered back into the drawing-room with our coffee, and Bill showed us his grandfather's battered dusty cabinet of treasures. There were little drawers of fossils and minerals, all labelled, and drawers full of pinioned butterflies and moths, and dried leaves from the rare trees in the pleasure gardens. Bill said he preferred the minerals. He had added specimens of his own, some of them collected at Lyme. He loved Lyme. He said I should go there one day.

At Bill's suggestion, we took a turn in the gardens. It was hardly dark, but Bill courteously took my arm as we stumbled through the undergrowth. There were nettles waist high, overgrown rhododendrons, Himalayan balsam, wild garlic. It was a wilderness. The mild air was heavy, rank, lush, erotic, sad.

We went back to the house for a last glass of wine. Bill told us that he was leaving the country. There was, he said, no freedom for him here. Penny, who was not hearing this news for the first time, said nothing. She watched a spider walk along the wall. They had two daughters, both at boarding school in Exeter. There would be no more Kellynch Elliots. A Shropshire Bridgewater Elliot was next in line, would inherit the title and the debts. Bill said he was off to Alaska, to a place called Anchorage. I asked why. 'Because it sounds safe there,' he said, and we all laughed. He said that he had been there once, briefly, changing planes on the way to Japan. He had liked it. It was as far from Kellynch as you could get. It was all snow and minerals. He would study minerals there in the long nights. He had sold a couple of paintings – a flood-damaged Hudson, a doubtful Reynolds – to finance his expedition. You could live for ten years in Anchorage on a gentleman in brown velvet, a lady in blue satin.

I did not know whether he was being whimsical or speaking the truth. It is difficult to know the difference with that kind of person.

On parting, he kissed my hand. The gesture was more intimate than a peck upon the cheek. 'Dear girl,' he said. 'Goodbye. Wish me well.'

Rose was very quiet on the way home. I think she had once been a little in love with him.

I heard no more of Kellynch for seven years. I somewhat lost touch with Rose: she sold her farm and took off to the South Seas to do a book on tropical flora, and this broke the rhythm of our friendship. In those seven years much happened. My imprudent early marriage came to a final end in divorce, but my career prospered. I had been no more than a promising actress in those early days, and not even I had thought I would be able to do more than scratch a living: but a lucky break in the form of a film role – as Juliet in a freely adapted version of Fanny Burney's *The Wanderer* – had come my way and since then I had been able to pick and choose. Tragic heroines from rustic romances were offered to me regularly, and most of them I declined. I had become well known and lonely.

I was sitting one evening in my flat off the King's Road reading a Thomas Hardy screenplay when the phone rang. I picked it up – which I might well not have done – and an unfamiliar voice said 'Is that Emma Watson? Emma? You won't remember me, but this is Penelope Elliot. Do you have time for a word?'

Of course I remembered her. I could see her face as though it were yesterday – her silver-yellow hair, her pale high brow, her girlish Alice band, her freckled nose, her little breasts, her faded jeans, her long thin bare feet.

'Penny,' I said. 'Yes, of course. How are you?'

She was well. The girls were well. Bill was well. She had left her fish man and married a lawyer. She knew I was well as she had seen me on TV. She was ringing about the Dower House. Bill's picture money – did I remember the picture money? – was running out, and he was thinking of letting the Dower House. They seemed to remember I was rather taken with it, and Rose had thought so too. Would I consider renting it for six months, for a year? Would I like to ring Bill in Calgary, or should she get him to ring me?

Whatever is he doing in *Calgary*? I asked. Oh, she said, he has fallen in love with the mountains and the everlasting snows. He says that Somerset is full of putrefaction.

We both laughed, and she gave me Bill's number. I tried to work out what time it might be in Calgary and what hours a man like Bill might keep, but I do not think I got it right because he sounded way out of all things when I spoke to him. Nevertheless we struck a bargain. I would take Kellynch Dower House for six months, renewable at six-monthly intervals. He said it had been done up slightly since my last visit. Not *too* much, I hoped. Oh no, he did not think I would find it over-restored. Any problems I could put through Penny and her husband. So useful to have a lawyer in the family.

This time I could detect the irony.

He was right in assuming I would not find the Dower House too much modernized. There had been attempts at improvement: the roses that had climbed in through the windows had been cut back, the roughly hacked dog-door had been blocked, the kitchen range had been given a coat of black lead, and loose covers had been fitted on some of the chairs. There were two new lavatories, though the bath still stood on claws in the centre of a three-doored bathroom. There was a second-hand refrigerator and a washing machine in an outhouse.

I was enchanted by my new retreat. How well I remember my first night there, as I stared at the flames of the log fire I had finally managed to light, and listened to some early Italian opera on the crackly radio. (Reception was never very good in that deep valley.) I was as safe as Bill in his snowy eerie.

As I sat, a strip of wallpaper, disturbed by my presence,

slowly unpeeled itself. A quarter of an hour later it began to rain and the chimney began to smoke. Rain fell down the chimney and onto the hissing logs. Smoke billowed at me. Coughing, I left the room, and found a rivulet of red water running through the back door, across the red tiles, through the hallway and out again under the front door. I opened the door and saw the water disappearing into a grate partly blocked by twigs and moss. I cleared the grate, and watched with satisfaction as the bloody trickle drained away.

I was by now muddy, so thought I would take a bath. The hot water was boiling, and gushed forth bravely. But alas, the cold pipes had developed an airlock. I sucked and blew but to no avail. I had to wait for the water to cool. I assisted it with ice cubes. When I got to bed, I could hear the sound of scrabbling in the rafters. Rats, mice, pigeons, owls, squirrels, doves? I fell asleep, content.

Each day brought some new disaster. It is extraordinary how many faults an old house can develop. I lived as in the nineteenth century. I became expert with bellows and stirrup pump, with mop and bucket, with toasting fork and balls of string and clothes pegs. Electricity cuts occurred almost daily. At times, tormented by the cooing of a hundred doves, I thought of buying a shotgun, but contented myself by throwing stones.

I arrived in a wet March, and stayed through most of the summer. My agent despaired of me and sent me threatening messages. Friends came to see me, were appalled by the discomfort, and went away. I wandered the hedgerows, climbed the hills, lost myself in the woodlands. I trod in the footsteps of the Wordsworths and Coleridge and Lorna Doone, I made my way through a thousand pages of *The Glastonbury Romance*. I studied the landscape and its history. I discovered that one of the oak trees in the avenue was the second tallest in Britain – *Quercus petraea*, thirty-six metres high, and more than six metres in girth. Once I went to Bath, but I did not like it there – it was full of young men drinking beer from cans, and the car parks were crowded and expensive. I never got to Lyme. I made acquaintances – a young woman up the valley called Sophy Hayter who kept goats, a retired vet who told me where to watch for the red deer. I dined with the Wyndhams at the Elms, had a drink with Dominic the blacksmith, and spoke, once, to the vicar. I often called in the church to see the Elliot ancestors. One lay helmeted and cross-legged on his crumbling sandstone tomb. There was a plaque to the Lady Elliot who had been so ill for so long.

I was on good terms with the people who ran the Hall, who said I could take my guests round whenever I wished. The Elliot coat of arms, with a date of 1589, was engraved over the three-storeyed porch of the south front, and the great magnolia still blossomed. Occasionally I would wander in to admire the lofty plaster ceilings, the polished floors (which smelt more of the schoolroom now than of the country house), the quantities of gilt-edged looking glasses, the paintings, the charming light rococo staircase. It was hard to think the house unworthily occupied and fallen in destination as one watched the peaceful pursuits of the students who came on botany or geology or painting courses. Some of them were very mature students, grey-haired, tweed-suited, rain-bonneted. They were usefully employed, and they kept the roof on, which was more than the Elliots had done. The whiff of carbolic and shepherd's pie was a small price to pay.

Sometimes I indulged a fancy that Bill Elliot was walking down the grand staircase with a new bride upon his arm, but this image derived more from Daphne du Maurier than from the house's own history. I could not help wondering how he felt about the place, and my proximity to it. Since I had become his tenant, he had taken to sending me enigmatic postcards. One mentioned the Chicken-of-the-Woods; he had drawn a little map of its whereabouts, so he too had remembered the details of our meeting. I did not have an address for him, so could not have responded had I wished.

There was a portrait of Bill in Kellynch Hall, by an undistinguished member of the St Ives school. He was wearing a sailor suit, and had gold ringlets.

In my Dower House, there was another portrait that interested me almost as much. It was of a woman dressed in the style of the 1820s, wearing a blue-and-yellow-striped dress with a low neck. She stared out of the frame boldly and with a certain effrontery. Her hair was auburn, her smile slightly crooked. Her largish hands – not well painted – were clasped in front of her bosom, holding a posy of primroses. I liked her. I wondered if she had been banished from the big house, or stolen thence by one who loved her. She seemed to smile at me with encouraging complicity.

In August I wrote to Bill's agent in Taunton renewing my lease. I was growing more and more attached to my solitude. I dreamed of Bill quite often.

One fine evening in late September I took myself up to the deserted kitchen gardens behind my house in search of rosemary. Some of the more tenacious herbs still grew there, though the beds were overgrown, the espalier fruit trees untrained, and the glass of the greenhouses broken. Mr Shepherd at the Hall told me that once fourteen gardeners worked there, growing asparagus and beans and lettuces and peaches for the Elliots. Why did they not put the gardens back into cultivation, I asked, to provide food for the students? Nobody would do such work these days, he said. It was cheaper to shop at the supermarket. Why did they not run a course on kitchen gardening, I suggested, and let the students grow their own supper? A good idea, he said. But I knew nothing would happen.

So I was the only ghost who haunted the garden. I came down with my handful of herbs, watching the evening light slant and flatten over the cedar of Lebanon, the tall hollies, the yellow Bhutan cypress, possessed by a luxury of self-pity and self-admiration so intense that I was consumed by it. I almost ceased to exist. And as I stood there, in a trance, I heard someone speak my name. I started with surprise – yet I was not wholly surprised, for was I not always expecting an audience, and did I not know that I was, that autumn evening, after a summer of fresh air, in particularly good looks?

'Miss Watson?' I heard, from the terrace. There was a man standing there, my binoculars in his hand. I had left them on the little writing table in the outdoor alcove, along with my book, my pack of cards and my glass of whisky – a glass covered, alas, inelegantly, by a postcard, to protect it from the flies. He had been watching my hawk.

'Yes?' I hazarded, a little coldly. Was he some intruder from the world of commerce, some angry messenger from my agent? But no, he was a gentleman.

'Miss Watson, I apologize for my intrusion. I could not pass without seeing the old house, and I was told I would find you here. And then I saw you, up in the walled garden. So I waited. Please – ' he stretched out his hand – 'let me introduce myself. I am Burgo Elliot.'

'Ah,' I said. 'You must be Burgo Bridgewater Elliot. From Shropshire.'

'Indeed, from Shropshire.'

We shook hands. I was in some confusion. For this was the heir, and I was the usurper.

In the circumstances – which included my glass of whisky – I felt obliged to offer him refreshment, to invite him in to see the improvements. Yes, he would like that, but perhaps we could sit first for a while in the garden? So we settled together in the alcove, I with my whisky, he with a sherry (he was lucky there, I do not often have sherry in the house) and a bowl of Bombay Mix between us. I inspected him, and he inspected me. He was, if anything, younger than Bill, so perhaps there was not much chance of his inheriting anything unless Bill fell down a glacier quite soon. Was he married, did he have sons, and would the estate be entailed to them when Bill died?

Such thoughts, which were quite unlike any I had ever had before I came to Kellynch, buzzed around in my head with as much determination as the wasps buzzed around the sherry. Where had they come from? Were they bred by the red earth itself, by the crumbling stone? They were not *my* thoughts at all. They had slept deep in the ancient masonry and had crept out at last into the late sun.

Burgo Elliot did not seem to hold me responsible for the neglect of the gardens, the peeling wallpaper, the smoking chimney, the laundry-cupboard door. I was a paying guest, and apologies were due to me, not from me. But it saddened him to see how run down things had become. Did I not find it too melancholy?

No, I said. It was the melancholy I loved. I did not care for fresh paint. I was a romantic.

He smiled. This was fortunate, he said.

We moved indoors, and he made the tour, even glancing into my bedroom with its embroidered counterpane. He stroked the scarred kitchen table, patted the settee as though it were an old family dog, and sighed. He said he had not been to Kellynch for years, not since he and Bill were boys. Poor Bill, he said. Did I know Bill well? No, I said, hardly at all, though even as I spoke I knew this was not quite true. I did know Bill Elliot. I had invested in him, and he had lodged in me.

Burgo Elliot was, like his cousin, a handsome man, though in a different style. He was darker, he was taller, he had grey eyes, and a Roman – perhaps a Norman – nose. He was also very thin. His head was a fine skull of sharp planes and bone, he had worn thin with time like an antique silver spoon.

He was, it appeared, a bachelor. He denied wife and progeny. He also denied Shropshire: although he was indeed one of the Shropshire Bridgewater Elliots, he lived in London. As, he believed, did I?

We sat indoors and he spoke affectionately of the old days. Here they had played, he and Bill and Henrietta. He had been an only child, and had looked forward to his summer holidays, though Lady Elliot had been a sad lady, and the old man a monster. He it was who had let the Hall go to its final rack and ruin. He had stoked the fire with priceless manuscripts, buried the family silver in the pleasure gardens without marking the spot, and shot the local policeman. He had done nothing to restore the Hall after the war years, and in the bitter winter of 1947 the tanks had burst and the rococo staircase had been a cascade of ice. So Sir Henry and his lady had moved out to the Dower House, evicting old Boniface, who had been squatting there as the sole remaining gardener, and they had camped like gypsies. The children had learned to fend for themselves. Bill had shot rabbits for the pot, and cooked them in the garden on an everlasting bonfire. They had made great cauldrons of oatmeal and nettle stew. The last of the staff had deserted, and the empty Hall had crumbled. When the old man died and Bill came of age, it was too late to rescue it. Lady Elliot had gone into a nursing home in Chard.

It was growing late, and my lamb cutlet would not feed two. So I fell silent, and he, being a gentleman, at once took his leave. He was on his way to see friends in Devon, who would be expecting him, he said.

He was lying. He would go no farther that night than the Dalrymple Arms or the Egremont at Uppercross. But I accepted his fiction and let him go. I knew I would see him again. And I wanted time to think about his apparition.

How could I not have been stirred by it? It would have taken a dulled, nay deadened fancy not to have been stirred by Burgo Elliot.

Why, I wondered, had he remained single? In my experience there were two likely explanations – one, that he had liked those of my own sex too much, the other, that he liked them not at all. I pride myself on having a good eye in these matters, but Burgo baffled me.

He had spoken with great fondness of Bill. Had he been in love with the beautiful boy? Or had it been his own childhood he mourned?

Bill, he said, had always loved the inanimate. He had thought it safe. When I had finished my cutlet, I went and knelt down by the little cabinet and looked at the weathered fragments of ammonite, the fossilized starfish, the swaying stone flowers of the sea, labelled in Bill's childish hand. And where was Bill now, perched on what ledge, huddled in what remote crevasse, while Burgo Bridgewater Elliot slept between clean sheets in a warm inn?

I became obsessed by Burgo Elliot. Had I dreamed him up? Even his name seemed false. Burgo – surely a name for a novel, not for real life. A name for a rogue and a villain?

Let me make this plain. Until I went to Kellynch I had no interest in what is called family. My own family – well, I have said they were lower middle class, but by the time I was born they were middle middle class. My father worked for an insurance company in Newcastle, my mother was a schoolteacher. He reads Trollope, she reads Jane Austen. They are sensible, hard-working people, but they have no connections and are proud of it. Nevertheless, my mother can never resist a temptation to tell the story of her meeting with the Duchess of Northumberland. It is a pointless story but she will tell it. My ex-husband, with more reason but as little excuse, likes to let it be known that his maternal grandmother was a Dalrymple. He reveals this fact in order to mock it. But nevertheless he reveals it. And am I not now letting you know that I married into the Dalrymples?

The Elliots and the Bridgewaters were much more interesting to me than the Dalrymples. How could I find out more about Burgo? I was too ashamed of my curiosity to ask anybody, and it was a happy moment when I remembered the books in my own back parlour. They were a deeply unattractive assortment of old bound volumes of *Blackwoods* and *Punch* and the *Spectator*, redolent of Sunday afternoons of ancient boredom, foxed and mildewed and spotted with birdlime – jackdaws often came down the chimneys and one of my occupations was to chase them away. I had never thought of browsing in this dull library, but now was its moment – and yes, indeed, there was exactly what I was looking for. There was the *Baronetage*, a heavy purplish folio volume with gold lettering on the spine.

I lugged it onto the kitchen table. I was not the first to consult it. The pages fell open, as I might have predicted, upon the Elliots of Kellynch Hall. It was clear that the entry had been much perused. There were two whole pages of Elliot this and that, but I could soon see that they were only of historical interest, for the last entry, added to the Gothic print in fine copperplate hand, read 'Heir presumptive, William Walter

Elliot, Esq., great grandson of the second Sir Walter.' We were back in 1810. This was no use to me. I needed something more modern.

I dug around, and at length found a 1952 volume of *Burke's Peerage*, which also fell open upon Elliots. And here they were, my very own Elliots. There was Sir Thomas, there was his son and heir William Francis Elliot and his daughter Henrietta. I read the names again and again, hoping to wrest some occult significance from the very words. There was no mention of Burgo Bridgewater Elliot. I could not find him anywhere. I needed a sequel, published after Sir Thomas's death.

In the morning I rang an old friend who I thought might help, and to whom I did not mind revealing my interest. He is himself a baronet, though he does not like this to be mentioned as he is also an actor and he hopes (so far in vain) not to be typecast. He was currently appearing in *Lady Windermere's Fan*. James seemed pleased to hear from me and delighted by the nature of my query. The Shropshire Elliots, I wanted? Well, first of all I must forget about the Shropshire bit. People do not come from where they say they come from. Does the Duke of Devonshire live in Devonshire, the Norfolks in Norfolk, the Bristols in Bristol? Certainly not. Now I am James Winch of Filleigh, he said, but I don't even know where Filleigh is, I think it is the home of some cricket team where grandfather once got a hat trick while touring with the Myrmidons . . .

I checked his flow and asked him to look up the Shropshire Elliots, to see if they had any money left. 'Why, thinking of marrying one, darling?' he said, and went off to consult his reference library. He came back in triumph, I knew he would have the right books. People like that always do, however much they dissimulate.

Yes, he said, here were the Elliots of Kellynch. William Francis, m. Penelope Hargreaves, 2 d., marriage dissolved 1978. And the heir was kinsman Burgo Bridgewater Elliot, of the Shropshire branch. He looked up Burgo, and told me that he was a company director of Felsham Metal Frame Windows. A very good prospect, said James. I should marry him if I were you, and not that other fellow. Or would you like to marry me and take a turn as Lady Filleigh?

I thanked him for his gallant proposal and rang off. I was shaking slightly and almost poured myself a vodka. I was shocked by my own curiosity. I could not shock you more than I shock myself.

Burgo reappeared in the spring. I had wintered in London, avoiding the dark nights and obliging my agent by doing some work. But in March I was back at the Dower House with the primroses, to find a postcard from Bill that had been waiting for me for weeks upon the red tiles. Rain had flowed over it, intruding cats had stepped inkily upon it, and its message was hardly decipherable, but I think it said 'With love to my fair tenant. Have you yet heard the nightingales?'

On my first evening the phone rang. It was Burgo. This was not much of a coincidence, it seemed, as he said he had been ringing me all winter. Where had I been? In London, I said. Ah, so have I, he said. But now he was in Somerset. Could he call and take me out to dinner at the Castle Hotel in Taunton?

And so it was that Burgo Bridgewater Elliot reopened negotiations. And, over his subsequent campaign, I remained as much in the dark as ever about his nature and his intentions. Never have I known so opaque an admirer. Never did he touch me, save in the way of courtesy – a hand at greeting, a hand to help me into the car or over a stile or to disentangle me from a bramble. Yet he was in his way translucent. He was worn thin with a lonely pain. One felt one could see through him and beyond. Like one of those elegant thoroughbred dogs that appear to have no space for normal bodily organs, he seemed to have nowhere within him to live a natural animal or emotional life. He was all stretched tenuous surface. Bill, in comparison, had been a solid man.

Perhaps, I sometimes thought, it was the place that Burgo came to see. It had cast its spell upon him, as it had upon me.

Was I falling in love with Burgo? I could not tell. I had nobody else to love, and at this moment in the history of my heart a second attachment, and to so eligible a gentleman, might have seemed a natural sequel to a somewhat unfortunate first choice. (Not that I entirely regret the cad. He had his points.) Did I *want* to fall in love with Burgo? Again, I could not tell.

It was impossible to reject his attentions. My vanity would not have permitted it. He was the perfect escort, who increased my consequence in my own eyes even when there were no others to watch, and he escorted me gallantly through all weathers. I dragged him up hill and down dale that spring, that summer, curious to see how far I could lead him. One day I decided to take him to Lyme.

I wanted to look for fossils. Bill had sent me a postcard of a dinosaur's egg from the Rockies, and I determined to try to find some small dull long dead creature of my own to add to the Elliot collection. I informed Burgo of my plans, and we fixed a date for our excursion. I had bought a little hammer, and I told Burgo to bring his boots. I was becoming imperious with him, but he seemed to like it.

The weather did not look promising, and we wondered whether to cancel our trip, but out of stubbornness I would not. Burgo did not disobey. It rained as we set off. I insisted on going in my car. I said it would clear but it did not. We drove along twisting lanes, the windscreen wipers working, the windows misting, and on the high ground as we moved into Dorset there was fog and I had to put on the headlights. Burgo sat there without a murmur of complaint. What was he thinking of my folly and my obstinacy? I spoke to him of the Black Ven Marls and the Blue Lias and the Green Ammonite Beds. I could not even tell if he was listening. I did not know what I was talking about. I wondered if he knew I did not know. Maybe, with Bill, he had searched those beaches as a child, had been there many times before. Why was he so docile towards me?

Lyme is a steep little town, not friendly to the motor car. Various signs ushered us towards parking places, and we ended up at the bottom, down by the Cobb. The rain had settled into a steady downpour, but despite this there were a few bedraggled persistent holidaymakers huddling their way along the streets. There was a smell of vinegar, fish, harsh false sugar and fried onions. There was even a pair of lovers embracing on the end of the Cobb. There is always a pair of lovers embracing upon the end of the Cobb. I made poor Burgo march along the Cobb, and we stood there and looked at the boiling water beneath us dashing against the rocks. It was very slippery underfoot. My trousers were soaked. Burgo, still looking every inch the gentleman, was wet through.

Even then I would not relent. I dragged the poor man off to the fossil cliffs – and you can guess the rest. We survived the Cobb, but the Black Venn Marls got us.

It was my fault. I was a bloody fool. But Burgo by this time was not behaving very sensibly either. There is something dementing about that landscape. The dark raw caked sliced earth, the ribbed ledges, the steaming fissures, the stunted trees sticking out of recent landslips, the dreary trickling of small black waterfalls, the dreary pounding of wave after wave upon the wet curve of the beach – I had never seen anywhere so desolate. As we walked along the beach, a great chunk of cliff the size of a packing case dislodged itself and fell with a mournful thud behind us. We should have turned back, but we went on. We both went on.

It was Burgo that saw the devil's toenail. His eyes are sharper than mine. He should never have pointed it out to me, but I should never have scrambled after it. I had not realized the black stuff was so friable. In short, just as I grabbed hold of the fossil, I slipped, and in slipping I dislodged a small avalanche, and thus it was that I did whatever I did to my leg.

I could not believe it. I am tough as well as stubborn. But I could not walk. There was nobody else in sight. Burgo would have to carry me back. I was covered in black mud, I was in pain, and I thought the tide was coming in. It was not a good surface for walking on at the best of times, and with the burden of a muddy lady Burgo must have found it agonizing. I kept apologizing. And still Burgo did not lose his temper.

I ended up in Weymouth General Hospital with my leg in traction. I was there for two and a half weeks. I had plenty of time to think. At the end of the first week Burgo asked me to marry him. I asked him why. He said it seemed to have been intended, and who were we to struggle against our destiny? If we found we didn't like it, he said, we could always get divorced. I was bold enough to ask him why he hadn't got married before, and he said that the black blood of the Bridge-waters had made it seem unwise, but maybe I wouldn't mind taking the risk? I seemed quite robust, he added.

I was quite pleased with myself, as you can imagine. Every-thing was going according to plan.

I told Burgo I needed time to make up my mind. He was far too much of a gentleman to retract his offer, I thought. I still did not know whether he wanted to marry me, thought he wanted to marry me, thought he ought to marry me, thought I wanted to marry him, or was in such despair that he didn't much care what happened. Or maybe he was up to some other game altogether?

My game by now is, I imagine, quite clear. I want the Dower House. I want it more than I have ever wanted anything. As I sit here, flying over the Rockies on my way to negotiate with Bill Elliot, I feel faint with desire at the thought of it. It is in my reach. Burgo says he will buy it for me, if Bill will let us have it. We shall see. If Bill won't let me have it, maybe I will marry Bill instead of Burgo. I feel such a sense of my own power as I sit here above the clouds. I can move mountains. A very small south coast avalanche was enough to bring Burgo to his knees. The Rockies look more formidable, but I cannot believe that they or Bill Elliot are impervious to my intentions. Bill has been waiting for me for eight long years. He will have something to say, surely, when we meet on the shores of Lake Louise.

Love of person, love of property. It is not as simple as that. What if I were to substitute the romantic word *place* for that cold Augustan word *property*? Would you then think so harshly of me? For the Dower House is worthless, as property. It is its own history. It is Bill and Burgo and Henrietta eating rabbit in the garden. It is the hawk and the Chicken-of-the-Woods and the red rain. It is the dead jackdaw in the bookcase, it is the avenue of oaks, it is the smiling woman with her primroses. She approves of my determination. So, too, incidentally, does Henrietta – she and Binkie and I get on *very* well. She thinks I should probably marry Burgo, but on the other hand she thinks it is time Bill came home, and I should try to get him back to the old country if I can.

I do not know what will happen. Emma Watson's story had no ending. Who knows what awaits me, down there on earth?

(1993)

12

The Caves of God

Biography, as the philosopher said, has added a new terror to death. It was in the spring of 1985 that Hannah Elsevir recognized that this aphorism, with which she had long been acquainted, might have an application to herself. The occasion of her fear was the posthumous publication of the diary of the father of an old friend of her ex-husband. Lord Reader had been a semi-eminent politician, on the periphery of public life for decades, but it was not the gossip about Cabinet and colleagues that alarmed Hannah Elsevir. It was his off-hand remarks about his son and her ex-husband.

This was the first: 'Giles has invited Peter Elsevir for the weekend. What a pretentious little prat. The boys talked of nothing but Burroughs and buggery. Is this the reward for an expensive education?' And again, three years later, a quick flip through the index revealed: 'Giles seems to have scraped a degree, God knows how, and so has that bit of bad news Elsevir', followed by 'Giles married today; speech by Elsevir as best man pretty offensive but not I suppose actionable.' Hannah Elsevir felt a hot chill prickle through her wrists and neck as she surreptitiously read these words in Waterstone's, and began to dread that everybody in the bookshop would turn to stare at her. How much more of this was there? The index offered several more references: how damning would they be?

She felt obliged to purchase the book, although it was not the kind of work she would wish to be seen reading, and she carried it off concealed in a plastic bag to the privacy of her own home by the canal. There she waited until seven o'clock, poured herself a stiff gin and tonic and addressed the volume. Her alarm was justified. The footnotes were ominous. Their precocious and summary dismissal of the undead Peter Elsevir was calculated to give pain: 'Elsevir, Peter, b. 1941, educated Borrowburn and Gladwyn College, Oxford. Achieved a brief notoriety in the 1970s with his organized "happenings" at the Boxed Garden in Fulham. Married in 1968 to the geneticist Hannah (Blow) Elsevir, divorced 1976. Now lives in California.'

Hannah stared at this brief life with dismay. At least there was no qv attached to her name; that was a mercy. But the implications of these few lines were unpleasant. She had not seen Peter for years, and had herself remarried and once more separated since their divorce. She felt no ill will towards Peter, or so she at first bravely told herself, and was not wholly surprised to see his name bob up. But if it bobbed up here, so tangentially, so insignificantly, where else might it appear? And what else from her past might emerge to claim her? Even now a network of letters and diaries and biographies was closing in upon her. Peter himself had seemed a long-forgotten threat, safely exported to another country; his own memories were surely lost in the amnesia of alcohol, but other recorders were nearer, more alert, more coherent. She must watch out.

She finished her drink and poured herself another. Then she sat down to think. She found herself obliged to confront the uncomfortable knowledge that it was possible, indeed likely, that one day somebody would want to write about her life. She would not be allowed to rest in the decent obscurity of a footnote. There were people out there (she gazed, nervously, across the black dimpled water at the lighted houses opposite) who would spy on her. This prospect she found both implausible and unpleasant, but she knew she had to face it. What had seemed like a natural modesty had persuaded her, since her rackety years with the drunken Peter, to lead a discreet, an almost hidden, existence, but her work had necessarily brought with it a certain kind of fame. One cannot win a Nobel Prize and remain utterly unknown. Particularly if one is a woman. Not many women have won a Nobel. Biographies of female achievers are hot properties.

Women and fame have a peculiar relationship. Women believe themselves undervalued and ignored and powerless, and indeed most of them are, but a consequence of this, reflected Hannah, is that those who achieve eminence are more visible than men of the same rank, and are subjected to a more prurient curiosity. Hannah's first husband, Peter, whose all too memorable and elegant name she had so unfortunately if understandably adopted in her career, had been a self-publicist of the most blatant sort, unhappy unless his name was in print and on lips. Hannah had reacted against this cheap glitter and had lived a life of quiet industry and secret sex. Her second husband she had suppressed from her *curriculum vitae*; he had been a mistake made on the rebound. But even he, unknown though he was, had connections. Even he could be used against her. He too had stories to tell.

Hannah Elsevir had received her Nobel with discreet dignity. She had been photographed and interviewed, and had even appeared on television, but she had given little away. She had been a disappointment to journalists, who had been hoping for something a little more sensational from the woman who had discovered what they dubbed 'the Vanity

Gene'. Surely the scientist who had added so much to our understanding of peacocks and paradise birds, of gender and display, ought to be willing to display herself a little more? But Hannah, quiet brown peahen, had kept her feathers well tucked in.

Nobody, at that period, had thought to ask her about the wild and handsome Peter, who had had so much of the peacock in his nature; he had disappeared into another world, leaving only his name behind him. His drab successor had been edited out. Hannah had appeared to the world's press as a dedicated professional woman, uncomfortable in the limelight. She had worked hard at this lack of image, for she had impulses towards confession, even towards a certain flamboyance. But now she was unsure that discretion would save her. She would have to work harder at dullness if she wished to be thoroughly ignored.

She resolved, on that evening, to make herself preternaturally dull. She would become so dull that nobody would dare risk pursuing her. She would sacrifice even her genius to obscurity. She would pass off her work as the work of others. She would hide forever behind a reputation of nonentity. Anything, anything rather than an exploration of her relationship with Peter Elsevir. For, as she sat there, she was forced to realize that it was the resurrection of Peter that would alarm her most. He was her secret, her buried skeleton, her murdered sexuality. He must remain entombed at all costs. Let science falter, let discoveries remain undisclosed. She would not publish, she would not divulge. Her name would fade from the records. Others could claim her credits. She would unmake herself and her past.

She set about this project with characteristic determination. Over the next few years, she nursed and encouraged her young underling, Brian Butterworth, to answer all queries on her behalf, and to take as much credit for their research as he reasonably could. Brian was a fine geneticist but an innocent in worldly matters, and he did not seem to realize that he was being manipulated – and anyway, reasoned Hannah, why should he care? His reputation prospered as hers remained static. Rumours began to circulate around the Institute that Hannah Elsevir was finished, that she had lost it, that Butterworth had been covering for her for a decade, that Butterworth should have got the Nobel. This was satisfactory.

Less satisfactory were her attempts to appear undistinguished. She had in her youth been possessed of her fair share of vanity, and as she matured had watched her diet and dyed her hair, as middle-aged women do. Now, as she embraced ordinariness, she decided she could eat as much as she liked and let her hair grow grey. The results of this new regime were odd. She put on weight, as she munched her way happily through buttered crumpets, roasted ducks, cream-filled cakes and Belgian chocolates, but the weight suited her. Her body billowed, and she had to buy flowing tents for dresses, but her face glowed with health and wellbeing. Her hair turned not a dull pepper-and-salt but a luxurious and brilliant white. She looked radiant. She had never looked so good. Hannah Elsevir might have lost the track of the hidden gene, people muttered, but she must surely have a secret lover. Who and where was he or she?

At first Hannah was indifferent to this gossip, as it was so wide of the mark, but in time it made her uneasy. She had become an object of curiosity, which had been far from her intention. But losing weight is more difficult than putting it on, and she found she could not revert to average dimensions. She was condemned to an outsized glow. And with the glow came energy. She had never felt so energetic in her life. She hardly knew what to do with the excess. She worked long hours, alone and unobserved, and she went for long walks. She swam length after length, she cycled round France, she climbed Great Gable. But wherever she went, she was highly visible. Heads turned in restaurants, cars slowed down to inspect her. What was she to do?

A kind of paranoia possessed her. She sensed that Peter Elsevir was about to resurface in her life, was about to return to undo her. This was all his fault. Could she blot him out, as she had blotted out her second husband? She would try. She began by going through all her papers and photographs and letters, searching for any reference to Peter, and systematically destroying anything that mentioned his name. She hesitated over her marriage certificate and her decree nisi, but they too went into the bin, with the wedding photos, the press cuttings, the snapshots of Peter as a baby. (She shut her eyes as she shredded some of the photographs, as Peter had been a very handsome man, but she shredded them just the same.) Then she turned her attention to public records. Was it possible to rewrite the past? No, it was not. She bought a bottle of Tippex and contemplated taking it to St Catherine's House, but realized this was folly and would only draw attention to herself; she satisfied herself with inking out his name and date in the *Who's Who* in her local public library. But the thought of all the thousands of libraries beyond her reach caused her much disquiet.

As she lay awake at night in her house by the canal she worried about the depth of the silence that came out of California. It was as though Peter Elsevir had disappeared from Earth. She had already taken to searching through the indexes of all memoirs and biographies that could possibly contain any references to him, and had discovered him lurking here and there – most dangerously, in a hostile and dismissive analysis of the Counter Culture by a critic from the New Right.

However, here too, he was laconically dismissed as only briefly notorious. She wrote to the author of this work under a pseudonym, from a false address, requesting any information about the subsequent career or whereabouts of Peter Elsevir, but received a not very helpful answer: he had, according to this source, left England in 1976 (well, she knew that anyway) and had gone to Santa Monica. Two possible contacts were suggested: she could try Elsevir's ex-wife, the geneticist Hannah Elsevir, or she could try to locate a religious sect called Icon, with which he had once been involved. That was the last that had been heard of him. Maybe he was dead. So many of that generation had died young. (And serve them right, the source implied.)

Hannah could find no references to this mystery sect. She drew a blank. She even thought of contacting Peter's family, through a third party, but dismissed this as too dangerous. She leafed her way through Elsevirs in international directories, even rang a few random phone numbers, but found nothing promising. Could she employ a private detective? She thought not.

Inspiration came to her as she was browsing yet again in the open shelves of the reference and biographical section of her university library – shelves which she had begun to haunt with conspicuous frequency. What about his old school? Peter Elsevir had attended a well-known, historic public school, to the memory of which, like many Englishmen, he had been attached by a sentimental hatred. Perhaps he had, against all the odds, kept in touch with it? Perhaps he still received its old boys' annual newsletter?

There was nothing as helpful as an address in the newsletter, but there was, miraculously, a sighting. Her instinct had been right. Peter's old pal Giles Reader had spotted Peter, by chance, in distant Anatolia. He had been, claimed Giles, in search of God. 'A much changed figure, of monkish austerity', wrote a shocked but admiring Giles Reader, himself now a successful financier.

They had met, it seemed, in a rock church in Goreme, staring at a fresco of the raising of Lazarus. They had exchanged a few words. Peter had not been forthcoming. He had not, he assured Giles, taken a vow of silence, but he claimed to be in semi-retreat, and out of the habit of conversation. Giles had respected this, and had moved on to complete his own theological art tour of Turkey and Syria. (He gave colourful accounts of Saint Eustace chasing the hart of Christ, of Saint Simeon the Stylite stinking on his lonely tower, of the Forty Christian Martyrs of Sebaste shivering and dying in their frozen lake, of the Thirty-five Salman Rushdie Martyrs of Sivas suffocating in their smoky hell.) 'This is a tormented landscape,' wrote Giles Reader in the *Old Borrovian*, 'a landscape of lonely extremes, of miserable pinnacles and underground cells. It tempts the traveller to hermit's dreams, to dreams of union with history and God.' But most of all Giles Reader had remembered the haggard features of his old friend, and his pale blue eyes, 'which seemed to see beyond this veil and pierce another world'.

From this unlikely eloquence it seemed that Giles Reader too was changed, and that he had been much shaken by this chance encounter with his old school friend.

Hannah stared long at this account, already three years old, and wondered if she should pursue the cold trail. There was something in Giles's description that assured her Peter had not merely been passing through Goreme. He had been there for some time, and was perhaps there still. Anyway, it was a beginning. A starting point. She had never seen the eastern regions of Turkey. She had never been east of Ankara. She thought she might visit Cappadocia in the spring. It was said to be an interesting region. She collected guide books and brochures, browsed her way through accounts of sculpted tufa, fairy spires, almond blossom, obsidian, apricots. She resolved to go in April.

There was pleasure in planning her trip. She could travel in style. She could join an exclusive art tour, as Giles had done. She could take a cruise with an art tour option. She could hire a car. She could hire a car with a driver. She could advertise for a tame archaeologist, or offer to lecture on Vanity in Trebizond.

She chose to travel alone. Over the past ten years she had taken several packaged excursions, sometimes as paying holiday-maker, sometimes as guest lecturer. She had spoken on her Gene in Kenya and the Galapagos, she had listened to the lectures of others in Egypt and Mexico. And once or twice, on these outings, she had met other single or divorced women whose lives too uneasily echoed her own. On one occasion, to their mutual chagrin, she and the archivist of her university library had found themselves sailing along the Danube together. They had felt obliged to share a table at dinner. They had cramped one another's style. She did not wish to risk such embarrassed proximity again.

And so, in April, Hannah Elsevir found herself driving along a straight road of uneven habit past rock and mountain and snow and stream towards the rock caves of Cappadocia, in pursuit of her vanished husband. The scenery was monotonous, or, more accurately, repetitive. Browns, greys, purples; the colours of infertile upland mineral earth. Was it the prevailing drabness that had goaded one or two of the villages through which she passed to paint their houses in a lurid, lively shocking pink and turquoise? Hawks circled high above her, watching from afar. There was not much cover on this barren high plateau. Where had Peter Elsevir gone to ground?

As she approached Goreme, after spending a night in a town that purported to be or to have been Caesarea, the landscape changed. A steep little winding valley, lined by trees hung with delicate pink bloom, led her to the strange and fantastic displays of shapes that had disturbed Giles Reader. Here there was cover, here there were hiding places. She parked the car at a tourist vantage point and surveyed the amazing panorama beyond and beneath her. And she despaired. For she could see that here a man might hide forever, here a hermit might embrace eternal solitude. Avenging armies might thunder, private detectives might track and pry, but here one could evade all pursuit. Each hollow hill, each towering turret was pierced by natural windows, by peep holes and arrow slits. Flocks of pigeons flew in and out of the thousand watching eyes of the rocks. This was the land of a myriad secrets. Where should her search begin?

She was booked into a pleasant small hotel in Urgup where her fellow guests included a couple of Bible-reading Americans, a Dutch family party on its Easter break and an Australian art historian. Over drinks in the heavily orientalized Harem Bar (surely she was far enough from home to sit and socialize incognito over a glass or two of raki) she listened to advice about sightseeing. She must visit the Church of the Apple and the Church of the Buckle and Sakli Kilise, the Hidden Church; she must see the Valley of Roses and the Red Dale; and, if not a claustrophobic, the Underground Cities where troglodytes had lived for centuries, safe from persecution.

Had Peter Elsevir become a troglodyte? Would she meet him peering at her from behind a grid in a wall in an earth-red cavern? Would he roll a stone down at her as she approached his cell?

For two or three days she explored the region, losing her

way amongst its scattered monuments, joining noisy parties with guides, eating alone in wayside cafés. Of an evening, she encouraged the barman and the hotel manageress to gossip about the tourist trade, and about the pilgrims of various faiths who came here – scholarly theologians, fundamentalists both Christian and Islamic, New Age mystics and, quite recently, an angelic choir which had travelled from Arizona to sing for the Resurrection on Easter Sunday. Had they heard, she enquired, of a sect called Icon? Did any of their visitors settle here? Were there still hermits walled up amongst those lunar mountains?

On the third evening, she was told of an Englishman who lived alone in a little village in the Valley of the Sword. She knew that this was Peter Elsevir.

The sun shone on her fourth morning. It was the hottest day of the year. Protected from the dazzle by hat and sunglasses she set off to the Valley.

Peter was sitting at a little yellow-painted wooden table on the pavement outside a small low rock-and-brick shack sticking out from the rock wall. He too wore dark glasses and an old straw hat perched on the back of his head, and he was reading a book. The bright light had brought him out of his hiding place. She parked her hired car across the road, and stared at him. Her heart thumped perilously.

He looked more beautiful than ever. How could this be true? Years of abuse and indulgence had failed to coarsen him; they had worn him thin and pale, they had refined him into an extraordinary elegance. Was this right, was this fair? His haggardness became him. His hair hung still in Sixties ringlets, its blond-grey touched gold by the sunlight. His nose was long and thin, his cheeks were hollow, his long bony hand languidly turned a page. And he smiled to himself, a secret smile. Would he sense that he was being watched? Dare she approach? Or should she drive away? The neck of his shirt was open to receive the springtime warmth on his thin chest. He had always had smooth, dry, hot skin. Gazing at it, at him, she was overcome by a pang of memory so intense she felt faint. She could feel that skin beneath her fingers. She could smell it from here.

She opened her car door, and crossed the silent deserted little road towards him, in the blazing noon day. He looked up at her approach. She could not read his eyes through his shades. He shut his book. He smiled, a puzzled, polite, delicate smile. He rose to his feet, taking off his hat to greet her. He had always been a gentleman. How had she forgotten these things?

She saw the moment of his recognition. He stood there, holding his hat, still smiling.

'Hannah,' he said. 'Is that you, Hannah?'

'Peter,' she said.

He shook his head slightly, in what seemed but a mild surprise, and gestured towards one of the other little chairs at the table. She sat. He sat.

'So,' he said. 'You hunted me down. I tried to hide, but you hunted me down.'

She was ashamed. She could find no words. She had loved this man. The memory of the feel of his hot skin assailed and reproached her. She had to reach out a hand to touch him. She leaned to him across the table, and laid her hand upon his. He burned with a pure dryness.

'Yes,' she said. 'I came to find where you had hidden.'

'I wonder why,' he said, smiling a gentle, quizzical smile.

'I suppose,' she said, 'I had come to think I had treated you badly.'

'No, no,' he said. 'It was I that did not treat you well.'

They sat there, drinking raki which he had brought forth

from his hut. The cloudy chalky white of bittersweet aniseed perfumed the air. They ate black olives, and slices of warm red tomato, and cubes of hard white salted cheese, and sharp dried brown wrinkled plums. Peter Elsevir said that he had embraced a life of simplicity. Not of austerity, but of simplicity.

He stared at his onetime wife, with measured appreciation.

'You look very fine, Hannah,' he said, as he poured her another glass of the strong clear spirit and added to it the transforming alchemy of water. 'You look large and fine. You have done well. You look quite opulent.'

'You too look well,' said Hannah, thoughtfully. 'I had not expected you to look so handsome still.'

They went indoors and lay down together, in the afternoon heat, on his narrow monk's bed, and talked. They spoke of their adventures, their discoveries. A fly buzzed in the dry silence. Hannah laid her hand on Peter's smooth chest, then lowered her head over him and deliberately inhaled his refined odour. He smelled of sun and salt and resin. Preserved, purged, purified. She sighed, deeply. She had done well to track down this man. He was remission, he was forgiveness, he was resurrection. She would leave him now, she would in all probability never see him again in this life, but he would remain with her, her secret virtue, her secret strength. She breathed again, and took in a deep inspiration of her youth, her love, her innocence, her hope. All these things had been good. They were not to be buried, or despised, or forgotten. They held no shame. They were a treasury of great happiness. The past forgave her, and she forgave the past. They lay there, peacefully. Nobody would ever know of this moment. No biographer could record it, no friend could mock it, no footnote could catch and snag and snap at it.

He smelled of apples and of honey, he smelled of the virtues of the wilderness.

'Peter,' she said, sleepily, in the afternoon heat. 'Peter, you smell divine.'

(1999)

13

Stepping Westward:
A Topographical Tale

You must not imagine me as speaking to you in my own person. I speak to you as Mary Mogg, and it is her story that I tell. Imagine me as Mary Mogg, a schoolteacher past the middle of life and slowly nearing retirement. I look forward with a mixture of feelings to my pensioned years, and wonder where to spend them. Mary Mogg – a plain name for a plain person. Plain speaking, I hope I am, and reasonably plain living, though I am not a water drinker. By now I am plain of person, though I was not always so. I would not claim that I was ever pretty, but I was personable enough – had you been told I was plain, you might have found me pretty, and had you been told I was pretty, you might have found me plain. Now I look like what, in part, I am – a sensible, hardworking, somewhat solitary teacher of English Literature, who enjoys long walks in the countryside as an escape from the demands of trying to persuade restless sixteen-year-olds in a comprehensive school to appreciate Wordsworth.

The school is in Northam, in South Yorkshire, on the industrial non-Wordsworthian side of the Pennines. I am Yorkshire born, and I like the Yorkshire Dales, the North Yorkshire moors, the Peak District. But this year I had promised myself a half-term midsummer treat, an excursion to the West Country, in the footsteps of Wordsworth and Coleridge. I have been teaching the *Lyrical Ballads* and I longed to see again those landscapes of the West. I had not been there for many years, but I remembered from my youth the Quantock Hills, the combe behind Holford, the Somerset and Devon Coast Path, the Valley of the Rocks, the steep woods below and above Culbone church, the Bell Inn at Watchet, the brook at Nether Stowey, the muddy source of the River Tone high on the Brendons. One whole summer I spent there, with college friends, when I was twenty.

I cannot paint what then I was and how glorious that faraway world then seemed to me. To my Northern eye the woods and valleys of Somerset were as luxuriant and extravagant as the riches of Guiana had seemed to the astonished eyes of Sir Walter Raleigh and his crew. Ferns sprouted like orchids from the trunks of vast oaks overhanging the rapid rivers, ivy with berries like grapes rampaged up ash and beech in tropical splendour, and hollies soared towards the sky. Primeval lichens of grey and sage green and dazzling orange encrusted bark and twig and stone, and the red earth broke into bubbles of scarlet and purple and bright spongy yellow. The lush profusion and the variety of nature had far surpassed our Northern austerities, and, faithlessly perhaps, I fell in love with the profligacy, that excess. I was utterly seduced.

I fell in love, too, with one of my travelling companions, which was a misfortune, for although at first there seemed to be a mutual sympathy, I soon discovered that he was more attracted to another of our party. Indeed, he later married her, and not, I heard, very happily, though that is not, I think, part of this story. So, to me, as you will readily imagine, that summer was one of intense emotion, and one that I have lived through in memory many times. And I never returned to Somerset, choosing instead to walk in Scotland, in the Lake

District, in France, in Germany, in Northern Italy. I too have crossed the Alps. Did I associate his loss with the places where I knew myself to be in the same season, both finding him and losing him? Did I feel that nature had betrayed the heart that loved her? I cannot say. All I can say is that until this year, I did not step westward.

But this year, I returned. I was prompted partly – and I know this is ridiculous, but my mentor Wordsworth has taught me never to be afraid of bathos – by the National Curriculum. It is commonly acknowledged that many if not most schoolteachers have been suffering from stress and demoralization over the past decade or so. I have fared better than some, but I too have felt constraints. I am getting older, and I do not understand the young as once I did. Teaching literature was once my pleasure: I felt I could at times awaken interest, catch the imagination, change lives for the better. Of late I have not felt this. A sense of defeat has been creeping over me. Literature is no longer valued, in the classroom or out of it. Literature has been relabelled Heritage – safely dead, and dressed in period costume. You can imagine my feelings when I discovered that the only poem by Wordsworth included in that government-sponsored anthology – since prudently dropped – was – you have guessed it – those 'Daffodils'. That poem has done immeasurable harm to Wordsworth with the young. It is not a poem for children. I have had innumerable disputes with students about that poem. It stands like a tombstone on the grave of his reputation. Most of the young just shut their ears and switch off when they see it. A few of the cleverer ones, like Shakira Jagan, tell me it is politically incorrect, because daffodils are a symbol of colonial domination in India and the West Indies (she is Guyanese) – and when I try to get her to read about Toussaint L'Ouverture instead, she just laughs at me. Heritage! None of the people who go on about Heritage have ever read a poem in their lives – or not since they yawned their way through the 'Daffodils' at school. I know there's nothing new in complaints about English teaching being sterile – remember that Victorian *Punch* cartoon of the two elderly gentlemen in frock coats walking through a wood, with the caption

> 'O cuckoo, shall I call thee bird
> Or but a wandering voice?'
> 'State the alternatives preferred
> With reasons for your choice.'

But it is getting worse. What would Wordsworth have thought of a generation of children encouraged to learn his 'Daffodils' by rote, because they are part of 'Our English Heritage'? Wordsworth, who with Dorothy encouraged little Basil Montagu's insatiable curiosity by directing him towards 'everything he sees, the sky, the fields, trees, shrubs, corn, the making of tools, carts, etc. etc. He knows his letters, but we have not attempted any further step in the path of book learning. Our grand study has been to make him *happy* . . .'

Well, it is a hobbyhorse of mine, and I get carried away. I apologize for this polemic digression. It is because I grow old and out of date. But at least I still feel *something*. And these reflections are not unconnected with my excursion, to which I now come.

I decided that the time had come, after three decades and more, to brave re-entry to that magic land, and I planned to spend three days walking from Nether Stowey to Lynton. I would forget Shakira Jagan and all the rest of them – and frankly, compared with the rest of 5B, Shakira is a genius, though don't tell anyone I said so. I would revisit old haunts, and see if they were still there. If *I* was still there. A dangerous enterprise. By chance I found I had chosen the dates on which the Wordsworths themselves were expelled from the grand paradise of Alfoxden, on June 25, 1798, and set off towards Nether Stowey, Shirehampton, the Severn and the Wye. Nearly two hundred years had passed since they moved on from Alfoxden: and nearly forty since I moved on myself.

When I said I would walk from Nether Stowey to Lynton, I didn't promise to myself that I would walk *all the way*. I would cheat a little. I am not as young as I was, and although much given to rambling around the countryside on foot in an unprotected situation, I have never had quite the stamina of the Wordsworths, of Coleridge, of Hazlitt, of Tom Poole. No, I would take my car, and book myself into bed and breakfast places, and spend my days in circular exploration. I would commune with the dead, and maybe with the living. In Northam one does not speak to strangers much these days, but in the countryside one may take greater risks. I am not, I hope, unduly loquacious – in fact I am rather shy – but occasionally, when walking, strange fits of boldness overcome me, and although I do not cross-question each child and beast I meet, I do enter into conversations that I would never embark upon indoors. Even the cheerful greeting of another walker – 'Good morning!' – 'Pleasant evening!' – 'Fine day for a walk!' – can lift the heart. The lonely communion of walkers, this I have valued.

Yes, you are right. I fear retirement. I shall miss 5B.

There is no obvious way to get from Northam to Nether Stowey, but I thought it was proper to pass by the gateway of Stonehenge. I had set off early and was driving quite fast along the A303 – it may surprise you to learn that my car is red and sporting – when I began to feel Stonehenge coming upon me through the great militarized and pig-rearing spaces

of Wiltshire, and I made a detour. It was not really very pleasant. Somebody should feel a little guilt and sorrow about the
state of the bunkerlike ladies lavatories. English Heritage
again, I suppose. English this, National that. I love England,
rather more, I suspect, than our ex-prime minister loved
poetry, however fervently she asserted that she did, but I do
sometimes think we set about our patriotism the wrong way.
My hobbyhorse again. Shut up, Mogg. I suppose there is no
harm in a café selling Megalithic Rock Cakes and Solstice
savouries, or offers of free Parker pens, but it is a bit sad that
most people seem to spend most of their time in the shop.
There were some Japanese children playing tag, and two
young men meditating on the grass, but most of my fellow
tourists were busy buying dishcloths or taking photographs.
And in the car park a car alarum bleaped insistently. People
watched it with suspicion. We are so nervous of one another
these days. You can see pickpocket warnings in the most
desolate corners of the British Isles, and once I saw a Neighbourhood Watch sign nailed to a tree in a remote field miles
from human habitation.

I made my way westward, tritely pondering the effect of
the growth of cities on human trust, and my next stop was
no more reassuring. I'd decided not to brave Bristol, as I
would be sure to get lost, but thought I'd try Shirehampton,
where William and Dorothy stayed with the invalid lawyer
James Losh on their way from Alfoxden towards the Wye.
This was a mistake. I took the wrong exit off the M5, and
was arrested by a policeman who thought I was trying to
invade the docks. He redirected me in a friendly enough
fashion and I retraced my route, but there was no sign of
Losh or Wordsworth in Shirehampton. It was all Boots,
Bingo, Spar, and Iceland. I could not bring myself to seek
its ancient core. I regained the motorway, and drove on,

ignoring Clevedon, and on to the Bridgwater exit. I had resolved to make my evening's walk to that little-known spot, Shurton Bars, in preparation for a more serious walk the next day. I checked in at my B and B, and set out again. My landlady had never heard of Shurton Bars or of Shurton, but I had my maps.

A little-known spot, and hard to find. This was where Coleridge, in September 1795, wrote 'Lines written at Shurton Bars', in the early days of his love for Sara Fricker. In that summer forty years ago we had visited Kilve, which I could see was slightly to the west, but I could also see that the place marked Shurton was inland, with no obvious route to the sea. I drove on, through the maze of little high-hedged country lanes, pausing to admire two rosy pink piglets in a field of blue cabbages, and an immobile heron standing on one leg in a pond, but I could not find Shurton. What I did come upon was the nuclear power station of Hinkley Point, which suddenly rose upon me, its regular hygienic blue and white boxes standing like a giant refrigerator, a palace of ice. It flew a thin flag of clean white smoke. I drove towards it, and was again arrested – the Visitors' Centre was shut for the day. I was informed I'd have to come back tomorrow if I wanted a guided tour.

I enquired about Shurton Bars. He looked foxed. He'd never heard of them. He wasn't local, he said; he thought there was a village called Shurton over towards Stogursey. If I asked those ladies just getting into their car to go home, they might know.

There were three ladies, attendants at the centre, wearing identical print summer dresses. Two of them shook their heads at my query, but the third smiled and said I was very near. I had to go back to a place called Knighton, not Shurton, and walk down the track to the sea. It wasn't far.

And I found Knighton, and parked my car in a farmyard, and with further help of a friendly lecturer from Bristol I found the right track. My spirits rose as they always do when I start to walk. The smell was delicious, of honey and of tansy. The grass-bordered track was wide and empty, and it rose gently through open farmland, waving with ripening wheat, or carved into ploughed blocks of glinting earth. I fell into a happy plodding rhythm, as I thought of Coleridge, and his friend Tom Poole, and of Tom Poole's brother who had lived at Shurton Court. In those days ferries crossed the River Parrett above Bridgwater, and plied their way along the coast: trading vessels brought coal and lime across the Bristol Channel from Wales to the lime kilns of the Somerset coast. What had the coastline looked like then? And then there was the sea before me, and the far sublime industrial shore of Port Talbot, and the island of Flat Holm to the east, and a little yacht, and a tanker, and the banks of lias and fossil. The turf was short and studded with flowers and flat thistles and the edge of the cliff crumbled, as I walked towards the flatter stretch I knew to be the Bars. It was a beautiful midsummer evening, and the points and promontories stretched on and on to the west in a dim blue-grey hazy hot light. I was all alone – or so I thought until I saw a man approaching. I had not yet cast off my city ways, for I felt a slight frisson of dismay at the prospect of an encounter with a stranger on so remote a spot, but it was only an old man with his dog, who greeted me civilly. And on the way back I met a boy on a bike who shouted 'Hi!' at me, in holiday mood, as he charged and bounced along the ruts.

The shingle had been covered in litter. Old wire, cans, plastic bottles, strands of orange plastic rope. And a flattened, rusted, battered car chassis.

I will not tell you where I spent the night for it was not

much of a success. My landlady was not from the neighbourhood, she assured me many times, she was from Sheffield.
This should have endeared her to me, as I like Sheffield, but
she was the moaning type of Yorkshire person who speaks
in double negatives. An artist in litotes. (Sometimes I think
I'm a bit like that myself.) She started to tell me her story as
soon as I arrived, and continued when I returned from my
pub supper – I had slipped out to the Plough at Holford. It
was a sad story and I was not in the mood for it. It was
marked by many deaths and illnesses. Her husband had been
made redundant in the decline of the steel industry, and they
had decided to leave the north and have a go at running this
little business, but, perversely, as soon as they had settled in
he had spitefully developed a fatal illness and died on her,
leaving her alone amongst strangers. She didn't like the
people round her and she didn't like her guests. They stole
soap and towels and sometimes wet the bed. On and on she
went as my eyes drooped, for it had been a long day, and I
was exhausted, but her story was in many cantos and she
had to tell it all. As I fell asleep between the flounced and
furry hot pink nylon sheets I wondered if she told this tale
to every guest. I bet she told it to one in one, but not one in
three. I felt sorry for her, but I am less patient than Wordsworth. Her lament lacked dignity, or so it seemed to me.

The morning cheered me. I planned to walk from Nether
Stowey, up Dowsborough, round the Iron Age fort, and on
towards Crowcombe Park Gate, where I would hope to find
the pool which inspired Wordsworth to write 'The Thorn'.
Then I would walk along the ridge towards Triscombe, and
back down through the woods to Nether Stowey. Ambitious,
but not impossible, and I could always cut it short if I was
tired. As I set off with my map and sandwiches and my battered
little Oxford green canvas *Lyrical Ballads*, I wondered if I

would have the courage to stop one in three and ask about Wordsworth. 'Have you ever read him, have you ever *heard* of him?' Such would be my questions.

But the characters I met were unpromising, and interrogation died on my lips, to be replaced by 'Lovely day!' There was a woman walking her Dalmatian dog to Stowey letter-box, and a girl on a pony, and two men on mountain bikes, and then, as the hill steepened, nobody. I got happily lost wandering round and round the twisted oaks and giant hemlock of Dowsborough, before striking off to Crowcombe – which Dorothy called Crookham. I was sure, from the map and from a description given by a Wordsworthian friend of mine (yes, I do have *some* friends) that the place marked as Wilmot's Pool must be the 'little muddy pond of water never dry' of the poem, and I resolved to eat my sandwiches there. I toiled up Frog Hill, leaving the dense vegetation of wood and combe, to the high ground of the Quantocks and its long views over the Channel. Here grew yellow tormentil, and pale silver yellow straggling cow-wheat, and early ripe bilberries, and wild strawberries. I passed a couple of ponies, which stared at me as the donkey had once stared at Wordsworth.

And here on the top were two men sitting in a Land-Rover, staring through binoculars at the opposite hillside. They lowered their glasses to greet me, and I asked them if they knew Wilmot's Pool – more for the sake of conversation than information, you understand. The younger, a ranger type dressed in army camouflage, shook his head, but the older said, 'Now what you call Wilmot's Pool is what we call Withy-man's Pool. You're on the right course. See that hummock? That marks the pool.'

'Why do you call it Withyman's Pool?' I enquired. But he did not know. He knew neither Wilmot nor Withyman. I asked him what they looked for, through their binoculars. He said they were looking for deer with calf. It was the season, and if I kept my eyes open I might see them too.

With further exchange of courtesies, I moved on. And there indeed was the pool, hard by the hilltop path. Wordsworth's measurement seemed on the conservative side, for this pool, as I paced it, was more like three yards long and three yards wide than three feet by two, and this was in a dry season. In wet weather it must have been far larger. Yet muddy indeed it was: he was right there. It was not mantled, or standing: it was just plain muddy. Rushes and tufted reeds grew in its marges (is the word *marge* an example of poetic diction, I wonder?) and there were little semi-succulent water plants of green and reddish hue growing from the dried whitened trampled mud. And there, too, was a hollow mossy circle of a tumulus that might well have been the grave of a baby – or indeed of a giant. The setting was on a grander scale than I had imagined, but then Wordsworth was not a one for hyperbole. More a meoisis or a litotes man. (We don't teach figures of speech these days.)

I sat on the tumulus above the pool and ate my cheese and chutney sandwich, as I reread 'The Thorn' for the hundredth time and more. I looked around for a thorn, but the nearest I could see was a good thirty yards away. When I had finished my bottle of water I went over to inspect it. This thorn, like Wordsworth's, was lichen encrusted, though not as extravagantly as Wordsworth had claimed – you could hardly call this 'a melancholy crop'.

> Up from the earth these mosses creep
> And this poor thorn they clasp it round
> So close, you'd say that they were bent
> With plain and manifest intent

> To drag it to the ground
> And all had joined in one endeavour
> To bury this poor thorn for ever.

And there I sat, alone, and recalled that lost summer, and its lost aspirations, and wondered what it was that had driven poor Dorothy to an old age of infirmity and obscenity. Perhaps you are waiting for me to say that I became pregnant that summer, and lost the baby, or had it aborted, or adopted. No, it was not so. The tale of Martha Ray is not the tale of Mary Mogg. I had no right to cry 'Oh misery! Oh misery!' This is a plain tale. The moving accident is not my trade. Yet tears rose to my eyes as I sat there and thought of the past. I had been young, and I had been happy, and my happiness was imprinted on these hills. Maybe I had seen this very thorn before. Thorns live long. The coppiced stools of oaks in the ancient woodland I had walked through had been there hundreds of years before Wordsworth, and he like me had seen the very hollies that still tower in Alfoxden Park.

Was I happy, was I sad? Who is to say? Old age, ill health, solitude – these lay before me. Wordsworth had written that poem, or so he claimed, to fix the thorn in his memory, to preserve forever its terrible aspect. He too feared to grow into 'a toothless thorn with knotted joints', and we know that Dorothy lost her teeth young. I have been saved from that by some fancy bridgework, but my mother, who died last year, had severe arthritis.

On such things I mused, as I walked over the moor towards the beech grove and the drovers' road to Triscombe, and as I walked I noticed that each low wind-battered bush of thorn or oak or holly was crowned with a small bird. The birds were not all of one species, but there they perched, in the afternoon heat, not singing, but chatting to one another, in a gentle, low, unexcited, friendly murmur of conversation.

As I descended into the wood, the notes of the birds changed, for it was turning towards evening, and they were now singing up in the canopy, just out of sight. I paused from time to time to listen, and during one of these halts I heard a louder rustling above me, where bracken grew beneath the trees. A deer with calf, I hoped, and I froze, half hidden – but then into sight came not a deer but a person, emerging sure-footed from the trackless hillside. She carried a canvas bag, and just before she reached the path she stopped, put down her bag, took something from it, and began to peer intently at the bark of the tree. Then she got out a little booklet and began to make notes. Then she moved on to another tree, and repeated the process. What messages did she read in the trees, what poems from them did she transcribe?

She was about my age, with thick streaked black and grey hair, and a handsome, ruddy, veined, wind-weathered face. She was wearing baggy dark red cotton trousers, and an earth-pink floppy shirt. As she moved from tree to tree, I followed her with my eyes, then took a step forward. Her hearing was acute. She turned at once. And she smiled as I approached.

'Afternoon,' she said, 'or is it evening?'

'Betwixt and between,' I said.

'Lovely day,' she said.

I wasn't going to let her get away with that.

'I've been watching you,' I said. 'Inspecting those trees. Do tell me, what *is* it that you do?'

Now you won't believe this but it's true. She laughed, a strange friendly hooting owl-like laugh, and said, 'You mean, how is it that I live and what is it that I do?'

'Yes,' I said. 'That is exactly what I mean.'

'*Well*,' she said, emphatically, 'I hope you'll pay proper attention if I tell you, instead of drifting off and daydreaming, like that other fellow. What was it that distracted him – "cold, pain, and labour, and all fleshly ills"?'

'I've done that bit,' I said. 'I'm ready to listen now.'

And we sat down together on a patch of green moss where the sun broke through the boughs, and she explained.

'I read,' she said, 'the messages of the forest. I decode the text of the trees. I read the lichen through my little lens.' And she passed me a small round hand lens.

'And what do the lichens tell you?' I asked.

'They tell us of the health of the woodland. They speak to us of acid rain from South Wales. Through the lichens we can monitor pollution year by year. Occasionally we use PH meters, but we can read much through the lens. Here, look, what do you see?'

I looked through her lens at the twigs she had collected, at the bark of the trees around us, and I saw revealed an extraordinary miniature world, of grey-green grottos and caverns, or armies of cactus spears, of seaweed fantasies, of orange spots, of starred and matted patternings, of black calligraphy on silver bark. 'Such a diversity!' I said. 'And in so small a space.'

But she shook her head. 'There's far less diversity than there used to be. We are losing species. Some cannot survive the changing climate. Some, which have grown for millions of years in the same places, are now threatened.'

'So lichen is a good indicator?'

'Oh yes, the more the better.' She laughed, entranced by her subject. 'I'm afraid Wordsworth got that wrong, when he said the thorn was being *dragged down* by the moss and lichens, or whatever it was he said. What did he say, exactly?'

I produced the poem, and we read it together, in perfect

happiness. And then we made our way down the hill together, talking of Wordsworth and of Coleridge – or rather she talked and I listened, to a dazzling flow of art and science mixed, and it was, for that space of time, as though the two cultures had never divided, as though they had flowed on together through the nineteenth and twentieth centuries, regardless of the National Curriculum. She spoke of Horner Wood and the Barle Valley, of Dowsborough Camp and Mounsey Castle, of Nettlecombe Park and of Kellynch Hall, of the lepers who lived below Culbone church, of the mineral railway and Tom Poole's tannery and the charcoal burners and the lime kilns. She was impressed that I had discovered Shurton Bars, where they used to land the coal from Wales. Not many people know about that, she said. And dear God, she even knew the poem, for it prompted her to an aria on the green radiance of the vanished glow-worm, and the electric flame of the marigold. You remember the lines, perhaps –

> 'Tis said, in summer's evening hour
> Flashes the golden-coloured flower
> A fair electric flame:
> And so shall flash my love-charged eye
> When all the heart's big ecstasy
> Shoots rapid through the frame!

(Not perhaps his best lines; but his footnote on electricity is superb.)

We had a beer together in the Castle of Comfort, and we exchanged names and addresses. Her name was Anne Elliot, and she was of an old Somerset family that had owned Kellynch in grander days, though now she lived mainly in Shropshire – 'In fact, I live all over the place,' she said, 'and wherever I find lichens I set up my camp.' She invited me to supper with her at the Kellynch Field Study Centre, but I declined. I did not wish to impose.

The next day, after a quiet night with a silent, disapproving, well-bred landlady, I decided to skip a projected visit to 'wicked Watchet' and move on to Porlock Weir, to walk the coast path, in pursuit of the forests ancient as the hills and deep romantic chasms which Anne had assured me were still there. A gold-spotted lichen had been growing in those woods for seventy million years, she said. Could I have remembered that right? Seventy *million* years? The weather held and my heart sang.

I parked in the car park at the Weir, and bought myself a bottle of water in the little shop. I would take my knapsack and some money and a toothbrush, for it occurred to me that if I wanted I could walk on to Lynton and the haunted Valley of the Rocks, and spend the night there, to return by bus in the morning. I mentioned this plan to the person in the shop, who was clearly the guardian of the neighbourhood, and she said it would be quite safe to leave the car in the car park, but I must beware of landslides. 'You look like a sensible person,' she said, in a somewhat admonitory tone, 'and I'm sure you know what you are doing.'

And off I set, up behind the pink Anchor Hotel, through fields of Jacobs sheep, past a little folly of a tollhouse, past the ruins of Ashley Combe, under the red deeps of a tunnel, and up the steep path to Culbone. I visited the little grey church, with its many tombstones of the Red family – there is one, believe it or not, to an Ethel Red – and noted (would I have noted this quite so keenly the day before?) the extraordinarily brilliant orange of the lichens that grew upon them, and then I went on up the path behind, steeply up to Silcombe. It was hot, and the air hummed. I emerged from woodland on a high-banked, open track, knowing and feeling that I was within half a mile of the fount of Kubla Khan. There were white cattle standing in a spring of red water, and farther on a field of large lambs. Most of them scampered off, but one stood its ground to speak to me, and thrust its nose through the fence at me. I reached out a hand and it nudged me with its little hard hot woollen flat head. It was bored, and it was pleased to speak to me. Do not mock the pathetic fallacy. I know a bored lamb when I see one.

And on I went, until the path rejoined the coastal woodland. I could see what my friend at the Weir had meant by landslides, for since Coleridge's day much of the path had slipped into the sea. Even my recent Pathfinder map was out of date. Below me were fallen tree trunks, some gallantly sprouting in their ruins, some dead as matchsticks. And far below them, the sea.

It was on this stretch that I embarked on my own folly. A gate informed me 'Danger: Road Closed: No Through Way: New Route', but I could see beyond this gate a particularly enticing Coleridgean jungle. The track looked good enough, and I am very sorry to say that I left the prescribed route and *deliberately* took the wrong turning. I told myself I would go only a little way – I thought I could hear the sound of a waterfall which called out to be inspected – but I should have known myself better, for each twist of the track revealed some new and wondrous prospect, of birch trees, of hart's tongue ferns, of great slabs of wet rock, of mossy caverns, of dappled glades. On I went, recklessly. And all was well until I came to a place where a little dry watercourse crossed the path. It was no kind of a jump – only a couple of feet, and certainly not a brook too broad for leaping – but I landed heavily on my right heel, and at once felt a shooting pain up the back of my calf.

I stood there on one leg like a heron in astonishment. I had never felt anything like this before. Gingerly, I tried to put my foot down again. The pain was intense.

I hobbled over to a tree trunk, sat down and tested my toes. *They* were fine. Everything was fine, except for the fact that I could not stand on my right leg.

I sat there, and philosophically ate a sandwich, and wondered how far I was from any human being and from my poor red car.

I had damaged a tendon, or torn a blood vessel. Such things happen. I ate another sandwich.

I felt quite calm. It was a pleasant spot. All the same, I admitted I had been a fool, and a fool whose best hope was to be caught out in her folly. Otherwise I should have to limp on, or back. I wondered which was wiser? The map showed a farmhouse not much further on, but then I knew I could not trust the map. The farmhouse might have fallen into the sea.

I decided to hobble back. It was not easy. I had to pick my way with great care, and I had travelled about a hundred yards when I heard, as I had heard the day before, a rustling in the woodland. I hoped and cried out.

'Anne!' I yelled. 'Anne!'

And it was indeed she, for who else could it have been? She emerged from the undergrowth, as she had before, her lens and her little booklet in her hand, and exclaimed in delight which quickly turned to dismay.

'Oh Mary,' she said, as though she had known me all her life. 'Oh Mary, Mary Mogg! What *have* you done? What a mercy I dropped by!'

She produced at once a plan of campaign. I was to hobble not back but on, towards the farm called Tasketts, which was, she assured me, still there. She would scramble back up the hill to her car, which was parked higher up on the drive, and meet me there, and drive me back to safety. 'Not to worry, Mary,' she said, 'the track's quite safe as far as Tasketts, it only gets dodgy after that.'

So off she scampered, and off I stumbled, and we met at this lost place perched in a deep combe halfway between sea and sky.

'Let's go in,' she said, 'and make ourselves a cup of tea. We deserve one. Don't look so alarmed, I know the people. They're old friends, but they're away.'

And she took the key from the soot drop by the door and let herself in. Indoors smelt of damp and moss and wood smoke. She put the kettle on and opened a carton of long-life milk and made us a pot of tea. She wrote a note to our unknown hosts, saying, 'Dear Bears, guess who's been drinking *your* tea?'

'*What* an adventure,' she said. 'Now you'll have to come back and spend the night at Kellynch with me.' And she laughed her hooting woodland laugh.

I gave in. What could I do?

The next twenty-four hours were like an opium dream, induced by nothing stronger than a few glasses, over supper, of Bulgarian red. I had stumbled into an enchanted realm. We reported at Porlock Weir, where my friend of the shop tut-tutted over my accident and said, 'Well, at least you had the sense to tell me where you were going,' and Anne drove me to Kellynch, twenty miles away. It was an old house, eighteenth century on a sixteenth-century foundation, once the Elliot family seat, but now filled with aspiring botanists on weekend courses. Anne was staying in the stable courtyard, in what had been the old estate offices. She had an entourage of fellow lichenologists – a young man from the Natural History Museum, a professor from a Scottish university, a part-time poet from Iceland and a gold panner from Guiana.

I have never spent such an evening. In that long, high room, surrounded by old Elliot trophies – birds in glass cases, a coal scuttle with a coat of arms, a chemical retort, an old printing press – we sat and talked and shared our mysteries. From time to time Anne would leap up to consult a book from the heaped shelves, for this room was also a library, and such a library – a librarian's dream, a librarian's nightmare. Here were sixteenth-century herbals, and first editions of old topographical poems, and hand-tinted tomes on lichens and butterflies. We spoke of Humphry Davy and Sir Walter Raleigh and the albatross. I even told them of the brilliant Shakira Jagan and my high hopes for her, whereupon the Guyanese gold panner told us that his mother had always claimed to be descended from Toussaint L'Ouverture himself. He spoke of his journeys up the Demerara and the Orinoco, he spoke of the wonders of the jungle, and the Icelandic poet told us of the secret places in Iceland where no harm comes, where the air is pure as in the Garden of Eden. The log fire crumbled to red ash, and still we talked.

At last I was put to bed, in a walled and panelled closet in the corner of the room. Anne shut its doors on me and I slept as I have not slept in years.

In the morning Anne asked me to stay on. 'This cedarn shade your prison,' she said, gesturing to the vast tree in the pleasure gardens below us, and the pretty little pink Dower House beyond it – rented, she told me, to a romantic actress. 'Stay here and recover!' But I knew that if I stayed more than one night I would turn into a pumpkin or worse. I had to go, I had to get back to school, I said, I would ring a taxi and rejoin my car. Nonsense, she said, she would first take me to see her doctor, and if he said I was fit to drive, if I insisted, she would drive me back to the Weir.

On the way to her doctor, who lived on a remote hillside

covered in goats, we were trapped for a while behind an agri-
cultural monster embedded in the hedge. In no time at all a
queue of cars accumulated, there, in the middle of nowhere
– first us, then two nuns in a Honda Civic, breathless not with
adoration but from ceaseless chatter, then a gentleman farmer
with a fine moustache, then a young man in glasses wearing
a red shirt – anarchist or hunt saboteur, we speculated – then
a turbanned Sikh, then a yellow mobile library. Truly the
English countryside is strangely peopled.

Well, I am back in urban Northam now. This is where I
belong, and when all is said the manners of the people suit me
better here. I will not make the mistake of transporting myself
in retirement, as my first landlady had done.

My leg is better. The doctor gave me some magic muscle
pills. I limp no more.

I am back at work, and my excursion seems like a dream,
but I am changed, I am fortified. You may by now have
suspected that after that Somerset summer of forty years ago,
after graduating, I fell into a profound depression. For a year,
I did not care whether I lived or died. I slept weeping, and
weeping did I wake. I recovered, slowly, with the help of
Wordsworth, finding in him, as had John Stuart Mill in similar despair before me, at first 'the real and permanent
happiness of tranquil contemplation', and then, at last, 'an
increased interest in the common feelings and common
destiny of human beings'. But like a coward I had feared,
with the approach of age and enforced idleness, a recurrence
of that despair. I stepped westward to test my destiny. And
I found there Anne Elliot, with a wild gleam in her eyes at
sixty.

She has said we must keep in touch, and who knows, maybe
we will. And maybe we will not. We are stubborn and mistrust-
ful of new friends, we Yorkshire folk. My real and sober life

is here, but I no longer fear the future as I did. The untravelled world still gleams. And Shakira Jagan has read Wordsworth's sonnet to Toussaint L'Ouverture, and she concedes that it is good. Or not half bad, as she put it, in her Guyanese-Yorkshire style. So I brought some magic back with me, and it will keep me through the winter.

(2000)

PENGUIN MODERN CLASSICS

JERUSALEM THE GOLDEN
MARGARET DRABBLE

Brought up in a stifling, emotionless home in the north of England, Clara finds freedom when she wins a scholarship and travels to London. There, she meets Celia and the rest of the Denham family: brilliant and charming, they dazzle Clara with their flair for life, and Clara yearns to be part of their bohemian world. But while she will do anything to join their circle, she gives no thought to the chaos that she may cause...

In this captivating story of growing up and moving on, Margaret Drabble explores what it means to leave a disregarded childhood and family behind.

Winner of the James Tait Black Memorial Prize for Fiction

'An extraordinary work' *The New York Times*

'Drabble excels at describing the minute detail of human behaviour' *Independent*

PENGUIN MODERN CLASSICS

THE NEEDLE'S EYE
MARGARET DRABBLE

Simon Camish is an embittered, timid barrister, too busy with his own problems to take note of Rose Vassiliou across a dinner-party table. But only a few
years before, Rose had frequently been in the news, an heiress who turned her
back on family money in the name of independence. Now she is a single parent
in a decaying house, trying to raise her three children while her ex-husband
takes legal action against her. When Simon finds himself drawn into her af–
fairs, he will discover – despite what Rose may wish - that the power of money
is ultimately inescapable.

'An extraordinary work: it tells a story deftly, beautifully' Joyce Carol
Oates

PENGUIN MODERN CLASSICS

THE SEVEN SISTERS
MARGARET DRABBLE

Candida Wilton has been ignored by her husband and children for years, before being displaced by a younger woman. Moving to London, alone, divorced and without much money, it seems she will now enjoy a life only of small pleasures: trips to the gym, visits to her reading group. When she receives an unexpected windfall, Candida gathers together six travelling companions – women friends from childhood, from married life and after – and maps out a journey she has long dreamed of, around Tunis, Naples and Pompeii, where her grey city life can blossom into one of colour and adventure.

In *The Seven Sisters*, Margaret Drabble captures the wonder of second chances with dry wit, honesty and immaculate observation.

'Elegiac, offbeat and moving' *Mail on Sunday*

PENGUIN MODERN CLASSICS

HEAT WAVE
PENELOPE LIVELY

Pauline is spending the summer at World's End, a cottage somewhere in the middle of England. This year the adjoining cottage is occupied by her daughter Teresa and baby grandson Luke; and, of course, Maurice, the man Teresa married. As the hot months unfold, Maurice grows ever more involved in the book he is writing - and with his female copy-editor – and Pauline can only watch in dismay and anger as her daughter repeats her own mistakes in love. The heat and tension will lead to a violent, startling climax.

In *Heat Wave*, Penelope Lively gives us a moving portrayal of a fragile family damaged and defined by adultery, and the lengths to which a mother will go to protect the ones she loves.

'Extraordinarily good, intelligent and perceptive... very moving' Susan Hill

PENGUIN MODERN CLASSICS

ACCORDING TO MARK
PENELOPE LIVELY

A respected literary biographer, Mark is working on the life of Gilbert Strong – a writer about whom he thinks he knows everything. Happily married, and apparently dedicated to a life of letters, he nevertheless falls in love with Strong's granddaughter Carrie, a vague and unsophisticated young woman more interested in bedding plants than books or passion. As Mark's obsessions develop over a hot, complicated summer, he begins to understand that nothing is ever what it seems; not Gilbert Strong, and certainly not himself.

According to Mark is a witty and moving look at love, literature and the dangers of middle-aged folly.

'Any time spent with Penelope Lively is a joy' *Observer*

*Contemporary ... Provocative ... Outrageous ...
Prophetic ... Groundbreaking ... Funny ... Disturbing ...
Different ... Moving ... Revolutionary ... Inspiring ...
Subversive ... Life-changing ...*

What makes a modern classic?

At Penguin Classics our mission has always been to make the best
books ever written available to everyone. And that also means
constantly redefining and refreshing exactly what makes a 'classic'.
That's where Modern Classics come in. Since 1961 they have been an
organic, ever-growing and ever-evolving list of books from the last
hundred (or so) years that we believe will continue to be read over and
over again.

They could be books that have inspired political dissent, such as
Animal Farm. Some, like *Lolita* or *A Clockwork Orange*, may have
caused shock and outrage. Many have led to great films, from *In Cold
Blood* to *One Flew Over the Cuckoo's Nest*. They have broken down
barriers – whether social, sexual, or, in the case of *Ulysses*, the
boundaries of language itself. And they might – like *Goldfinger* or
Scoop – just be pure classic escapism. Whatever the reason, Penguin
Modern Classics continue to inspire, entertain and enlighten millions
of readers everywhere.

'No publisher has had more influence on reading habits than Penguin'
Independent

'Penguins provided a crash course in world literature'
Guardian

The best books ever written

PENGUIN (🐧) CLASSICS

SINCE 1946

Find out more at www.penguinclassics.com